HOLLYWOOD
IS LIKE
HIGH SCHOOL
WITH
MONEY

HOLLYWOOD IS LIKE HIGH SCHOOL WITH MONEY

ZOEY DEAN

GRAND CENTRAL
PUBLISHING

NEW YORK   BOSTON

Grand Central Publishing
Hachette Book Group
237 Park Avenue
New York, NY 10017

Visit our Web site at www.HachetteBookGroup.com.

Printed in the United States of America

First Edition: July 2009
10 9 8 7 6 5 4 3 2 1

Grand Central Publishing is a division of Hachette Book Group, Inc.
The Grand Central Publishing name and logo is a trademark of Hachette Book Group, Inc.

Library of Congress Cataloging-in-Publication Data

Dean, Zoey.
  Hollywood is like high school with money / Zoey Dean—1st ed.
     p. cm.
  Summary: "Young professional Taylor Henning must attempt the impossible: staying in touch with her inner mean girl while staying true to herself"—Provided by publisher.
  ISBN 978-0-446-69719-4
  1. Hollywood (Los Angeles, Calif.)—Fiction. 2. Motion picture industry—Fiction.
3. Chick lit. I. Title.
PS3604.E1547H66 2009
813'.6—dc22
                              2008037868

Book design and text composition by L&G McRee

For my mom,
who got me through high school
and all the years since

HOLLYWOOD
IS LIKE
HIGH SCHOOL
WITH
MONEY

CHAPTER ONE

Dear Michael,
You'll never guess where I am.

I paused and turned the postcard over to look at the picture of the iconic Hollywood sign, stark white and enormous against the bumpy range of the Hollywood Hills. As I chewed the end of my pencil, I realized, belatedly, that the sign pretty much gave my location away. Really, where would Michael Deming think I was—Peoria? I sighed but kept on going. After all, it was only a postcard.

Got the job I mentioned last time. Moved out here from
Middletown just last week. L.A. is crazy and weird, and I
love it!!

I hesitated for a little while over what to say next. Michael Deming had never once written me back, though I'd sent him probably three hundred letters and notes over a period of nine years. Some people, like my friend Magnolia, would say this made me a kind of epistolary stalker, but I knew it just meant I was a fan. A really, really big fan. Kind of a really, really creepy fan, Magnolia would say, but of course I wouldn't listen to her. And anyway, what did she know? As much as I loved her, she was still trying to figure out what she wanted to do with her life, while I was here, at a movie studio, getting ready to start *doing* what I wanted to do with my life.

Will keep you posted, I wrote. *Love, T.*

Probably the "Love" business was a little much, but I sort of felt like I could say anything to the guy. It's easy to be yourself when no one is actually paying you any attention. Also, I'd never signed my whole name—for some reason I'd always just put T— and the anonymity made me bolder.

I tucked the postcard into the *Fodor's Los Angeles* that I kept in my purse and glanced up at the sleek, black-haired receptionist talking quietly into her headset. The wall behind the white crescent of her desk was a waterfall, with sheets of chlorinated water splashing endlessly down into a basin filled with shimmering rocks. Wind chimes tinkled in the corner of the room, and every once in a while a mist of gardenia-scented air wafted out from some invisible vent. Some interior design team had gone to a lot of trouble to make the lobby of the creative department at Metronome Studios look like a very expensive spa. And it was definitely impressive, although the sound of the water made me feel like I had to go to the bathroom, even though I'd just peed.

Michael Deming would hate it, I was pretty sure of that. He'd fled Hollywood years ago and now lived in a log cabin without running water or electricity in the San Juan Islands. Or at least that was the rumor. Michael Deming—director, auteur, genius—was the J. D. Salinger of the film world, except that he'd only ever made one studio movie, which had been a flop. But a lot of people had been obsessed with *Journal Girl*, including me. I'd seen it for the first time at age fifteen, as the clueless new girl at Boardman High School in Cleveland, Ohio. By the time the credits rolled, I had discovered what I wanted to do with my life: I was going to make movies.

At first I thought I'd act, but as it turned out, I had terrible stage fright. I also developed a weird stutter whenever I had to say a word that started with the letter *S*. The summer before my senior year, my parents sent me, at my insistence, to Director's Camp, but I didn't do so well there either. I was terrible at telling people what to do, I had no "unifying vision," as my counselor put it, and I couldn't work an editing machine to save my life. Luckily, I ate some bad shrimp, got food poisoning, and was sent home early.

Despite such setbacks, I did not give up. I focused instead on how to make movies without having to be in front of the camera or manage heavy equipment. Four years in the film department at Wesleyan convinced me that I had the talent to pursue my dreams; two years interning for a beloved professor, shadowing him as he made a brilliant movie only a handful of people would ever watch, convinced me I wanted to work on movies that might actually get *seen*. Hence my presence in this lobby, waiting to start my first day of work as an assistant to an assistant at a major movie studio.

Thank you, Michael Deming. You are my inspiration, even if you've never even bothered to write me a single note of encouragement. Even if, at this very moment, you are wearing dirty overalls and eating squirrel meat in some backwoods hovel, cursing Hollywood as a nest of vipers, phonies, and sellouts.

I took a sip of the iced mocha I'd bought from the café down the street from my apartment—technically Magnolia's apartment, but she'd been kind enough to let me and my boxes move in—and cleared my throat, hoping the receptionist would notice me. She sighed and pushed a curtain of black hair back from her admirably high cheekbones. "Taylor Henning?" she said breathily.

I stood up obediently, my heart pounding in my chest.

"You can go in now. Here's your ID." The receptionist pushed toward me a laminated card that read METRONOME STU-DIOS in intimidating block letters. I picked the ID up and saw a grainy version of my narrow face and light blue eyes staring back at me. My hair was sort of flat, and my nose was a little shiny, but I'd certainly seen worse pictures of myself. My Ohio driver's license, for example, which I hadn't bothered to change in six years of living in Connecticut, made me look like a felon.

"I'm sorry—where again?" I asked. "I can't remember."

"Last corner office on the southwest side." The receptionist opened an *Us Weekly* to a spread of Ben Affleck pumping gas into his car. "Stars—they're just like us!" the headline proclaimed.

Right, I thought—just like us, only richer, better looking, and constantly hounded by photographers. As I walked away, the receptionist called, halfheartedly, "Good luck."

I turned around and smiled my best, most grateful smile. "Thanks," I said, but she was no longer paying any attention to me.

I swiped the ID through the silver card slot, and the glass doors slid open with a hiss. If the waiting room was a spa, the interior of the creative department was a luxury space station.

Below the high white ceilings, the illuminated walls gradually changed color, like a pulsing screen saver, from vivid orange to deep magenta to purple and blue. It was . . . not tacky, exactly, but not subtle either.

Through open office doors, I could see the creative executives, intimidatingly busy on their BlackBerries or laptops or iPhones. Their assistants sat at desks outside the CEs' offices, guarding their doors, acting as secretaries, factotums, and girl/guy Fridays. And in about five minutes, I was going to be one of them.

The last corner office on the southwest side was a sleek glass cube buffered from the hallway by an intermediate room, half office, half reception area. A shiny placard announced that I was entering the domain of Iris Whitaker, President of Production. Iris Whitaker, my new boss. In the outer room were two sleek black desks, two bookcases lined with scripts, a NASA-quality laser printer, a low white couch, and a single window that looked out onto the courtyard and fountain in the middle of the studio lot.

I set my bag on the smaller, empty desk and looked around, feeling my pulse beating hard in my neck. The other desk, which mine faced, was decorated with a cluster of silver photo frames, votive candles, and a porcelain vase of pink tulips. That would be where Kylie Arthur, Iris's first assistant, sat. Up until very recently, Kylie had been the second assistant, but now she was basically my boss too. I'd never met her, but Iris, during our interview last month, had assured me that we would get along.

I would have been able to see into Iris's office but for the tangle of tall plants along the glass wall that separated her from us, her minions. There were several towering cacti, a bunch of lush, ferny things, and even a miniature orange tree. Through the green fronds I could only make out the occasional flash of a white blouse. But I could hear Iris's gravelly voice, and though I didn't want to eavesdrop, I couldn't help it.

"*Quinn,*" Iris said. "I don't care what your father says, you know the drill: shopping on Third Street on Saturdays only. Now don't make me get into it again." She paused, then cackled. "Nice try, kiddo," she said. "I'll see you tonight. I love you."

I waited another moment until I was sure that Iris was off the phone and then approached the threshold to her office. I could already feel my cheeks flushing, the way they always did when I was nervous. (This was why I never wore blush—overkill.) I unclenched my fists, smoothed my hair, and tried to think calming thoughts. I knocked on the doorjamb.

"Come in," Iris called, and steadying my breathing, I entered.

Iris Whitaker sat behind a desk cluttered with paper, typing furiously into her computer. The vast rear window of her office looked over one of the ocher soundstages toward the skyscrapers of downtown, which were, unsurprisingly, obscured by an orange brown smog. Hesitantly, I moved a few inches further into the room, stepping onto the sheepskin rug and admiring the marble coffee table and the slate gray minimalist sofa with its shantung throw pillows. The office had the strange but not unpleasant smell of potting soil and expensive leather.

Iris's computer pinged—e-mail sent—and then she turned to look at me with her dark eyes. Copper-colored curls fell to her shoulders, and her arms were Pilates-toned. She was in her forties, but she looked about twenty-seven—hardly old enough to be the mother of Quinn, who Iris had told me was a junior in high school. "Taylor!" she said warmly, standing up. "Welcome—come on in."

I leaned over the desk to shake Iris's hand. She was angular and nearly six feet tall, and her handshake was as firm as a man's.

"Hi," I said. "Thanks." Then for some stupid reason I wished her a happy Monday.

Iris smiled, not dismissing my silly remark but not responding to it either. "Please, pull up a chair. Actually, not that one—it's holding up that cactus there. So you made it here in one piece, I see."

I sank so deep into the black leather chair I'd chosen that my head was barely above the desktop. "Yes," I said. "I've been here a whole week." I tried to sit up very straight, but what I really needed was a booster seat.

Iris twisted a large opal ring on her right hand; otherwise she wore no jewelry. I'd heard that she'd been married to a high-powered producer but that there had been a messy divorce. He'd run off with a starlet—someone young and malleable, not tall and fierce like Iris Whitaker, the seventh most powerful player in Hollywood. That was what *Entertainment Weekly* had called her; I'd read it on a plane trip to Florida to see my grandparents. Or at least that was what I thought I'd read. I'd had a couple vodka tonics—I do *not* like to fly the friendly skies—and so I couldn't be 100 percent sure.

Iris was smiling at me but not saying anything, and it's awkward moments like this when my verbal floodgates tend to open. "I just have to tell you how thrilled I am to be here," I said. "I know I said this in the interviews, but this is all I've ever wanted to do, and I can't believe I get to be doing it. I know how lucky I am, and I want you to know that I'm grateful too. I mean—it's just incredible. And so I want to say thank you. Thank you for

the opportunity." I managed to stop myself then by biting my lip.
Hard.

Iris raised her carefully plucked eyebrows. "That's great to
hear," she said a beat later. "You're welcome."

"Movies are my passion," I barreled on. "And I plan to be
here for the long haul. I'm not in it to hang out with celebrities or
drop names. I don't want to party all night at Chateau Marmont
or anything. I'm in it because I've never wanted to do anything
else but make great movies."

Clearly I needed a better strategy than lip-biting to shut me
up this morning. Maybe a muzzle would do it.

Iris smiled. "*Great* is a tall order, you know," she said, not
unkindly. "*Profitable* is often about the best we hope for. But we
do look for great stories here, of course. If I'm doing my job
right—and if you're doing yours too—that means we're reading
every script out there, plus every magazine article and every
book and every blog that might be a hit. We don't want to miss
anything that might translate to the screen. We're prospecting
for gold, Taylor, and we sift through every pebble in the river to
find it." She paused. "There! That's my recruitment speech. Not
that I need to persuade *you* of all people. You seem to have drunk
the Kool-Aid already. Not to mix metaphors or anything."

"Of course." What she said was true—I needed no convincing.

"It's not an easy job," Iris continued, still twisting the ring.
"You need to make yourself available to us around the clock—
which is where the BlackBerry you'll be getting comes in," she
said with a wink. My stomach tingled with excitement. Not that I
relished the idea of middle-of-the-night e-mails (*I'll need that
script on my desk at 8 a.m. sharp!*), but knowing I'd soon have my
very own BlackBerry—like a doctor's pager, I thought—made

me feel high powered and professional. And God knows my battered old Nokia could use an upgrade.

"Of course," Iris added, "I do lean on my assistants to help me prospect."

"Absolutely," I agreed. It was why I had wanted the job so badly. At Metronome, assistants weren't just cappuccino fetchers; they were asked their opinions while they delivered the cappuccino. At the agencies, you started out in the mail room.

"Enthusiasm comes in handy. But it can sometimes cloud someone's judgment," Iris continued. She pointed her BlackBerry at me. "Not every movie deserves to be made, you know."

"Oh no," I agreed. "Of course not. I mean, half the movies that do get made don't deserve to get made, it seems. Like that one where Owen Wilson played the one-legged horse trainer with the pet monkey, what was that called? I'd like to meet whoever thought *that* was a good idea."

"Actually," Iris knit her brows, "we considered that script."

"Oh," I stammered, "I'm sorry—I mean, I'm sure it had great potential. I think—"

There was a knock at the door, and I sat back in the chair, immensely grateful for the interruption. In two more minutes, I would have talked myself right out of my new job, and then what? I'd have to go back to Middletown and beg Eckert Pinckney, the professor who'd already paid me out of pocket for the last two years, to take me back. Not that I'd left on bad terms; he was the reason I even got this job, anyway. Of the handful of people who actually saw *Gray Area*—the gritty but beautiful film I'd helped him make—Iris Whitaker was one of them. Opportunities like this only came along once in a lifetime, as my mother was fond of reminding me, and I wasn't about to screw it up.

A lithe blonde slid into the room on a pair of kelly green ballet flats. "Morning, Iris," she said. "Bryan Lourd said twelve-thirty at Cut. I told them that was too late, but he insisted. Also that weird DP called again."

The girl cocked her head while she waited for Iris to respond. She stood by the cactus, not looking at me at all. She reminded me of Sienna Miller in the film *Factory Girl*, playing Edie Sedgwick, except that her hair was long and wavy and dark gold, with butter-colored highlights that framed her face. A jumble of silver chains around her neck tinkled as she shifted her weight from foot to delicate foot. Her perfume smelled like lilies—really expensive ones.

"Thanks, Kylie," Iris said. "Kylie, this is Taylor. Taylor, this is Kylie Arthur, my first assistant. She had your job until a week ago, when Christy got promoted to CE."

I'd met Christy Zeller when I flew out to L.A. from Middletown last month. I'd stayed for just two days, with Magnolia, and interviewed at Metronome. Christy had been just an assistant then, and now she had her own office and her own assistant. At Metronome, they nurtured talent and they hired from within.

I heaved myself out of the chair, but Kylie didn't offer her hand. She just stood there in her skinny jeans and her silky polka-dot tunic top and smiled. "Hi," she said. "Welcome to Metronome." Her eyes flicked up and down the length of my body, taking in my black wool-blend pants from Banana Republic and my blue ruffled shirt from Forever 21. "Cute shoes."

Involuntarily, I glanced down at my Nine West–but-look-like–Michael Kors black pumps. "Thanks," I said, unsure if she was being snide.

"Taylor just moved here from Connecticut," Iris noted. "She

was working with Eckert Pinckney on that film I told you about, the one about star-crossed lovers and domestic violence?"

"Oh," Kylie said, playing with one of her chains. Finally she looked me in the eye. "How are you liking L.A. so far?"

"Well, there's a lot of smog," I said. It was the only thing that came to mind.

"Right," Kylie said, looking at me blankly through her long, mascaraed lashes.

There was an awkward pause, which Iris finally broke. "Kylie's one of the best assistants I've ever had," she said. "If you have any questions, she's the go-to person." She turned to look at her e-mail. "And I guess we'll have to move my two-thirty so I'm not late from Cut."

"No prob." Kylie nodded briskly and vanished behind the plants into the outer office.

"Kylie'll get you situated," Iris said, dismissing me. "Good luck."

"Thank you," I said. I thought that maybe I should shake Iris's hand again, but she was already scrolling through her BlackBerry screen. As I passed the jungle of plants on my way to my new desk, I felt a mixture of elation and mortification. I had gushed like a seventh-grader, I was wearing imitation designer shoes, and I'd summed up my feelings about my new home with the word "smog." *But still,* I thought, *I'm here. I made it.*

I straightened my shoulders and sucked in my stomach. At twenty-four, I was ready to start living my life. But first, I really had to pee.

CHAPTER TWO

Some people say that being a second assistant is kind of demeaning," Kylie said, touching a lit match to one of her votive candles. "But it's not. It's incredibly important. I'm actually going to miss it a little." The wick sputtered, then caught the flame. Kylie looked up. "I hope you don't mind." She blew the match out. "It's soy-based and aromatherapeutic. It helps my concentration."

"No problem," I said quickly, suppressing the urge to make a joke about fire safety. I wanted to ask Kylie what she was going to miss—the photocopying? the fetching of nonfat lattes? sitting at the smaller desk? Don't get me wrong, I was thrilled to be at Metronome, but I knew there were going to be parts of my job that weren't actually thrilling. That was the way things went: you paid your dues, and then you got to do what you came for. So far I'd been second assistant for half an hour, and all I'd done was log into my computer, put my notebook in my desk drawer, and wait for Kylie to tell me what I ought to be doing with myself.

Kylie tossed the matchbook onto her desk. "Chateau Marmont" was written across it in loopy script. "So here's the deal with being Iris's assistant. We're on all her calls and we do her schedule. We also make sure she only speaks to the people she needs to and that she's never surprised by *anything*," Kylie said, ticking an imaginary list off her fingers. "If she knows about it, *we* know about it. Here."

She held out a stapled packet, which I walked over to take from her slim, manicured hand. "This handbook is your bible," Kylie said. "Also known as the employee manual for assisting the president of production. It has everything: passwords to check voice mail, the private numbers of all the top agents, private numbers of her favorite restaurants, and a list of callers you should *always* put through. It also has her daughter's schedule, a few lines about proper attire, and the recipe for her spirulina smoothie."

"Wow," I said, flipping through the pages; there was a baffling array of lists and diagrams. "This is great. You know, I saw an employee manual for carnival workers once. You know, carnies? The rules were all like, do not sleep under cars. Do not be too drunk to respond to a customer's needs. Do not pee in public."

Kylie stared at me.

"I know this is totally different! I was just trying to be"—I paused—"funny," I said softly.

"Right. Now, I don't know how much real assistant work you did with that professor of yours?" Kylie asked, peering at the screen of her Mac Pro.

"Not much, actually," I admitted. "I was more of an assistant *creatively*," I added, a little proudly. Okay, so maybe I was more of a shadow, occasionally voicing my opinion on the story, the script, the way the film could be shot. And yes, there was some dirty work—scraping together our paltry funding, figuring out how exactly we'd be able to shoot the thing on such a tight budget. But I didn't think Kylie needed to know about that.

"Right," Kylie said, dragging her eyes away from her screen and back to me. "Well, being an assistant at a studio is a little different. Actually, being a *second* assistant is a little different. It's a little more"—her head bobbed from side to side as she searched for the most flattering word—"logistical. Filing, copying, errands, making reservations. That kind of thing."

"And reading scripts," I said. I opened the handbook. *Iris's favorite herbal tea is Tazo's Wild Sweet Orange,* someone had scrawled in the margins, *and while she likes Irish breakfast tea, she does not like English breakfast or Earl Grey.*

"Scripts?" Kylie repeated. When I looked up, Kylie was watching me with two tiny slash lines of a frown between her green eyes.

For a moment, Kylie reminded me of Melanie Pitts, who was in all my film classes at Wesleyan. Melanie had this annoying way of looking at you that made you feel like you were a tiny mouse speaking Spanish: small and unintelligible. A lot of people in my classes spoke to me that way, though, because nobody in film studies took me seriously. Even as all my classmates wore funeral-attire black, smoked cigarettes between classes, and refused to go to the multiplex when the latest blockbuster came out, I constantly referenced my Midwestern upbringing, wore Gap jeans and Nikes, and continued to see every new Ron Howard movie. But then when it came time for all the seniors to show our short films, and I screened my Fellini-meets–Judd Apatow piece, my classmates suddenly took notice. Melanie, whom I'd spent the last four years praising but who never deigned to say more than, "Um, thanks," even asked me out to coffee to "discuss my work."

"Yeah, reading scripts for Iris," I prodded, shaking off the memory. "She was just telling me that it's part of the job."

"That's sort of more of the *first* assistant's job," Kylie corrected. "She probably meant in the future you would be doing that."

Before I could ask her to clarify, her computer made a bell-like sound.

"Sorry, it's just an IM from my boyfriend"—Kylie turned to type a reply—"hang on."

I leaned back in my new chair. It made a squishy, new-car noise. I turned the knob to adjust the lumbar support. "Is he at a studio too?"

Kylie seemed to hesitate. "Actually, no. He's not in the industry."

I imagined a banker, a real estate mogul, an ad man—someone who could keep Kylie well stocked in Louboutins. He probably wore shiny shirts and a Princeton ring on his finger and picked Kylie up after work in a yellow Porsche Boxter. "What does he do?"

"He teaches tennis in Beverly Hills." Kylie gave her hair a small, almost defiant toss. "He could totally act if he wanted to, though," she added, and I wondered if she was slightly embarrassed by her boyfriend's job. "Everyone always says how charismatic he is."

I would have offered up something about my boyfriend in return, just to be friendly, but I didn't have one. I wondered if I should make one up—some dashing, dark-haired fellow pining for me back in Middletown. Instead there was only Brandon, who certainly wasn't missing me. Unless you counted the fact that he couldn't wait to see me crawl back there with my tail between my legs. Brandon Rogers was another person who'd suddenly joined the Taylor Henning bandwagon during senior year. He went from the cute, unattainable guy whose neck I'd always liked to stare at in Advanced French Film Theory to my number-one fan. We dated for the two years after graduation, while I was working with Professor Pinckney and he was a production assistant at a small New York company that made edgy documentaries. We broke up when I took the job at Metronome. On the flight to L.A., I kept replaying our good-bye in my head: the lingering kiss on the cheek, and then, "Call me in a few years, when you're making *Superman 7*."

Suddenly our phones rang simultaneously. I looked in confusion at all the NASA-like buttons on mine.

Kylie slid a little headset over her blond waves. "Iris Whitaker's office," she purred. "Oh yes, of course she'll be attending. Yes, with a plus one. No, thank *you*." She took the headset off again and smiled at me. "See? Nothing to it."

"An RSVP," I offered brightly, trying to seem like I knew what was going on.

"Mmm. A Women in Film fund-raiser. Drew Barrymore is co-chairing, and Iris has known her practically since *Poltergeist*. She used to babysit Iris's daughter. But anyway, let's take a quick tour, and then we'll get you acquainted with the Xerox machine." Kylie slid out from behind her desk and motioned me to follow. "This floor is all the CEs, plus all their assistants," she said, leading me down the hall past framed posters of all of Metronome's hits.

Creative executives ranged in importance from freshly promoted junior execs to executive vice presidents, and even I could tell which was which by the size of their offices and the costliness of the furniture in them. But whether they were lowly or powerful, they all had one singular and crucial mission: to find the raw material to make movies. Once they did and a script was bought, they shepherded that script through the obstacle course of preproduction: they found directors, attached actors, hired new writers to punch up the script, and picked locations. Development people were like fortune-tellers. They were the ones who could see—in the spare white pages of a screenplay, a few thousand words of a magazine article, or the unpublished galleys of a novel—an audience sitting in front of a thirty-foot screen, in rapt attention. They were the kind of people who helped Michael Deming make his masterpiece.

As Kylie walked me around, I eagerly took everything in. The Metronome offices were arranged like a bull's-eye, with the outer ring of big, windowed offices belonging to the bosses, to people like Iris. In the next ring sat their assistants, ready to answer to their bosses' every whim. The junior CEs had a cluster of offices on the north side of the building. And in the light-deprived inner sections of the office were the kitchen, the copy room, and the cubicles for various lower-level assistants.

"There's the VP of marketing's office," Kylie said, "and that's his assistant, Margie; over there is Peter—he's a scout."

I was trying to take in all the names, but I could feel them fading from my mind seconds after Kylie pronounced them, like hastily memorized equations after a math final.

A guy our age in a silky shirt and a retro skinny tie came jogging down the hall past us. "Hey, Kylie," he called in passing. "IM me—I've got gossip."

Kylie let out a little squeal. "In a sec!" she cried. Then her voice flattened again. "That's Wyman. He's another assistant. Here's the kitchen, the bathrooms, the nap room——"

"Nap room?"

"Yeah, some consultant came in and told us that naps improve productivity, so Metronome made a nap room in what used to be a janitor's closet, but no one's ever actually gone to sleep in it. It just doesn't look professional, you know?"

When we returned to our desks, Kylie held out a script. "Three copies, please. Third door on your left, as I'm sure you remember."

I took the pages and started down the hall, past the desks of other assistants busily answering phones for their own bosses. One girl with short black hair looked up at me as I passed, and when I smiled, she flashed her teeth in return, but it was more a grimace than a smile. I tried to smile back—isn't that what karma's all about?—but faltered. People here weren't going to go out of their way to welcome me, that was for sure. But, I reminded myself, that was okay. I'd spent four years feeling like the underdog in college, and look how that had turned out. L.A. was different, certainly, but winning these people over couldn't be any harder.

The copy room was lit with a cold fluorescent light, and inside were two Xerox machines, two fax machines, and a giant color printer. I put the pages into the feeder, realizing as I did so that it was Paul Haggis's new script. I felt a little thrill of excitement. Take that, Brandon, I thought. For all his talk about how American cinema was dead, I knew he'd secretly kill to get his hands on a Haggis screenplay.

As the machine spit out its pages, I picked them up and began to read, scanning through paragraphs of stage directions describing long tracking shots. It was a slow start, but by page twenty-five, I was fully absorbed in the story of Jack Tharp, a small-town lawyer who slowly comes to realize that the life he's living is an utter sham, and I didn't realize for another ten pages that the machine had jammed.

"Shit," I said. I tossed the script on the counter and began opening various drawers and hatches in the copier and slamming them closed again in a rising panic.

"Um, are you trying to kill the copier?" said a voice.

It belonged to the girl who'd grimaced at me earlier. Her black hair was cut in a sleek bob—very Catherine Zeta-Jones in *Chicago*—and she was leaning in the doorway, looking vaguely amused. *Very* vaguely.

"It jammed," I said desperately.

"I can see that. Here." The girl took the remainder of the Haggis script and fed it into the other copier. "This one still works. When you get back to your desk, you can call the copy guy."

"Thank you so much," I said.

"Whatever," the girl said mildly. "It's your first day."

"Is it that obvious?"

"Pretty much." Then she turned on her heel and walked away, which I tried not to take personally.

I stood with my hands on my hips, watching the rest of the script print out. For a moment, the copier seemed to pause, and I held my breath in consternation. But then it kicked into gear again, and I sighed with relief.

"So it's Ken from CAA?" I asked. It was only the sixth phone call I'd dared to answer, and I could feel Kylie watching me. I liked the headset—it made me feel like a travel agent or an infomercial hostess—but the connection wasn't very good, and I strained to hear.

"No, *Kent* from *UTA*," said the assistant on the other line, his voice rising. "How many more times do I have to say it? *UTA*, not *CAA*. Jesus!"

I typed Kent/UTA as quickly as I could on Iris's call sheet on her computer, then slugged down the rest of my Diet Coke.

"Right, of course," I said. "I'll let her know you called. Would you like to leave a number?"

Kent's assistant made a sound of disgust and hung up the phone.

"We have his number," Kylie told me when I took off my headset. "We have everybody's number."

I looked up at her guiltily. "Was that the wrong thing to ask?"

Kylie didn't even bother to respond, but by the afternoon, I felt like things were beginning to look up a little. I hadn't broken any machines for a couple of hours, I'd only hung up on one person, and Kylie had assured me that he was only a screenwriter, and not a very famous one at that. ("*Never* piss off an actor or a director," Kylie counseled, looking down her ski-jump nose, "but don't worry so much about writers. They're used to being snubbed.") Sometimes I thought I felt Iris's eyes on me, checking up on my progress, but it was impossible to tell through all the greenery.

The only problem was that no one had said anything about lunch. Kylie had vanished for a little while, but whether she'd eaten or not, I didn't know—she looked like the kind of girl who lived on Diet Cokes and celery with low-fat peanut butter. I'd already devoured the stale granola bar in my purse and was now relying solely on caffeine to keep me functioning. But my teeth hurt, and my leg was jittering more than a spastic Rockette's.

I was also hoping Kylie would talk to me more about what it was like to be at Metronome. What movies were they making now? Had she ever come across a really great script in the slush pile? Which famous people were nice, and which ones were assholes? Did Jack Nicholson really shower only once a week? Was it true that Vince Vaughn had a weird foot fetish? But Kylie generally ignored me and kept her nose buried in screenplays. Every once in a while her computer pinged, though, which meant she was IMing her tennis player or gossiping with the other assistants. Over the course of the last hour, shiny-shirt guy had passed by, offering her a knowing wink, and a tall, impeccably dressed brunette with Pantene Pro-V commercial hair had whispered something in Kylie's ear and then stalked off, seemingly satisfied.

I was reading through the phone log, making sure it didn't have any typos, when the phone rang, and Kylie interrupted one of her regular whisper-giggle sessions with yet another assistant (tall, coltish Cici, in this case, whom Kylie had barely managed to introduce me to) and said, "Oh God, don't answer it."

"Who is it?"

Kylie waved a dismissive hand and locked her arm through Cici's. "Back in five," she said, and then the two of them vanished around the corner, Cici's kitten heels clicking along the shiny floor. I told myself that Kylie must be a really efficient worker when she put her mind to it, because she certainly spent a lot of time socializing.

The phone continued to ring, and I was sure that I saw one of the ferns pushed aside and a dark eye gazing out at me. I couldn't let Iris see me sitting there like an idiot, failing to do one of the most basic duties of my job, so I put on the headset and pressed the button that said Talk.

"Iris Whitaker's office," I said, imitating Kylie's answer-purr. I loved the way it felt to say that. I'd even practiced in the bathroom: *Iris Whitaker's office, may I help you?* I could say it all day—which was convenient, since it was a big part of my job. The fern in Iris's office shifted back to its place.

"Hi, this is Dana McCafferty." The girl sounded like she was in junior high, except that I could sense a very unchildlike confidence from just her introduction. "I'm calling about my script. I sent it to Iris a few weeks ago. *The Evolution of Evan?* Can you tell me if it's been read?"

"I'm not really sure," I said. "I just started working here."

"The last girl I spoke to said she'd get back to me soon," Dana said. "And that was a week ago. So I'm just following up."

"Just a minute," I said. I glanced at the shelf of scripts. It could be anywhere. "I should probably take your number and call you back."

"Actually, it would be really great if you could just take a look and see if it's been read, or if it's in the script log. You do have one of those, don't you?"

Yes, we did, but I couldn't remember where it was on my computer. I wasn't sure if I thought Dana's pushiness was annoying or admirable. If I could just find the script in one of these piles, though, I could tell her that much. "Hang on," I said. I felt proud of myself for my initiative.

I took off my headset and walked over to a pile of scripts on the floor. If Kylie wasn't interested in talking to Dana, she probably hadn't been all that interested in her script either. In general, studios looked down on scripts from unrepresented writers. But everyone had to start somewhere, I reasoned. Maybe Dana's screenplay was the next *Casablanca*. I dug down among the pages, each ignored screenplay the product of someone's best and dearest dreams. It was sad, but also a little funny: *Pyscho Killer Pigs* was the title of one script, and *Alien Gunfight* was another. (But hey, not every movie could be a sensitive indie comedy.) I was just about to give up when I saw it: *The Evolution of Evan*, tucked between the story of two ninja warriors who don't know they're brothers and what seemed like a *Sideways* rip-off. Like the others, it didn't look touched.

I went back to the phone. "I found it," I declared. "I don't think anyone's gotten to it yet."

"Okay," Dana said, taking this information in stride. "So can *you* read it?"

I hesitated. My first thought was to say a polite no and hang up. But there was something desperate in this girl's voice, and it was a desperation I recognized. It was how I might have sounded had I ever been able to get Michael Deming on the phone. And I did want to start reading screenplays—wasn't that part of the job? Prospecting for gold?

"Please," Dana said. "I think you might like it."

"All right," I heard myself say. "I guess."

"So you'll give me notes?" Dana asked. "I can come to your office next week. Monday? How's Monday?"

Now this was something else entirely. "I'm going to have to check—" I began.

"I'm sorry, I'm just trying to move this along. You have to understand."

Just then I looked up to see Kylie walk back into the office holding another bottle of Diet Coke.

"Fine, I'll see you then," I said and hung up the phone.

"Don't tell me," Kylie said. "Dana?"

I nodded.

"You've got a lot to learn," Kylie said. But instead of sounding annoyed, she sounded almost pleased.

CHAPTER THREE

I t's official," I said, pulling my new BlackBerry—which Kylie had given me at the end of the day with an it's-no-big-deal shrug—and a stack of freshly cut business cards out of my purse. "You are looking at Taylor Henning, card-carrying employee of Metronome and BlackBerry-wielding second assistant to Iris Whitaker, vice president of production."

"Ooh." On the bar stool next to me, Magnolia grabbed one of my business cards and turned it over in her hands. I'd spent the last ten minutes telling her about the office, Iris, and Kylie, but I'd waited until now to break out the big guns. "You're special." She grinned. "So tell me honestly—scale of one to ten?"

"My day? Six," I said, grabbing another fistful of wasabi peas from the dish on the bar. "Would have been an eight if I weren't such an embarrassment to myself."

Magnolia put down the business card and contemplated her gimlet. "Six isn't bad," she said. "As far as first days go. But that

Kylie girl sounds a little alpha to me. Just stay calm and assertive. Alphas can totally handle that."

"Mags, you make it sound like she's a dog I've got to train. If anything, it's the other way around. *She's* not the one who walked into the men's bathroom."

Magnolia was obsessed with dogs, dog trivia, dog training, and *The Dog Whisperer*. She could eat an entire pan of brownies in a single sitting, and she was happily oblivious to fashion, celebrity, and her own sex appeal. We'd been assigned to be roommates freshman year, and while I'd always been a little mystified why the housing committee thought we'd get along, they wound up being right. In college, we each had our own group of friends, but we always managed to keep up with each other. She grew up in L.A. with her hippie parents and moved out here after graduation, getting her own place. She worked two jobs to pay for it: in the mornings, she walked the dogs of the rich and famous in Sullivan Canyon, and in the afternoons, she put on a pink smock and waxed starlets, porn stars, and the occasional hirsute gentleman at a salon called Joylie. It was sort of a weird combination, but Magnolia was sort of a weird girl. Brilliant, certainly, but weird.

"Kylie's been helpful, really. I think she didn't want to baby me too much. She wanted me to learn the ropes on my own."

"Right." Magnolia rolled her blue eyes. "We had a girl like that at Joylie. She gave me one of her customers my first day, and I thought she was being nice, but it was just because the guy had more hair on his back than a yeti. I used a whole *vat* of wax on him. Oh, hi, two burgers," Magnolia said to the bartender, a Vincent Gallo look-alike who'd been giving her the eye ever since we sat down. "Medium-rare, one salad, one fries. We're splitting, right? You're not going to make me eat all the lettuce by myself?" she asked me.

I nodded. I was glad to be living with someone like Magnolia—someone who wasn't afraid to eat a hamburger or wear jeans and flip-flops to a bar. Even though she grew up here, L.A. hadn't gotten to Magnolia, and I admired that. I didn't want L.A. to get to me either, the way it had clearly claimed Kylie—though I wouldn't mind feeling a little more confident. I also wouldn't mind a few new pairs of shoes and some nice highlights. Or a cute little Prius, but let's not get greedy.

"I'll be right back," Magnolia said and smiled as she turned down the hall to the ladies' room. "Don't hook up with anyone while I'm gone."

I watched Magnolia walk down the hall, and so did the bartender.

"Don't worry," said a voice on my left. "The first day's always the hardest."

I turned to see a startlingly cute guy in a pin-striped suit standing beside me. His eyes were a warm dark brown and he wore his hair in that scruffy, slept-on style that I couldn't help liking, even though it probably meant he spent half an hour in front of the mirror just to make it look that way.

"Sorry, I couldn't help overhearing," he said. "I've been trying to get the bartender's attention, but he's just been ogling your friend this whole time."

He smiled at me and leaned in a little closer, and suddenly I felt pretty sure he was flirting with me. I blushed and ducked my head. I hadn't flirted with a guy since Brandon and could barely even remember what it felt like.

"I'm sorry for eavesdropping, but it was only in the most discreet and polite way." He grinned and held out his hand. "Mark Lyder. With Ingenuity. And congratulations. Iris Whitaker's office is pretty impressive."

Ingenuity was one of the biggest talent agencies in L.A. It took me a moment to follow through with a handshake.

"I'm Taylor Henning," I said. "But I guess you know everything else about me."

"I don't, really," he said, moving still closer. "But let me take a stab at it. You're from the Midwest, but you went to college on the East Coast. You're new to L.A. It kind of freaks you out, being here, but you're totally excited. You're an optimist by nature and a very nice person. Your boyfriend back East misses you terribly." He smiled, watching my reaction. "Am I close?"

"God, is it that obvious?" I brushed my bangs back from my forehead, alarmed at being spotted so easily for a newbie. I decided I really ought to see about those highlights and contemplated getting a spray-on tan too. Maybe I'd even get a new driver's license picture while I was at it.

Mark laughed. "It's one of my party tricks." He gestured around the bar, to the black leather couches and the only marginally hip people sitting on them. "This place really shouldn't be one of your first impressions of L.A. I'm only here because my friend lives around the corner, and I can't get him to go anywhere else. We ought to get you to a cooler place." He turned to the bartender, who had finally wandered over. "Two Maker's, one rocks, one neat."

"We?" I asked, trying to sound flirtatious.

"I meant me," he said. "Assuming the boyfriend won't have a problem with it."

"There's no boyfriend," I said quickly. He was so cute that I didn't mind admitting this.

The bartender placed his drinks on the bar, and Mark threw down a twenty. "How's Koi?"

"Um, Koi's great."

"Okay, then. Tomorrow night." He dug into his jacket pocket and produced a thick, embossed business card. "Six-thirty. You eat sushi, right?"

Before I could answer, he pressed the card into my palm. "I can't wait to hear about the second day," he said, walking away. "I hope it's a nine."

Magnolia, who had been lurking at the end of the bar, plopped down eagerly in her seat. "What happened?" she asked.

I looked at her with wide, surprised eyes. "I think I just got asked out."

"By who?"

"He's over there in the corner. Don't look now!"

Magnolia ignored me, squinting prettily into the dim light.

"I think he's an agent," I said.

Magnolia wrinkled her nose. "He's good-looking," she said. "But if he's an agent, I'd be careful. They're jackals, you know— or hyenas, actually. Hyenas are bigger. And you, Taylor Henning, are a darling little Lhasa apso."

"Shut up," I said, pretending to be annoyed. But really I felt quite pleased with myself. My day had just gone up at least one point.

CHAPTER FOUR

Good morning, everyone," Iris announced, slipping a pair of tortoiseshell glasses onto her aquiline nose. "Let's get started, shall we?" It was ten o'clock on Tuesday morning, and the creative department was gathered around the gleaming conference table for its weekly meeting.

I rubbed my eyes—I'd had a hard time sleeping the night before. Partly it was the excitement of my second day on the job, and partly it was the lumpy mattress I'd bought on serious markdown at a discount furniture store. But I readied my pen and paper while the creative execs stopped whispering and put away their BlackBerries.

Iris scanned the checklist I'd just printed out for her. "Where are we with *Camus's Nightmare*? Does *anyone* want to direct this for us?"

From my seat along the wall, I eyed the other assistants, who also sat with notepads on their laps, facing their bosses' backs. To my immediate right was Amanda, the raven-haired girl who'd helped me in the copy room but who had yet to be actually friendly. Next to her was Cici, whose uncle was a famous screenwriter who had given up movies for writing rum-fueled diatribes for the *Huffington Post*. And past Cici was Wyman, who had traded yesterday's skinny tie in for a pair of thick, purposefully nerdy-looking glasses. He was the only one of the assistants with an actual graduate-school degree in film. He wouldn't let us forget it, either; every sentence out of his mouth referenced his time at Tisch.

It had become clear to me that Kylie, who sat in a cloud of lily perfume on my right, was the undisputed queen of the assistants. The others came by at least once a day and hovered in front of her desk, gossiping, and if they didn't have any good dirt about which creative executive at Columbia was sleeping with which junior executive at CAA, they'd just talk about *Project Runway* or *Rock of Love*. To me it seemed like wasting time; Kylie said they were "monitoring the shifts in contemporary popular culture."

"*Camus's Nightmare* has been a tough sell." This came from Tom Scheffer, a bald but extremely fit man in his late thirties. He set down his sludge-colored smoothie on the conference table with a thunk, as if to punctuate this speech. "Turns out an existential thriller set in Algeria isn't exactly pulling in the A list. We've got feelers out for Brett Ratner, but he seems pretty overcommitted. And Ben Stiller might be interested."

Iris wrinkled her nose. "Ben Stiller?"

"But then he'd have to star," Tom said.

"Well, if he thinks he can play a twenty-three-year-old jujitsu champion, then more power to him," Iris said dryly, and everyone chuckled. "But really, let's be serious. What about

Holden?" Iris continued, turning in the other direction. "Where are we with him? Lisa?"

Holden MacIntee was *Vanity Fair*'s newest cover and Hollywood's latest obsession. After starring in a small independent film that happily showcased his smoldering green-eyed gaze and Olympian physique—not to mention his not-inconsiderable talent—the twenty-three-year-old star was suddenly on everyone's short list for the next summer blockbuster.

"Spoke to Kevin yesterday," said Lisa Amorosi, a frizzy-haired executive vice president, in her Brooklyn-inflected monotone. "He said Holden is *so* sorry for canceling lunch the other day—"

"As he should be," Iris said, raising her eyebrows.

"And he likes the script, but he has reservations."

Development people hated "reservations." They usually seemed to preface some outrageous demand, like an entire script rewrite, or an additional trailer for the star's pet guinea pig.

Iris slid her glasses off her nose. "What kind of reservations?"

"He doesn't want to be typecast as, you know, a 'hunk,'" Lisa explained, applying a pair of air quotes to the word.

Iris snorted. "Has he looked in the mirror lately?"

Lisa rolled her eyes. "You know these kids. They all want to be Daniel Day-Lewis when they're really just Zac Efron."

Everyone laughed, but Iris's face had darkened.

"This isn't funny," Iris said sternly. "We need to figure out next summer *now*," she continued. "We are *not* going to be part of another *Variety* think piece on why movies are dead or mentioned in some snarky *New York* magazine story about how no one can make a decent film anymore, let alone one that critics like and people actually pay to go to."

"Did you read that Manohla Dargis thing in the *Times*—," a

young man in a linen blazer began, but Iris silenced him with a glance.

"I'm not asking for miracles, people, I just want a decent goddamned movie. Actually, that's not true. I want a great script and an A-list star, and I want them wrapped up in a package with a big red bow."

On the pad on my lap, I scribbled *Great Script/Star.* It didn't really seem all that helpful.

Iris put her hands behind her head and sighed; everyone else in the room sat up straighter. "What I do *not* want is this movie about a young boy growing up and coming to terms with his sexuality in the Dark Ages, a project which for some baffling reason has been the talk of nearly everyone I know and which Metronome is going to pass on with a sense of great satisfaction and confidence," she said. "I don't care how talented a director James Foreman is, it'll never make any money. And Andy Marcus, the screenwriter, is a demented Neanderthal. Any questions?"

I wanted to laugh, but Iris didn't look like she was in the mood for humor. I wrote *No demented Neanderthals* on my pad of paper, and beneath that drew a hairy apelike face with a big X through it, for clarity's sake. The rest of the meeting had to do with a marketing campaign for Metronome's latest kid flick, which involved a nine-year-old, a Shetland pony, and a time machine, and I admit my mind sort of drifted. There were some crassly commercial parts of this job, I realized. But hey, Hilary Swank had to have her *Next Karate Kid* before she got her *Million Dollar Baby*.

After the meeting was over, Kylie, wearing a very expensive-looking trapeze dress over another pair of skinny jeans, sidled over to my desk. "So you're going to have to do phones most of the day—Iris wants me in the Wes Anderson meeting," she said. "I hope that's cool."

I smiled and nodded, though of course I wished I could go to the meeting too. "Sure, of course. Is it all right if I leave at six?"

"Six? You got a date or something?" Kylie raised a playful eyebrow.

"We . . .," I said, a little embarrassed.

Kylie grabbed me by my wrist and pulled me into the kitchen so fast I almost slipped on the polished tile.

"Tell me everything," Kylie smiled, her voice low and coaxing.

I felt myself flush. "I was at a bar last night and this guy, he's an agent at Ingenuity, just asked me out." I felt weirdly proud of myself then—not for being asked out by a cute boy but for having a chance to impress Kylie. Not like it was such a feat, but within the world of this office, I had nothing enviable: no designer clothes, no gossip to offer up. It felt kind of nice to have some currency.

"*Who?*" Kylie squeezed my hand tighter, her perfectly manicured nails digging into my skin.

"Um, his name's Mark Lyder?"

Kylie dropped my wrist like it was suddenly hot. "Well!" she said. "Check *you* out."

"You know him?"

"Of *course.*" She waved a hand, as if it were the stupidest question she'd ever heard. "Does he know you work for Iris?"

"Yeah, he overheard me talking about it."

"Where's he taking you?"

"Koi."

"*Quel surprise.* That means 'what a surprise.' Well, don't be nervous. It'll just feed his ego. Just go in there and talk about work stuff. And *don't* go home with him, whatever you do," she said, wagging her finger like a protective mother. "You'll never hear from him again."

"Um, okay." I smiled slightly. It was kind of nice to see Kylie get all mother hen, even if I was a little old for the advice. "But what do you mean, talk about work stuff?"

"You know, bullshit. Trade info." Kylie opened the fridge and took out another Diet Coke, her fourth of the day. "Tell him about how we passed on the Dark Ages project, that kind of thing. Doesn't Ingenuity rep the writer?"

"Is it cool to say things like that?"

Kylie looked at me over the top of her soda. "Contrary to what you might think, honesty is pretty much always the best policy."

"Really?" I'd watched enough episodes of *Entourage* to know that Hollywood had its own, sometimes logic-defying, set of rules. It was just a little surprising to hear that honesty was one of them.

"Taylor." Kylie placed a hand on my arm, her green eyes suddenly softer. "You're *supposed* to talk about what's going on here. Especially with people like Mark. You give him some dirt, he'll give you some dirt. That's how this business works." She winked. "Plus, it'll make you look like you're kind of a player, you know?"

I nodded, feeling strangely pleased. I had no idea that Mark might be someone *important*. Or that he might think *I* was.

⟡

I was nervously watching the clock and chewing my finger-nails, ruining the manicure Magnolia had given me to celebrate my first day of work. It was almost 5:45, and Kylie and Iris still weren't back from their meeting with Wes Anderson. Today hadn't been a nine, as both Mark Lyder and I had hoped. It had been a seven, maybe seven and a half. On the plus side, I'd bought lunch in the commissary instead of letting my stomach basically digest itself like it had yesterday. But on the minus side, I'd eaten my sandwich surrounded by tables of people who all knew each other and who didn't seem to notice me at all.

On a piece of scrap paper, I'd made a list:

GOOD THINGS
Learned how to forward calls to other extensions.
Entered in most of the unsolicited scripts into script log.
Cut back on Diet Cokes—only had four. (They're free!)
Getting the swing of typing on BlackBerry's tiny keys.
      (Seriously, who has hands that small?)
Got Kylie to talk about boyfriend; she might be starting
      to like me. (Name: Luke Hansen. Sign: Cancer.
      Apparently he's "very sweet.")
Made Iris her spirulina smoothie; Iris claimed to like it.
Successfully faxed Jude Law's agent. Jude Law!

BAD THINGS
Got Weinsteins mixed up—Harvey currently bearded.
Brought up the carnie handbook again—Kylie not
      amused.
Kept big agent on hold too long; he told Iris, who was
      not happy.
Did not make any friends.
Realized never called copier repair guy.

I was trying to think of more good things to make me feel better when Kylie and Iris finally came in, looking pleased with themselves.

Iris disappeared with a wave into her jungle of an office, but Kylie sighed dramatically and collapsed into her Eames chair. "Oh my God, Wes Anderson can talk," she said. "And he's so small! It's like he's a ten-year-old boy. *Très bizarre.*"

I raised an eyebrow.

"Very strange," Kylie clarified. "I spent a year in France, and I like to keep my language skills fresh." From her desk drawer, she pulled out a bag of soy nuts and shook three of them into her hand.

"Ah." French was definitely not standard in my Cleveland high school, and while in college I thought it might be cool to understand what Truffaut's characters were saying, subtitles served me just fine, thank you very much.

Iris reemerged from her office, a Birkin bag that probably cost more than my Honda Civic slung casually over her shoulder.

"And *now* I'm off to meet with Paul," she said to Kylie. "I wish I had more time to talk first, but what'd you think?"

"The script?" Kylie sat up a little straighter in her chair. "Well," she said carefully, "it's not *Crash,* but at least it isn't a war movie."

"Oh, the Paul Haggis script?" I blurted, realizing what they were talking about.

Both women turned to look at me.

"That's the one," Iris said. "Why?"

"I read the first act while I was photocopying it," I explained, wondering if it was okay to admit that.

"And?"

I glanced at Kylie, who didn't seem to be blinking. "For starters, it's too long," I said. "The setup takes forever. It's going to need some serious cuts. Starting with the stage directions.

What director wants all his shots laid out for him already? Or her, of course. And I don't think the paraplegic guy is a very sympathetic character. I mean, okay, he's got a bum deal, but he doesn't have to go around throwing rocks at puppies."

They both just stared at me, and my heart thumped wildly in my chest. I'd said the wrong thing *again*.

Then Iris chuckled. "That's funny, I thought the same thing," she said. "If you have any idea on how I can say that nicely to him, call my cell," she said. "Good night, girls."

Something else to put in the "Good Things" column, I thought, my heartbeat slowing down. I put my computer to sleep and stood up. "Well," I said to Kylie, "I guess I should get going too."

Kylie offered me a little frown. "Why?"

"I have a date, remember?"

Kylie shook two more soy nuts into her hand, popped them in her mouth, and then froze in midchew, a stricken look in her bottlegreen eyes. "Oh my God," she said. "Oh my God."

"What?" I put down my purse.

"I completely spaced. Quinn's driver is sick, and someone has to take her to her math tutor's tonight." Kylie chewed again, slowly, still in shock. "I can't believe I forgot."

"Isn't she sixteen?" I asked. "Shouldn't she have a Mercedes of her own by now?"

Kylie shook her head. "She doesn't have her license yet. Oh, Taylor, can you . . . ?" She left the rest of the sentence to my imagination.

"But," I said, feeling desperate, "I have to meet Mark."

Kylie gestured to the legal pad on her desk. "And I have to type up all these notes for Iris's breakfast tomorrow with the chairman. He's going to ask her about this meeting." Kylie flipped the pages with her fingers. "Look at all this," she said helplessly. "Taylor, I'm really sorry I forgot. But you can postpone a date, and I can't postpone tomorrow's meeting. I mean, this is just one of those things . . ."

"Okay," I said quietly. "That's fine, I guess."

"Just call Mark and tell him you'll be a little late," Kylie said. "He'll respect that. Besides, it'll keep him on his toes." She lit the candle on her desk and took a deep breath with her eyes closed. "And make sure you Google map everything," she said. "When you're new here, there's nothing worse than getting lost in L.A."

CHAPTER FIVE

By the time I got to Iris's house in Beverly Hills, it was already almost seven. Even with the directions printed out, I'd gotten turned around on Santa Monica Boulevard and had to double back, with everyone honking at me because I had the audacity to drive the speed limit instead of twenty miles over it. But I was proud of myself for not getting too profoundly lost; as my dad liked to say, I had the directional abilities of a four-year-old.

Iris's house was a sprawling Mediterranean with a freshly painted stucco exterior and a tiled terra-cotta roof. The air was sweet with the smell of September flowers. In the center of the front lawn was a majestic fountain in the shape of three very beautiful, very busty nymphs. Rudolph Valentino would approve, I thought, climbing out of my Civic and wincing as the front door made its habitual loud squawk.

I'd bought the car, a 1999 model, for two grand from a guy on Craigslist, and so far, barring that hinge (and the fact that it lacked a GPS system, which I really could have used), I was very happy with it.

I picked my way up the flagstone path to the front door, past an orgiastic cluster of roses and the burbling fountain. I rang the doorbell and waited. I thought I could hear music from inside, but no one came to answer. After two more rings and almost three minutes, I felt myself starting to get annoyed. If Quinn had to get to her math tutor's so badly, wouldn't she be ready with her protractor, or at least be somewhere she could hear the bell? I paced around in front of the door. I took a deep breath and turned the door handle.

"Hello?" I called.

When still no one appeared, I tiptoed down a long, narrow foyer, past black-and-white line sketches in heavy gilt frames, following the music, which sounded suspiciously like Salt-N-Pepa. I almost smiled. Quinn was into old school! Though she probably only knew about them from *I Love the '80s* on VH1.

Eventually I came to a large, dimly lit den. Deep cream-colored sofas flanked a huge fireplace ringed in Italianate tile. In the corner, *The Hills* flickered on a flat-screen TV, and from invisible speakers came the unmistakable chorus of "Let's Talk About Sex."

"It's *totally* brutal," a girl was saying. "He was like, going to talk to her about it or whatever, but then she just tells him straight up—yeah, I totally hooked up with Chas and I want to do it again. So he goes straight for his dad's gin and his mom's Vicodin, you know what I mean?"

The voice was coming closer, and so I stood there, waiting to be discovered, hoping I wouldn't scare the girl to death.

"I know, he was a total wreck. I was like, um, I'm sorry, I totally feel for you and everything, but you've really got to grow a pair. . . . That's not harsh! She's obviously a first-degree slut."

The girl, when she came around the corner, caught sight of

me, and her mouth fell open. Like her mother, Quinn was very tall, and she had the same auburn hair, which she'd swept up into a carelessly tousled knot and secured with a pencil. But there the resemblance ended. Her eyes were a startlingly pale shade of blue, her lips were large and full, and her nose was . . . the word I kept thinking of was *fierce*. Or *proud*—that was nicer, wasn't it? She was not what you'd call pretty, but there was something commanding about her, something much older than sixteen.

I lifted my hand in a little wave. From across the room, Quinn's wide-set eyes met mine with an intense, seemingly instinctual dislike. She rubbed one bare foot against her calf, showing off navy blue–polished toenails.

"Um, can I call you back?" she whispered into her iPhone. "There's somebody, um . . . *here*. Okay. Later." She clicked off.

"Hi, " I said, "your mother—"

"Who are you and how'd you get in here?" Quinn held her head very high and proud on her long neck.

"I'm Taylor, your mom's new assistant. I rang the bell and no one answered, so I let myself in. I was told that I needed to take you to a math lesson."

Quinn's eyes slithered over me coolly, and she put a hand on her hip. "Where's Kylie?"

"She couldn't make it tonight," I said. "She sent me in her place."

"Right, she's not the second assistant anymore. I bet she loves that." Quinn smirked. "So do you like eavesdropping on people? Is that a job skill these days?"

Iris seemed to glow whenever she mentioned her daughter, so I was rather taken aback by Quinn's aggressive tone. "Really, I didn't hear anything," I promised. Except that her friend Chas liked to mix gin and Vicodin. When I was in high school, the craziest combination I ever tried was Bud Light and clove cigarettes.

Quinn stopped balancing on one foot, walked into the room, and flopped down on one of the cream-colored sofas. "You don't really look like the Metronome type."

"Well, we can't all look like supermodels." I shrugged. Then I worried that Quinn would take offense at that—like, she might think I was implying that neither of us was pretty. Because actually, maybe Quinn could be one of those slightly odd looking supermodels.

Quinn snorted. "*Kylie,*" she said. "Personally, I can't stand Kylie."

I was startled. She and Quinn seemed like they'd be BFFs. "Why not?"

"Because my mother loves her and today I hate everything my mother loves. Also because I think she's secretly a raging bitch." She idly opened and closed her phone. "Most people are, you know."

I couldn't help myself. "You're a little jaded for someone in high school."

Quinn stuck her feet in the air and wiggled her blue-painted toes. "I'm just a realist."

"I don't know. When I was your age—"

"Spare me," Quinn said, slicing a long-fingered hand through the air. "Please."

I blinked, slightly wounded. Well, it wasn't Quinn I had to impress, I told myself; it was Quinn's mother. And Mark Lyder, if I ever made it to my date. All I had to do now was get Quinn to her tutor's.

I took a step toward the door. "Should we get going? Your tutor's waiting."

Quinn waved her hand again, this time nonchalantly. "Maybe I'll cancel," she said.

"You can't," I said. "It's too late."

Quinn pulled herself up off the couch then and flounced past me toward the front door, where she slipped on a pair of daisy-printed flip-flops and shouldered a studded white leather bag. "Are you coming?" she said. "God."

Outside she sniffed disapprovingly at my car and slid into the backseat. I would have thought that I'd outgrown that whole high school insecurity thing, but as it turned out, taking flak from a snide sixteen-year-old was still a surefire way to feel like crap. And Quinn wasn't even *born* when Salt-N-Pepa were popular. Somehow that made me feel even worse.

Traffic was bad on Santa Monica Boulevard. Most of the time Quinn was busy with her phone, interrupting her texting only to ask me to change the radio station or complain about how slow we were going. I tried to engage her in a little friendly conversation but was quickly made to understand that she had very little to say to me. She wasn't rude, exactly; she just made it clear that she thought I was a complete and utter nobody. It was all very *Mean Girls*.

But when we got to her destination, she suddenly reached out and touched my shoulder.

"Thanks," she said. "You're way better than Kylie."

I didn't know how or why she'd come to that conclusion, but I was happy to take it and run.

CHAPTER SIX

Welcome to Koi. May I—"

Before he could finish his sentence, I shoved my car keys into the deeply tanned valet's hand and dashed past him toward the restaurant. When I'd called, Mark hadn't seemed to mind postponing our tête-à-tête, but I'd told him 7:30, and now it was 8:00.

I ran past the velvet rope and the bouncer and up the steps to the teak and bamboo patio. A cluster of girls in minute skirts giggled over pastel-colored drinks in tall glasses. I knew that Koi wasn't the hot spot it had once been, but it was still a far cry from the diners on Middletown's main drag. The restaurant looked like a Japanese garden as imagined by some modernist sculptor, its soaring ceilings and airy rooms somehow still intimate, dim, and leafy. Candles flickered on every flat surface, lighting everyone (including me, I hoped) with a flattering glow.

Across from the hostess stand, three tanned girls with caramel hair and pouty lips leaned against the wall, drawing carnivorous

looks from a couple of guys in open-necked shirts sipping im-
ported beers at the bar. To the guys' left was Mark, perched on a
teak stool, busily tapping into his iPhone. I tried to slip by him on
my way to the bathroom to make sure I looked less harried than
I felt—he could wait three more minutes for me to put on a little
MAC Creme de la Femme, couldn't he?—but he looked up and
saw me.

"Hey, tardy," he said, standing up. I swear his brown eyes
twinkled as they took me in, and a dimpled smile crept across his
face. He leaned in and kissed me once on each cheek, and I could
feel the tickling brush of stubble against my skin. He was even
cuter than I remembered him being, and younger looking too. In
his slightly too large suit, he looked less like an agent and more
like a college kid playing dress-up.

"I finally made it," I sighed, wiping imaginary sweat from my
brow. "Thanks for waiting."

"I was starting to get worried you'd found another tour
guide."

He scanned the room behind me, as if he were looking for this
imaginary tour guide. I saw him notice the three girls by the
hostess stand.

"You think they're triplets?" I asked, nodding to the girls.
"Or do they just have the same hairdresser and the same plastic
surgeon?"

"You're funny, tardy," Mark said. He glanced over at the Barbie
look-alike behind the bar. "One pitcher of cold sake and some
edamame." He smiled back at me. "You drink sake, right?"

"Right now I would drink anything," I said, leaning back on
my bar stool.

"I thought we agreed today was going to be a nine. Tell Dr.

Mark what happened," he teased, easing into his seat. "What was exciting?" He took a final swig of his beer and pushed it away.

I looked up at his open, smiling face. He seemed genuinely interested, and I was grateful to him.

I shrugged, trying to remember what I'd even done today. I was still feeling rattled by my car ride with Quinn, and work seemed like ages ago. "I worked the phones by myself while Kylie was in a really long meeting."

"Well that's something," he said. "But it's not exactly what I'd call *exciting*."

"Me either," I admitted.

The bartender placed a stoneware pitcher between us, along with two tiny ceramic cups. Mark splashed a little sake into each, and we raised them in a toast. I tilted my head back and let the clear liquid slide down my throat. The sake tasted like rubbing alcohol and burned on its way down. I had to stop myself from making a face—I didn't want Mark to know I'd never had sake before. I was more of a wine and vodka girl. But really, I thought, why would anyone drink this? Iris's nasty green smoothie probably tasted better.

"Cheers," Mark said. "Now you've got to tell me something juicy. You must have at least one good story."

I took another sip of sake. It didn't taste any better, but I thought if I kept drinking it, maybe it would. That usually worked with cheap red wine, anyway, and I had the obligatory lamp-shade-on-my-head pictures to prove it.

"Well, there's this project you might be familiar with . . ." I could tell I'd piqued Mark's interest by the way he sat back, looking only vaguely curious. Bad poker face, I thought. Or maybe he just wasn't worried about fooling me.

I told him what Iris had said about the Dark Ages project, and the terrible writer. "I actually drew a picture of a Neanderthal with an X through it," I laughed. "As if I'd ever forget."

Mark laughed, but I could tell he was surprised, and maybe a little bit bummed, by the news—after all, if Ingenuity repped Andy Marcus, Mark probably did feel some loyalty to him. He refilled my cup, lost in thought. To change the subject, I asked him what he was working on.

He pushed the edamame bowl at me. "Here, have a little protein. I can't eat too much soy. It makes dudes grow breasts."

I looked at the little green pods, sitting innocuously in their ceramic bowl. "You're lying."

"Scout's honor." He put a hand to his pin-striped chest, and the funny but endearing image of Mark Lyder as an actual Boy Scout popped into my head. "But anyway, since you so politely asked, I'll tell you that I'm working on the next *Mission: Impossible*."

"Literally? Or, like, you're just working on an impossible project?"

"It's more like *Mission: Impossible* meets *Casino Royale* meets *Ocean's Eleven*. Think Will Smith, the Afflecks, Jake Gyllenhaal, Colin Farrell, and George Clooney." Mark ticked the names off an imaginary list.

I chewed a few edamame. "Are there any women in it?"

"Women?" Mark said. He knit his dark brows.

"Yes. Like, people without a Y chromosome?"

He took some edamame out of the bowl, inspected the little green pods thoughtfully, and then placed them on his napkin. "Jessica Biel has a small part, I believe. But this is a heist-kidnapping-action thing—it doesn't need women, unless you count female extras with large breasts in tight dresses they're only too happy to take off. It needs good explosions and fast getaway vehicles, which it's got in spades. I predict two hundred mil at the b.o."

"Sounds . . . blockbuster-y." I couldn't help but think about *Journal Girl,* which had no big stars, a budget of seven million, and scenes that could still make me cry even though I'd seen it fifty times and knew every line of dialogue forward and back.

"That's the plan. So why were you so late tonight, anyway? Did you break the copier again?" His eyes were laughing but in a flirty way.

"Oh, no." I took another small sip of sake, wishing I could subtly send a *Call copier repair guy* e-mail to myself on my BlackBerry. "It's just that Kylie totally spaced and sprang this errand on me at the last minute."

Mark was looking past me toward the door again. The surgically enhanced triplets were gone, replaced instead by two girls who could have been their cousins. "I'm pretty sure she didn't space."

"What do you mean?"

His BlackBerry—yes, I realized, he had a BlackBerry *and* an iPhone—rang on the bar. After a quick glance at it, Mark turned it off, but its red message light blinked on and off like a warning. "She did that on purpose," he said lightly. "She didn't space."

I frowned—I had a hard time imagining Kylie being so devious. And after all, she did have those notes to type up. "How are you so sure?"

Mark smiled, as if I were extremely amusing. "Hollywood is like high school," he said gently.

"What are you talking about?" I asked, confused. After all,

according to Hollywood, even *high school* wasn't like high school. I mean, really, did pretty boys like Zac Efron dance around in your hallways?

"It's one of those clichés that's actually true," Mark said. "The jocks and the cheerleaders rule the school. They're the ones who get their movies made. They find the best projects, they sign the best clients, and they end up on top."

I raised my eyebrows. I wasn't really buying it. "What about everyone else?"

"They don't survive. They get weeded out." He took a long sip of sake.

"So you're saying that people don't succeed because they're not cool?"

"Because they're not *tough*," Mark corrected as he poured both of us more of that rubbing alcohol they were trying to pass off as a delicious Japanese beverage.

"But what about talent?" I asked. "Isn't that why people get ahead?"

Mark shook his head. "Most of the time talent's not that important, Taylor. Sometimes it's not important at all. Attitude is where it's at. And a sense of style doesn't hurt either." He looked, rather pointedly I thought, at my humble mall garb.

I considered his argument and quickly dismissed it. "But at Wesleyan——," I began, ready to share my "they come around eventually" theory, but Mark cut me off with a laugh.

"I know what you're going to say, and yeah, I went to Vassar, but Hollywood's a different world. The self-righteous b.s. doesn't work here. You went to school with people who were losers in high school. Now you're with the popular kids, and they do care about things other than talent." He pronounced the word *talent* like it was a ridiculous, outdated notion, like I'd just asked about the tooth fairy.

"You're just being cynical," I said finally. "Also, come on. What about the AV nerds? Don't they get to become camera guys or something?"

Mark laughed again. "Look, you seem like a nice person, Taylor, and that's only going to hurt you. You've got to be tougher and a lot less nice. Take it from a captain-of-the-football team type."

I raised an eyebrow, amused. *Is that what you think you are?* And if he was captain of the football team, what was I?

The fact was, I had never been all that cool. I wasn't *uncool*, but I wasn't homecoming queen either. In fact, I hadn't even gone to my own prom. If there were two types of girls in the world—those who were nice and those who were not—I'd always been in the first camp. I'd been friendly with almost everyone in my high school class, even the goths and the loners and the kid who wore a suit to school because he traded stocks on the Web in his free time.

"I just had a thought. I live right around the corner from Mulberry Street. Best pizza in L.A. You want to get out of here?" Mark's eyes searched mine as if nervously gauging my reaction. But the look behind them said he didn't doubt for a second I'd say yes.

"Thanks," I said carefully, "but I should probably be getting home. I have another big day ahead of me. Hopefully it'll be a nine." I smiled tightly. The idea of going back to Mark's place—even being in the *vicinity* of Mark's place—was about as appealing to me right now as sitting through two hours of every action star on the planet blowing stuff up. With a wet dog on my lap.

"Okay," he said shortly, standing up. "Then we'll do it another time."

He kissed me again, but this time it felt forced. And he only
hit one cheek. As I threaded through the crowd, I was already
imagining the letter I'd write to Michael Deming. *Remember that
joke you told on Letterman? How the difference between a pit bull
and a Hollywood agent is just jewelry? I thought of that tonight. Not
that the guy was a pit bull, really. He was more like a Lab—you
know, sort of enthusiastic and undiscerning—crossed with a . . .*

God, I said to myself, you sound like Magnolia.

As I exited Koi and the cool September air hit my cheeks, I
almost—*almost*—felt a little sorry for Mark. How often did the
captain of the football team get turned down by the head of the
yearbook committee?

CHAPTER SEVEN

ris Whitaker's office, can you hold for a minute?"

I hit the orange hold button and ripped open the packet of Advil with my teeth. My head felt like someone had put it in a vise and was slowly and maliciously turning the lever to tighten it. Sake, it turns out, is dreadful to drink and worse to recover from. I'd only had a couple glasses of it, but I should have eaten something besides a handful of edamame if I wanted to avoid a hangover.

It was still early, before eight-thirty, and Kylie wasn't in yet. I picked up the line. "Thanks for holding, may I take a message?"

The line was dead. "Shit," I said. Dropping a call was even worse than saying Iris was out of the office. I'd heard of people getting fired for that, though maybe that was Cici trying to scare me.

Then I heard high heels clicking down the hallway toward me. Iris. She was early—usually she came in at nine-thirty—and, from the sound of it, in a serious hurry.

I put a bright smile on my face as Iris blew into the room like a well-heeled hurricane. "Good morning," I said as cheerfully as possible.

Iris didn't smile back. "Can you come into my office please?" she said flatly, then disappeared behind her wall of plants.

I panicked, figuring she'd somehow found out I dropped the call. But how? Maybe she had the room on surveillance camera, or maybe she had a special superpower that alerted her whenever one of her assistants did something stupid. Though admittedly, if that were true, she'd have called me into her office long before this morning. Besides the copier incident, I had also a) walked into the men's room *again*, b) lost half a script that I'd talked Kylie into letting me read, necessitating a slightly embarrassing call to the agent repping it, and c) called Tom Scheffer "Tim," much to his dismay. Anyway, I stood with some difficulty—the Advil sure wasn't kicking in yet—and entered the jungle of Iris's office.

She sat behind her desk, calmly reading the *Los Angeles Times*. "Close the door," she said tonelessly, her eyes on the paper.

I obeyed her, closing it with a gentle but ominous click. "For some reason the phones have been going crazy this morning," I said, "but I've almost gotten everything on the call sheet."

Iris looked over at me. Her eyes seemed especially glittery this morning, cold and hard like agates. "I've been an executive at this company for fifteen years," she said, carefully folding the Calendar section. "Longer than even I expected. Do you know how many assistants I've had in all that time?" She cocked her head slightly.

It was a rhetorical question, but the eerily composed tone of Iris's voice made it seem important. I tried to do the math. "Twenty-five?"

"Almost thirty-two." Iris smiled faintly at the number. Then she leaned forward and clasped her hands, as if she were about to share a secret. "Sometimes they leave of their own volition. But most often they are *asked* to leave."

I gulped and could almost feel the Advil still lodged in my throat. I didn't like where this conversation was going at all.

Iris stood up and walked to the window, looking out over the soundstages, her back facing me. In a dark tailored suit, she cut a crisp silhouette. "Did you tell someone at Ingenuity that I said Andy Marcus was a deranged monkey, or whatever it was I said?"

Demented Neanderthal, I thought but didn't say. And yes, I had. Oh God. Mark Lyder. That sake-drinking pretty boy with his Aveda hair and his too-large suit. He'd gone and blabbed what I'd told him.

"This business is run on relationships, Taylor," Iris said icily, still not facing me. "We have to preserve goodwill at all times. We never, *never* tell someone that we hate their project. We tell them that it's great but that we're overcommitted. We tell them that we love it but that we've got something similar in the works. We tell them it's genius but we're just not bold enough to pick it up. But we most emphatically do *not* tell people things that make them angry. We do not insult people to their faces, and when we insult them behind their backs, we expect that insult to remain confidential. Is that clear?"

I nodded, but then I realized that she couldn't see me. "Yes, Ms. Whitaker," I whispered.

"You're my assistant, Taylor. Of anyone here, I need to trust *you*. I thought you understood your responsibility."

"I'm so sorry," I said. "I didn't mean it. I didn't . . . ," I stuttered. I didn't know what else to say.

Still Iris faced out over the studio lots, her hands laced behind her back. And as I stood there, waiting for her to turn around and fire me, I felt a sudden swelling of self-defense. I *am* a nice person, I thought. I never would have said those mean things about Andy Marcus . . . if Kylie hadn't told me to. *Kylie*. Her moment of sisterly advice in the kitchen replayed itself in my head with a flash. *Trade info. Honesty is pretty much always the best policy.* I winced involuntarily.

But what pained me most about the memory wasn't Kylie's manipulation—it was how easy a target I'd made myself. She'd handed me the rope, but I'd tied the noose and brought my own step stool. How could I have been so stupid?

"You know," I said, my voice stronger. It was simple—I'd just explain to Iris what Kylie had said, and we'd start over. "It wasn't my idea. Kylie—"

"I don't want to hear it." Iris cut me off with a raised, steady hand. "I am not a referee, Taylor. And if the two of you can't get along, this is not going to work out." She let out a deep breath and finally turned to face me. "Now, I'm not going to fire you," she said calmly.

My heart lurched at the word, like a runaway roller coaster that at the very last second doesn't crash.

"But if you make one more mistake like this, I will let you go without a second's thought. Is that clear?"

I nodded. *Crystal.* I stood very still on the plush carpet, afraid to move, as if I were literally on thin ice.

"I have quite a day of damage control ahead of me," Iris said. A slight grimace came across her pretty mouth as she probably imagined all the sucking up she'd have to do today.

There was a soft, polite knock on the door.

"Yes?" Iris called.

Kylie's face appeared in the doorway. "Iris, Quinn's on line two," she chirped. Her alert, duplicitous green eyes bounced from Iris to me and back again. It wasn't hard to figure out what had just happened. For a second, she almost seemed to smile.

"All right, tell her one moment," said Iris, running a hand through her perfectly coiffed red hair.

Kylie ducked out, and had I had anything in my hands, I swear I would have thrown it after her. I had never felt so angry in my life, even when Magnolia's dachshund peed on my laptop freshman year. Kylie had tried to *ruin* me.

"Taylor, do we understand each other?" Iris asked, her eyes finally softening.

"Yes," I said.

"You can go. I have to speak to my daughter now."

I thought then about Quinn and her haughty, adolescent attitude. Quinn would call Andy Marcus a demented Neanderthal right to his face if she felt like it—I had no doubt about that. She'd enjoy crushing his ego. But she never would have fallen for a trick like the one Kylie had played on me. She was only in high school, but Quinn was way too sly. It had only taken an hour of sitting in traffic, trying to get her to her tutor's house, to figure that out.

But then, maybe that was exactly it. Hollywood is like high school. I walked out toward my desk, my mind racing. The Advil was kicking in, and I was starting to formulate a plan.

Dear Michael, I wrote on an imaginary postcard. *I'm learning things already.*

CHAPTER EIGHT

It wasn't hard to find Pinkberry; a line of teenage girls and yoga pants–clad moms snaked out of the front door and onto the sidewalk. I contemplated joining them—I could use a little snack myself. But I reminded myself that a) I wasn't here to eat, and b) I didn't even like Pinkberry. (All that fanfare when you could just put a Dannon in the freezer.) So instead I walked slowly along the length of the line, searching for a familiar face.

It was another gorgeous September day, and the stately oak trees and brick-faced buildings of Larchmont Village made me feel, for a second, like I was back in Connecticut, before I'd even dared imagine I'd move to L.A. But I was also aware of a kind of creeping anxiety that I'd never had back then. The stakes were higher now.

A few girls in the Pinkberry line gave me dirty looks; they probably thought I was hoping to cut in. Finally I spotted my quarry: three teenage girls in designer sunglasses and extremely short gray kilts, one blonde, one a brunette, and one the redhead I was looking for.

"Oh my God, I'm so in love with that server," the blonde said, tossing her hair over her shoulder.

"Adorable," said the brunette. She shrugged her distressed leather bag up higher on her shoulder. "He's like, twenty-two?"

Quinn snorted. She wore gigantic Chanel wraparounds and a tight purple T-shirt with an exploding heart across the chest. I was fairly sure that wasn't part of the Carleton School for Girls uniform. "Oh come on," she said, her voice low and deadpan. "You're going to date a guy who works at Pinkberry?" She stirred what looked like a white stew of crumbled Oreos and Cap'n Crunch and then put a spoonful into her mouth.

According to the schedule outlined in my assistant's manual (aka bible, handbook, and list of miscellaneous yet crucial information: the names of Iris's sister's children, for example, and her favorite place to get cupcakes), Quinn Whitaker got out of class at the Carleton School for Girls at three-thirty. Then, most days, she came here to Larchmont Village, a quaint cluster of shops, yoga studios, and restaurants, for Pinkberry and shopping. At five, her driver—providing he wasn't sick, of course, thereby forcing yours truly to perform his duties—picked her up and took her home. After telling Kylie that I had a doctor's appointment, I'd come here today on a mission. But now that I was in the same vicinity as Quinn, part of me wanted to crawl to my Civic and hide in the trunk. Now or never, I told myself and took a deep breath.

"Hey Quinn," I called out. "Can I talk to you for a sec?"

Quinn turned toward me and froze. So did her friends.

I slipped off my sunglasses. "It's Taylor," I said. "We met last night?"

Quinn still didn't move, and she gave no indication that she recognized me at all. *Remember how you made fun of my car?* I could ask. *Remember how you sat in the backseat and sighed at every red light?* Her friends had their hands on their hips and were probably giving me Medusa-like stares underneath their enormous D&G shades.

The brunette leaned over and whispered, "Was she at Hyde?"

Quinn apparently decided that playing dumb wasn't the answer. "It's my mom's assistant," she said with an exasperated sigh.

I played with the zipper of my purse, trying to ignore the fact that a sixteen-year-old had just referred to me as "It."

"Are you spying on me?" she demanded.

"No," I said in as firm a voice as possible. But really, my insides were quaking like a lactose intolerant who'd just been force-fed a tub of Pinkberry. "I just need to ask you a question."

Quinn slowly looked me up and down. With a desultory shake of her head, she ambled over to a newsstand a few feet away while her friends flounced down onto a nearby bench. A college-aged Help for the Homeless volunteer in a red vest followed her with his eyes, momentarily forgetting the petition he was trying to get passersby to sign.

"What is it?" she asked, pushing her wraparounds up to the crown of her head. Her eyes were even colder than her mother's when she was contemplating firing me.

I straightened my shoulders; I had to make my pitch count. "Okay, here's the thing," I said. "Last night you said I wasn't Metronome material. And you're right. I'm not. I'm *so* not that that I almost got fired this morning."

Quinn raised a carefully plucked brow, and I thought I saw

the glimmer of a smile play about her lips. Meanwhile her friends on the bench were staring at us.

"You said you know Kylie, right?" I said. "And you don't exactly, um, love her?"

"Yeah," Quinn said, sounding more amused. "What'd she do?"

"She tricked me into doing something—I won't go into it—but I think she's going to get me fired. She's certainly trying. And I can't let that happen. I just can't." I willed my voice not to break as I thought of how close I'd come today. I couldn't lose my job. I'd worked too hard and waited too long to get it.

Quinn crossed her arms in front of her chest. "What's this got to do with me?"

I took a deep breath. "Have you ever heard that saying 'Hollywood is like high school'?"

Quinn looked at me as if I'd just gotten up off Dr. Phil's couch.

"Okay, it doesn't matter. The point is, there are certain skills that my job seems to require—skills that have nothing to do with typing or answering phones—that I don't have. People skills. But not *nice* people skills. I think you could help teach me how to survive in this place. How to be . . . I don't know. Mean."

Quinn gave a short, hard laugh that sounded more like a bark. "Man," she said. "You must be desperate."

I nodded; I was. There was no use pretending.

She looked down at her quickly melting yogurt and swirled it contemplatively. "You've got it all wrong," she said after a minute. "It's not about being mean. It's about being confident. Not taking anyone's shit."

That certainly put a more positive spin on it. "Right," I said. "That's what I'm talking about."

Quinn was still calmly pondering her Pinkberry, swirling her Oreo bits around and around. Finally she said, "So what's in it for me?"

I chewed on the end of my plastic tortoiseshell sunglasses. I hadn't really been expecting that, but maybe I should have been. I mean, the whole helping-people-out-of-the-goodness-of-your-heart thing didn't seem all that popular here in L.A. I wasn't sure what to say. I couldn't really offer her money—for one, I didn't have any, and for two, she had *plenty*—and I could hardly offer to be her assistant too? One Whitaker was enough. And I was pretty sure she didn't need me to buy her beer or get her into an R-rated movie. What did a sixteen-year-old girl who has everything want?

"I'm not sure. Maybe if you ever need me to drive you somewhere . . . ," I said lamely.

Quinn rolled her eyes. "Please," she said. "I have a *real* driver for that." She paused. "I can come up with something better. How about we just say that you owe me a favor? Whenever I need one."

This seemed reasonable, and I began to nod. "Any idea what *sort* of favor?"

Quinn shrugged. "I don't know yet. But I'll let you know when I figure it out."

I heard a tiny voice inside my head murmuring a warning, but I happily quieted it. "Deal," I said, extending my hand.

Quinn ignored my hand and pulled the wraparounds back over her face like a mask. "We should get one thing straight," she said. "Nobody knows about this. *Nobody*. And you can't just come and find me when you want something. It's, like, stalker-y."

"Okay," I said, only slightly insulted. It wasn't like I was trying to *hang out* with her. I pulled my card out of my purse and rubbed my finger over the raised Metronome logo, the ticking line of the metronome running into the austere-looking M. I handed it to her. "Here's my e-mail, cell phone, address, everything. What about you?"

Quinn held up her palm. "I'll call *you*," she said, dropping the business card into her apple green Hervé Chapelier shoulder bag. Then she walked over to a garbage can and dropped her melted Pinkberry into the trash. "Are we done here?" she asked, and before I could answer, she sauntered, on her scuffed ballet flats, back to her friends, who were now hanging out in front of the LF store, looking snobbish and bored.

I squinted in the strong September sun with a mixture of relief and fear. Quinn had agreed to help me, but was it a batshit-crazy plan in the first place? And what if Iris found out? I couldn't think about that now, though, because right now I could see a tiny bubble of hope floating on the horizon.

I stared at the newsstand, where copies of *Vanity Fair* lined the eye-level shelf from end to end. Twenty shirtless Holden MacIntees with forty smoldering green eyes gazed back at me. Behind me, the Help for the Homeless volunteer was practically begging a woman to sign a petition. "It's a tough world out there, lady," the young man pled, "and everyone needs a little assistance!"

I slipped my five-dollar sidewalk sale sunglasses back on. I had to get back to the office soon, or Kylie would start to think the doctor had discovered something really wrong with me, like gout or syphilis. Not that she'd really mind that, I thought. In fact, she'd probably be pleased.

"Come on, give us a hand," the volunteer shouted as the woman walked away. "It's a crazy world!"

I marched back to my blue Civic with as much confidence as I could muster. Nowhere was as tough and crazy as Hollywood, I thought. I just hoped the help I'd recruited would be enough.

CHAPTER NINE

Magnolia!" I shrieked.

There was a little dog doing figure-eights on the faded blue carpet of my bedroom. It looked like a dust bunny or a filthy mop head come to life, except that it wasn't even as cute as that. When I yelled for Magnolia, it paused for a moment, gave me a querying look, and then went back to racing around the room with one of my socks in its mouth.

"Magnolia! What the hell is this?"

Its gray hair was long and greasy. From its general direction wafted up a scent so offensive that I was almost impressed. Our apartment building wasn't the cleanest I'd ever been to—the halls had dirty old Astroturf, and certain indigent West Hollywood men occasionally slept on our stoop—but this was taking things to a whole new level.

Magnolia appeared in the doorway in her bathrobe, her pretty heart-shaped face pink from a shower. "Oh, that's Cabbage! Isn't he cute?" she said, smiling at him with a look that could only be called loving.

"Cabbage?"

"Yes, he was found in the back of a cabbage truck—isn't that crazy? No one knows how he got in or where he came from. I just pulled him from the shelter. Sorry, I meant to e-mail you about it. It's just until the weekend," she said, casually scooping him up. "Until my friend has her adoption fair." She nuzzled his ratty, smelly head. "Do you want a bath, mister? Huh? Do you?"

I grabbed a bottle of perfume from my dresser and sprayed some into the room. Kate Spade's eau de parfum meets Magnolia's eau de rat-dog. "But what's he doing in my room?"

Magnolia looked up at me over Cabbage's odiferous head. "He just seems to like it in here," she said, as if that explained everything. She turned to cart the scrambling dog in her arms out of the room.

"I had a terrible day," I called, hoping for a little sympathy.

Magnolia made kissing noises into Cabbage's fur. "You know what they say," she said. "Some days you're the dog, and some days you're the hydrant. Oh, and your boxes arrived." Maybe this didn't seem sympathetic enough, so she added, "And there's Poquito Mas in the fridge."

I flopped down onto my bed, which Garbage—or Cabbage, whatever—had thankfully avoided. I'd have to hunt down the bottle of Febreze I'd bought last week, but right now I was just too exhausted. Ever since Wednesday, when I'd almost gotten fired, I'd felt like even more of an outcast at Metronome. No one spoke to me or smiled at me. Whenever I went to grab a Red Bull from the kitchen or to the bathroom (the last stall was good for a quick cry),

I felt the eyes of the other assistants silently watching, assessing me, looking for confirmation that my days were numbered. I felt like some kind of ghost. Like pretty soon some shaman or something was going to come along and exorcise me from the office. Kylie simply observed my struggles from her desk, mildly looking over her aromatherapy candle and occasionally murmuring falsely sympathetic things in French. *Tant pis,* I heard her say once when I lost a phone message I'd written on a scrap of paper instead of typing it into my computer. *Too bad.*

I pulled on a pair of Wesleyan shorts and the old tank top I used to play tennis in and dragged myself out to the living room to attack my boxes. What a way to spend a Friday night. There weren't that many packages, really—I'd been a ruthless editor of my possessions. As I cut the boxes open with a dull bread knife, it suddenly seemed as if I hadn't even sent myself enough to make my room here feel like my own. There were some books I'd thought might prove useful (*Independent Feature Film Production: A Complete Guide; Woody Allen on Woody Allen; The 101 Habits of Highly Successful Screenwriters; Leonard Maltin's Movie Guide*, etc.), a few trinkets (a framed still from *Gray Area* Professor Pinckney had given me; some pictures of my dad looking goofy and my mom looking patient, which were typical expressions for them both), some decorating items (curtains from Ikea; cute new pillows from West Elm), and the rest of my clothes, all of which looked cheap and unfashionable after a week at Metronome.

As I struggled to hang up my cheerful yellow curtains, I thought about what a crappy day it had been. Kylie had pawned call-rolling duties off on me so she could grab a leisurely lunch with a junior executive in production. Call-rolling was one of the most nerve-wracking duties of an assistant. It entailed sitting at a separate desk in Iris's office and lining up calls for her to return, one after another, with no breaks or waiting in between, because executives in the film industry had no time or patience for breaks or waiting. While on each call, Iris would communicate, via strange and sometimes baffling hand signs, to tell me when to get the next call ready. A circling wrist meant *About to wrap up*. A waving wrist meant *Get the next one on hold*. Wiggling fingers meant something like *Pretty soon I'm going to tell this person to shut the hell up*. It was incredibly stressful—I felt like a referee who didn't know the right signals. And God help me if someone got bored of being on hold and just hung up. That only happened once. Iris had simply said, "There's no one there, Taylor," and turned to her computer. But of course I felt horrible. Iris barely looked at me anymore. It was like I was a dumb, untrainable dog who wasn't even worth scolding.

I'd made a list of Good Things and Bad Things, but of course it didn't make me feel any better. How could it?

BAD THINGS
Kylie and Cici clearly talking about/laughing at me.
Iris's eyes like in that Foreigner song: cold as ice.
Broke copier again.
Cried twice. Blamed red nose on allergies.
Forced to admit had never heard phrase "lock picture."
    Can't they just say "finished movie"?

GOOD THINGS
Soup lady in commissary friendly to me. (Obviously she
    doesn't know any better.)

I put away the rest of the clothes I'd sent myself, hardly even bothering to fold them, and tucked the cute new pillows high on a bookshelf, just in case Garbage learned how to jump up on my bed. Because honestly, he looked like the kind of dog that would try to mate with my bolsters.

Then there was the box marked DVDs. I thought about how happy I'd been when I was packing them up. There I'd been, addressing this package to myself, so excited, so hopeful, so unbelievably naïve. I'd actually imagined driving down Sunset Boulevard in a convertible with the wind blowing through my hair. How unbelievably stupid was that? It's like I thought I was going to be *living* in a movie instead of trying to learn how to make one.

I unwrapped the few movies I'd deemed essential. The rest—there were hundreds—would gather dust in my old bedroom in Cleveland, where I'd shipped the rest of my belongings. There was *Say Anything . . .* (because I love that movie, cheesy Peter Gabriel song and all), *You Can Count on Me* (because not all love stories are romances), *Eternal Sunshine of the Spotless Mind* (because not all romances make sense), *Some Like It Hot* (because who doesn't love Marilyn Monroe and men in drag?), and of course there was *Journal Girl*. I had a beat-up poster of that too—though not a very big one—and I taped it up over the faded peach paint of my very first apartment, my junior year, on Warren Street.

Needless to say, Quinn hadn't called. Of course it had only been a day, but couldn't she see how desperate I was? I felt like I was back in high school, waiting for my sophomore crush to call me after we'd been assigned partners on a history project. (He never did. But we did get an A, no thanks to him.) Really, how pathetic was I, waiting for a spoiled sixteen-year-old to come rescue me?

Irony of ironies, I was supposed to meet with Dana McCafferty on Monday morning. How was I supposed to give her advice when I obviously didn't know the first thing about anything? How was it that I'd managed to screw up everything in a single week?

I stared for a while at the *Journal Girl* poster. Michael Deming had had a vision, and he hadn't let anything stop him from realizing it, I told myself. I tried to let that cheer me up. This meant I had to ignore the latter part of Michael's story, the one where he goes crazy and runs off to become Grizzly Adams in the Pacific Northwest.

❀

"Whatcha watching?" Magnolia asked a little while later, as she walked out of the bathroom with Garbage wrapped in a towel.

"*Journal Girl,*" I said. I was deep into a pint of chocolate mint ice cream.

"I should have known," Magnolia said with a wan smile as she plopped down on the sofa next to me. "The girl writes an imaginary person so many letters that she brings him to life, right?"

I nodded. I'd watched it so many times freshman year, it was a miracle Magnolia didn't have it memorized by now. She began to towel off the dog, rubbing him so hard, his fur stood on end. It looked like he'd stuck his nose in a light socket.

"I kind of did the same thing with the director," I admitted. I'd never told anyone about it in high school or college, worrying I'd sound lame, but really, what did I have to lose at this point?

"Or tried to. Michael Deming. He was sort of my pen pal." Minus the *pal* part, I thought but didn't say. "Back when I still had illusions that I'd have a career." I'd mailed him that first postcard with the Hollywood sign on it, but after that, nothing. I'd just imagined writing *Dear Michael, I had no idea I could be so clueless.*

"Stop being so hard on yourself," Magnolia said, squeezing the dog with the towel until his eyes began to look even more buggy. "That screenwriter thing wasn't your fault. Kylie set you up."

"I just wish I knew how to make it different." I went on excavating in my pint for more chocolate. "All day long I watch this girl pretend to be this amazing assistant, when I know she's in this for all the wrong reasons."

"What's she in it for?"

I thought about this. "I can't tell. But I think she's totally soulless. I think she just wants to gossip with the other assistants and suck up to Iris and go to parties and meet famous people and wear cute shoes. I don't even think she likes movies that much."

Magnolia patted my knee. "It's going to get better. Just remember: calm and assertive. Positive reinforcement for desirable behaviors. Right, Cabbage?"

The dog licked Magnolia's nose, then eyeballed mine. I shook my head at him. "No way, Trashcan," I said.

Magnolia sniffed. "He's much cleaner now," she said. "And now I'm going to take him for a walk."

After Magnolia and her beast trotted out of the apartment, the latter rubbing his electrified fur against one of my unopened boxes, I went back to my movie and let its familiar lines lull me into a kind of pleasant stupor. Sure, it was going to take a miracle to help me succeed in Hollywood, but I'd worry about it to-morrow. Right now I was going to worry about getting every last molecule of ice cream out of this tub.

I was half asleep when the doorbell buzzed. I jumped up, my heart in my throat and the empty pint of ice cream still in my hand, and made my way to the door. I threw it open, hoping it wasn't a serial killer. But then again, serial killers probably didn't ring the bell.

In a zebra-print tunic, black skinny jeans, and peep-toe suede stacked heels, Quinn stood on the doorstep, hand perched on her hip. Beside her on the floor was a gigantic Hefty bag.

Oh my God, I thought groggily. I am trash and she is bringing me *more* trash.

"Am I interrupting a binge?" Quinn asked, disdainfully eyeing my spoon and the spot of chocolate on my tank top.

"No, no, no," I said. "Come in." I wondered how bad my hair looked but figured there was nothing to be done about it now.

Quinn stepped carefully over the threshold, as if my apart-ment contained a toxic spill. "You were on my way to Hyde," she explained, dragging the Hefty bag behind her. "So I thought I'd drop some stuff off."

"Would you, um, like something to drink?" I opened the fridge. In the door was only half a quart of skim milk and a bottle of Ari-zona iced tea. I saw a barrette on the counter, though, and I clipped my hair back, hoping it made me look more presentable.

Quinn waved off the ridiculous suggestion that she would ac-tually linger. "I'm not here to hang out," she said. "My friends are waiting downstairs."

Reaching into the garbage bag, she pulled out a leopard print tunic. I read the label: Cavalli. Next she pulled out one black

Manolo wedge, and then a crushed velvet halter top in a deep burgundy, which she set on top of the TV. Finally she just overturned the bag, and filmy dresses, dark-washed skinny jeans, glittery handbags, and strappy gold sandals tumbled onto the couch. It was like Quinn was a tanned and skinny Santa Claus, but instead of toys, she was bringing me *style*.

"Oh my God." I leaned down to touch a gunmetal-gray Stella McCartney dress with fringe. "Is this stuff—"

"Mine," Quinn said, standing over the pile with her hands on her hips. "And some are my friends'. These are just all too last year."

I was trying not to dive right into the pile of clothes and kiss them. I fingered a Doo.Ri shirtdress, hardly able to speak. "Are you sure?"

Quinn shook the lustrous coppery hair out of her eyes, already glancing at the clock on the wall. "First lesson," she announced. "Fake it till you make it."

I looked up at her, still too fashion-shocked to parse her meaning.

She sighed, exasperated. "*Clothes equal attitude*. I know people are always saying that, but it's absolutely true. And there's *no* way you can have attitude in clothes from the Gap or whatever mall store you shop in." She pointed to the Stella McCartney dress. "Try that on."

Dumbly I obeyed, shimmying it up over my tank top and shorts. It was a little tight across the chest, but otherwise it was a perfect fit. I glanced at myself in the hall mirror and almost gasped. Already I looked like a different person. Put together. Decisive. Maybe even—if it weren't for the chocolate that was not just on my tank top but also *on my chin*—sexy. You know

·how when Julia Roberts gets a makeover in *Pretty Woman?* I felt like that, but maybe even better.

"Not bad," Quinn mused, walking up beside me. She adjusted one of my straps. "You'll have to go through it all, though. You might find something even better." She squeezed a tube of bubble gum–colored lip gloss over her lips. "All right, I have to go," she said. "But don't forget: fake it till you make it," she repeated.

"Thank you," I whispered, still awestruck. I ran my hands down the silky bodice of the Stella dress and sighed.

"Give me a couple months, and you'll be a new person," she said. "Oh, and here." She pulled a shiny black iPhone out of her purse and handed it to me. "We had an extra one lying around the house. From now on I'm going to be texting you, and I'm sure the phone you have is from, like, 2001 or something."

I didn't want Quinn to know how right she was—my old Nokia, now retired, was sitting in a shoebox under my bed—so I pulled my BlackBerry proudly out of my purse. "Actually, I have—," I began, but Quinn cut me off with a hand wave.

"No, I don't want you trying to contact me and accidentally contacting my mom. This needs to be OTR. *Off the record?*" She raised her eyebrows at my perplexed look.

Quinn stepped gingerly back toward the hallway, avoiding my boxes and trying her best not to touch anything. "You *do* know it smells like a homeless person lives in here, right?" I opened my mouth to explain about the wet dog, but she'd already closed the door behind her.

I surveyed the pile of clothes on the couch and then the sleek iPhone in my hand. I felt like Cinderella herself. Already the playing field between me and my wicked stepsister had leveled a little.

CHAPTER TEN

Morning," I called brightly to Shara, the Metronome receptionist, as she bent over her *Us Weekly*. "Happy Monday!"

Shara pushed back her shiny ebony hair and looked at me for a
long time. "Morning," she finally said, but she sounded confused.

That gave me pause. Had I spilled my triple nonfat latte no
whip on myself? Was the Stella dress too tight across my chest?
Did I look absurd, like a bear in a tutu? I rushed down the hall to
my desk, threw my purse into a drawer, and ran into the bathroom.

And there, in the cold, blue, unflattering light, I saw what
Shara had seen: the gunmetal gray dress made my eyes an intriguing blue gray rather than their usual light blue; the dress's
clean lines hugged my curves perfectly; I looked classy, polished,
and stylish. I looked so good, I almost didn't look like myself. I
breathed a great sigh of relief and offered a silent thank-you to
Quinn. I might have even texted her, but I didn't want to push
my luck. And besides, I really hadn't gotten the hang of typing

on my iPhone's tiny touch screen and would probably write *tgsnk tui* by accident.

At eight o'clock sharp, Shara called from the lobby to say that Dana McCafferty had arrived, and a few moments later the writer herself came hurrying toward my desk, all smiles and gratitude. She was short and what most people would call plain: her hair was cut in a straight brown bob, and wire-framed glasses somewhat enlarged her already sizable brown eyes.

"Thank you so much," she said to me, not even waiting for an introduction. "Really, it's such a relief just to know that someone has even read my work."

"Have a seat," I said, motioning to the chair I'd situated next to my desk.

She sank gratefully into it, crossed her ankles, and slid her Converse under her chair. Her feet barely touched the floor. "Nice offices," she said. "I like the whole pulsing colored wall business."

I smiled—it had impressed me too. "I really liked your script," I said, getting down to business. I'd brought it to bed with me last night, thinking I'd just read the first act, but had enjoyed it so much, I stayed up late to finish. "More than I thought I would." I flipped through the pages. "It reminded me of Cameron Crowe with a little Diablo Cody thrown in."

Dana flushed at the compliment but opened her spiral notebook and readied her pen. She looked like an eager student on the first day of school.

"The premise is great," I continued. "Guy needs to help his parents break away from him before he can break away from them. And you've got great dialogue. But you've got to focus the story. Right now I don't know who I'm supposed to identify with: the parents or the son."

I sipped my latte while she wrote, enjoying the quiet of the office early in the morning. I wondered if, among the piles of unread, unrepresented scripts on the bookshelf, there were any others as good as Dana's.

"And your second act kind of tapers off," I went on. "But that's always the hardest part. Raising the stakes as we get to know the characters. You know, like in *Juno*? She had to keep getting to know the couple a little better each time before the final scene when they break up?"

Dana nodded eagerly. Sitting there, her Converse sneakers dangling off the floor, she looked like an earnest ten-year-old— the Curious George T-shirt put her over the edge—trying desperately to get an A. Sometimes she interrupted me to ask questions, but mostly she just listened and wrote. The more I talked, the more confident I became—it was a relief to be able to talk movies with someone who was actually listening. It brought me back to the warm comfort of hours spent in small classrooms at Wesleyan, hashing out details of our favorite movies rather than breaking down complicated film theory. I told Dana that the meet-cute didn't quite work, the best friend character wasn't that interesting, and the dream sequence was a little too *Being John Malkovich*. All the while, she scribbled furiously.

Finally she looked up and pushed her glasses up her tiny nose. "Wow," she said. "This is so amazing. I can't thank you enough for taking the time to meet with me. I'm sure you must be extremely busy."

"You've got something good," I told her, meaning it. "I think you can have something great."

She blushed and ducked her head. It occurred to me then that she thought I was someone far more important than I was. Oh my God, I said to myself, *Fake it till you make it* was working!

I was feeling pretty pleased with myself until I heard the sound of Iris and Kylie's voices coming down the hall. Suddenly it seemed prudent to send Dana away as quickly as possible.

"Actually, Dana, I do need to get going," I said, nodding toward my computer. "Lots of e-mails to go through . . ."

Iris and Kylie breezed into the room. They came to a dead stop at the sight of Dana McCafferty, who blushed a deep scarlet.

"Hello," Iris said. She turned to look at me, and her expression was suspiciously cheerful. "Are we interrupting something?"

"Iris, this is Dana," I said politely, as if I were the host of an impromptu cocktail party. "She sent in a script, and I was just giving her some notes."

"Oh," Iris said, staring once again at Dana. "How nice."

I could see Dana swallowing, maybe trying to work up the courage to pitch Iris. I fervently hoped she wouldn't—really, we were both on thin ice—but whether or not she meant to, she lost her chance when Iris turned and ducked into her office. Kylie plopped down at her desk and booted up her computer, but I could feel her staring at the back of my neck.

Dana watched Iris's closed door for a moment and then reached for her JanSport. "So can I send you another draft?" she asked. "Incorporating your notes?"

"Sure," I said. With Kylie there, I was suddenly afraid to say more.

"Okay, great," Dana said, hitching her backpack over both her shoulders. "Thanks again."

The moment Dana was gone, Iris came out of her office again.

Kylie was giving me that special frown she seemed to reserve for me, but Iris's face was blank.

"I'm sorry about that," I said. "She called last week, I didn't really know what to say—"

"I told you to get her off the phone," Kylie supplied, adjusting the low gold belt she wore over a draped jersey dress.

"I tried, but she was kind of persistent, and I really didn't mind—"

Iris held up her hand. "Taylor, you know we're not here to give notes on spec scripts. This isn't a writer's workshop we're running."

I nodded. My heart did a swan dive into my stomach.

"Though I have to say, I am impressed with your hustle." Iris gave me a small wink. "But let's not get ahead of ourselves. It's only your second week."

"I understand."

Iris retreated into her office again, leaving me with Kylie.

"You're lucky she's in a good mood today," Kylie said. "That could have been ugly." She sat down delicately in her chair and crossed one tanned leg over the other. Then she lit her aromatherapy candle with her Chateau matches and closed her eyes and sniffed.

Casually I stood up, allowing her the full view of my new ensemble, and just as she was about to open her mouth to say something, I pulled out my new iPhone and looked at the screen.

"It's going to be hot today," I said, flashing her the weather page and smiling.

Kylie clamped her mouth closed again, and for a moment it was as if we'd switched places.

I didn't know much French, but I knew the word *victoire*.

CHAPTER ELEVEN

Um, where exactly *are* you?"

Even over the phone, Kylie's cool, imperious voice made my skin crawl.

"When I said run to Whole Foods, I meant the one on *Fairfax*. Not Bundy, for God's sake."

I balanced my iPhone between my ear and shoulder. "I'm pulling in now," I said as I made the turn into Metronome's black iron scrollwork gates. "I'll be in the office in two minutes."

"And you remembered to get the Toujours Jeune spirulina from France, not the generic kind, right?"

"How could I forget?" I asked, pouring sarcasm into my voice like sugar into coffee. Seriously, did she have to be so Shannen Doherty in *Heathers*? That morning at eight, a text had come in on my cell:

Need to do a run for spirulina at WF before work! Sorry I spaced!! ☺ K

That smiley face made me want to poke a hole in my new phone, even though I loved loved loved it.

A few minutes later, I walked, sweaty and annoyed, into the overly air-conditioned lobby of the creative department, grateful for the Alaskan temperature. "Hey, Shara," I called out as I swiped my ID. "What's Britney up to now?"

Shara chewed on the end of her pencil and looked even more confused than she had yesterday. But after a minute she smiled, which was encouraging; it was about as nice as anyone had ever been to me around here.

"See ya," I offered as I pulled open the glass door.

Wyman, the holier-than-thou Tisch nerd, came barreling out of his office with a stack of scripts in one hand and a supersized coffee in the other. He nearly ran into me, but even in my new red Weitzman wedges, I managed to duck out of the way.

"Sorry," he said without looking up. But then he did, giving me the once-over. "Well," he said, eyeing my tailored little plaid Marc by Marc Jacobs top and charcoal skirt. "Very Vanessa Redgrave 1966. You know, in *Blowup*?" He didn't wait for an answer, of course, but brushed past me on his way.

I took this as a compliment. I couldn't remember what anyone in *Blowup* wore, of course, but it was hard to imagine Vanessa Redgrave looking bad. After that I felt an extra spring in my step. I pranced down the hall, the Whole Foods bag swinging from my hand, practically dying for more assistants to run into. But not even Cici glanced up when I passed; she was too busy flirting with someone on the other end of the phone line.

When I walked into our office area, Kylie was at her desk, hunched over a script, and quick as you can say Shu Uemura, my mood shifted.

"We have an ideas meeting in ten," she said, her nose still buried in her script. "Put the spirulina in your desk this time. Also I hope you saved the receipt."

Maybe it was the new clothes, or maybe it was the three shots of espresso I had them drop into my venti mocha, but I had a momentary desire to wrap Kylie's pretty little chains around her throat until she turned purple.

When I didn't answer, Kylie looked up. And yes, she too looked bug-eyed at me. Apparently she'd thought yesterday's sartorial success was a fluke. Think again, Kylie, I said to myself.

"What?" I asked, fighting the smile that threatened to spread across my entire face.

"Nothing," Kylie said abruptly, turning back to her script.

I picked up my own copy, purposefully jangling my gold Me&Ro bracelets. I could see Kylie fighting the urge to look up again—the girl did appreciate jewelry. She was like a crow, attracted to shiny things.

A quick pound of familiar beats from a Timbaland song began to play in my purse. I plunged my hand into the loose wreckage of my bag, past iPod wires and Kleenex and my wallet. I pulled out my iPhone and was greeted with a snapshot of half of Quinn's face. Even blurry, her fierce, proud features commanded your attention. I turned my chair away from Kylie's curious eyes and clicked the green button on the screen to read the text from Quinn:

Lesson #2: Speak up in class.
When you're quiet, you're invisible!

I was a little perplexed. I had a hard time imagining Quinn raising her hand in geometry, but then again, what did I know?

"Girls, we ready?" Iris strode out of her office in a tailored cocoa-colored suit, clutching a legal pad and her BlackBerry. "Taylor, I'd like you to be in this meeting, so grab one of the interns to cover the phones." Iris didn't break her stride as she walked out the door.

I slid the iPhone back into my purse, hoping Iris hadn't seen me texting. "Interns? We have interns here?"

"Amanda's got one and so does Wyman," Kylie said exasperatedly, as if I'd just asked if Metronome had a roof or a floor. She punched an extension on the phone. "Hi, can you send Julissa in here right away? Thanks."

"Have we always had interns?" I asked stupidly. Because I could have really used them in the copy room, I thought. That copy machine had it in for me.

Kylie shot me a weary glance. "Of *course* we've always had them," she replied. "All you had to do was ask."

A moment later a freckled girl with bright pink cheeks and big hazel eyes bounded into the room. I'd seen her before, bouncing up and down the hallways in her red Pumas, her shiny brown ponytail bobbing behind her. I'd always thought she was some VP's daughter or something.

"Hi, I'm Taylor," I said.

"I'm Julissa," she said, her big eyes shining. She thrust out a small, eager hand for me to shake.

"Julissa, can you cover Iris's phone?" Kylie asked distractedly, pointing in the general direction of my desk.

Julissa nodded. "I've been waiting for you guys to give me something to do," she said, walking around me to take a seat at my desk. "But I just thought it seemed like you had everything pretty well covered."

"Yeah, pretty much," I lied, shooting an angry glance at Kylie. I couldn't believe she'd never told me that help was only a phone call away. From now on, I vowed, Julissa was going to make Iris's algae smoothies.

☙

We were in the conference room for our weekly staff meeting, listening to a pitch from Lisa Amorosi, the frizzy-haired executive VP from Brooklyn. She could have really used a visit from Ken Paves, I thought, or at least a lesson on how to use a flatiron.

"Zombie cheerleaders," Lisa said, twisting a hair elastic around her frizz. "A virus gets out in a suburban town. Everyone gets infected. Except for the high school cheerleading team. They fight back, and they also win the state championship. So it's *28 Days Later* meets *Bring It On*."

Iris jotted notes on a legal pad. I wrote too: *Kirsten Dunst! Never too old to play a cheerleader. Casey Affleck as head zombie? What about Gary Busey?*

From my seat against the wall, I searched Iris's face for any signs that she knew of Quinn's and my collaboration. For instance, was there a chance she recognized my shirt? But Iris never looked my way. She, like everyone else, was bent over her notes.

"So this is a comedy?" Iris asked, looking up with a somewhat dubious expression.

"A black comedy," Lisa corrected. "You know how zombie movies are. They're always tongue-in-cheek."

Tom Scheffer cleared his throat and seemed to flex his large muscles beneath his Thomas Pink shirt. "I don't remember there being anything funny about *28 Days Later*," he said.

"So the tone would be, what?" Iris asked, toying with her black fountain pen. "*Buffy*? Or *Blair Witch*?"

Kylie, who as first assistant had the honor of sitting on Iris's right, leaned in close. "I don't think you want to do *Buffy*," she cautioned. "I think this needs a more subtle irony."

Iris absorbed this but still searched the room for more opinions. "Tom?" she asked. "What's your take?"

"I would say that it isn't Metronome material," Kylie interrupted. "We're not known for blood and gore. Our catalog is much more sophisticated than that."

Iris nodded, and Kylie looked around the room proudly, as if what she'd said was brilliant. And then Quinn's text came to me. *Speak up in class.*

I sat up straighter in my seat and scooted forward so I was closer to the table.

"Actually, it seems like there's a way to get around that," I said. "If we really like the project."

Iris and the rest of the staff turned to me expectantly.

"What if Metronome were to create a special division for genre films?" I asked, searching their faces for signs of interest. "Look at all the money movies like *Saw* and *Hostel* are making for Lionsgate. True, they're not Metronome, but Miramax did the same thing with Dimension Films. Dimension released the *Scream* films, which made over a hundred million dollars. And then they used that money to make their artier Oscar films under Miramax."

There were close to twenty people in the room, and all of them were looking at me. Wyman, for one, was nodding, and I almost smiled gratefully at him. As far as the others went, who knew? I took a deep breath and kept going.

"So if we want to create a franchise in this zombie-cheerleader idea, then having a separate, smaller genre division would be the way to do it. Or if we wanted to parlay it into a possible television idea, like *Buffy*—isn't Metronome starting its own TV production division? I thought I read that a few months ago in *Variety*."

I stole a glance at Iris, who looked both surprised and pleased, as if I'd just completed an excellent tap-dance routine. She turned to Tom. "It's worth bringing this up again, don't you think?" Then she looked at me. "They've talked about it before, and it's not really revolutionary. That said, it's a good thing to keep in mind."

My cheeks, which I could just tell were bright and red, began to cool, and I breathed a sigh of relief. Kylie, on the other hand, looked as if she'd just eaten an extremely sour candy.

"So should we maybe call some agents for specs?" Lisa asked. Her voice sounded a lot more animated now that her project might stand a chance.

Iris glanced back at me. "Sure, okay." She gave me a small nod of approval then and shook her copper curls away from her face like someone who'd just felt a fresh spring breeze.

Okay, so maybe I didn't get an outright A, but I'd certainly caught the teacher's attention. As everyone else filed out of the room, I dug down into my purse to pull out a stick of Trident and my phone. *Got it*, I texted Quinn under the table.

CHAPTER TWELVE

If you want to make a memorable entrance someplace, you can sweep down a spiral staircase like Norma Desmond in *Sunset Boulevard*, or you can basically fall out of your Civic, hands covering your mouth in horror, as you watch the valet you just hit with your car door cradle his wounded knee in his hands. Needless to say, I did the latter.

"Oh my God, I'm sorry! Are you all right?" I cried, peering into the valet's agonized face. "Can I do something?"

He took a hand off his knee and held it out. "Fifteen bucks."

I unpeeled a ten and a twenty—extra for damages—from the paper-clipped bills inside my gold Anya Hindmarch clutch, another Quinn-me-down. He grabbed them and my keys and jumped into my car. I felt better, seeing his agile leap onto the fake leather bucket seat; clearly I didn't hurt him that badly, despite his dramatic reaction. Probably another aspiring actor.

I rearranged my cleavage inside my low-cut jade Ella Moss

halter top and pulled it down over my black A-line skirt. *All right*, I whispered to myself. *Here goes nothing*.

A few yards to my right, the red carpet ran like a gauntlet from the front door of Social Hollywood all the way to the night-club around the corner. The clicking camera lenses and the popping flashbulbs were even louder and brighter than I could have imagined, and there were so many photographers, cameramen, and reporters that I couldn't even see who it was they were after. It could have been JLo or Gwyneth, Tom Cruise or Daniel Craig. Hell, it could have been Carrot Top for all I knew. (Carrot Top? Was he still alive?) Above the fray, the art deco façade loomed like a fortress from a fairy tale.

Despite my nerves, I was thrilled. It was my very first movie premiere. The closest I'd ever been to something like this before tonight was watching Billy Bush on TV.

Around the corner from the red carpet was another entrance—for those of us who weren't worthy of the paparazzi, natch—and so that's where I took myself. I glanced down at my iPhone.

Lesson #3: Make one cool friend.

I'd had to ask Quinn for clarification on that, because really, if no one at Metronome would talk to me, how was I supposed to make friends with anyone? I could feel Quinn's impatience in her texted reply, my iPhone practically sighing in exasperation. *Meet someone at a party*, she'd typed. *Not invited to any parties*, I wrote back. *Crash one then* came her reply, and after that, there was nothing.

As I walked up to the side door, a slim girl wearing a futuristic headset and holding a clipboard stepped in between me and the entrance. Her headset flashed in blues and pinks—very *2001: A Space Odyssey*. "Name?" she asked coolly.

"Henn—um, Arthur," I caught myself.

Headset Girl glanced down at her clipboard. Fortunately, there was no possibility Kylie would actually show up. "Ugh, I'm so over James Bond," she'd said this afternoon when she'd come across the envelope. She'd tossed the invite into our communal trash can. Besides, tonight it was her boyfriend's birthday party at El Coyote, which I'd discovered by overhearing Kylie and Cici discussing what they were going to wear. Needless to say, I was not invited to that either. I waited as Futuristic Headset Girl scanned the second page of her list. What if she asked me for ID? She wouldn't do that, would she?

"Oh, here you are," she finally said.

She checked Kylie's name off with her red pen, and I breathed a sigh of relief as a hulking doorman with a bandage over his nose stepped forward to stamp my hand. He barely gave me a glance as I breezed past him into the club. I was *in*.

I'd read enough *In Style* and watched enough *E!* to know that studios spared no expense when they threw a party for a movie, especially when that movie might win an Oscar or—even better—make unfathomable amounts of money. But still, as I stood at the top of the staircase looking down onto the festivities, I just about had to pick my jaw up off the floor. Social Hollywood, a gymnasium built in the 1920s and reincarnated as an overpriced Moroccan restaurant/nightclub, had been transformed into Hawaii, the setting of the latest Bond movie. White sand covered the sunken main floor, and coconut trees swayed in a manufactured breeze. A gigantic volcano carved out of dark chocolate erupted in the corner, spilling mouthwatering rivulets of milk chocolate lava. Lights in pinks and blues splashed over the crowd like a tropical sunset.

Slowly I descended the stairs, aiming less for a memorable entrance than an invisible one. The dance floor was filled with gorgeous, confident people, all of whom seemed to know each other. I nervously snapped my clutch open and closed. Why had I thought it was a good idea to come here alone?

"Mai tai?" A waitress wearing a grass skirt and two coconut shells over her gravity-defying breasts offered me an umbrella-decorated drink.

When in Rome, I thought, and sucked half of it down in one gulp. Then I brought out my iPhone. I didn't want to be all Luke Skywalker, calling out for Obi-Wan every second or anything, but I really needed some advice.

I'm in, I wrote. *What's my target?*

A moment later the iPhone buzzed.

The most important looking person in the room. At your level.

I squinted at the message, as if, like Obi-Wan, it had secrets it hadn't yet revealed. *What's my in?* I typed.

Go for the bar. Sidle up and say This party sucks. Works every time.

I slipped the phone back into my bag and pointed myself toward where I thought the bar might be, wending my way through men in silky Hawaiian shirts and women in minuscule, shimmering dresses. It wasn't easy to walk on the sand, and I almost spilled the rest of my mai tai on a short guy in a white suit who looked like he'd stepped right off *Fantasy Island*.

The bamboo bar, which was strung with colored lights and flickering fake torches, was packed with people. As Kylie would say, *Quel surprise.*

I positioned myself at the back of what looked like a line, next to a boyishly handsome guy in a linen jacket, holding a martini glass. He wasn't much taller than me, with wavy dark hair, a prominent nose, and bright blue eyes.

"Is this the line?" I asked.

"It *was* the line," he replied. "About ten minutes ago, before people realized they have Grey Goose. Now it's just every man for himself. Top-shelf liquor brings out the worst in everybody." He held out his hand. His fingernails were cleaner, shinier, and more perfectly shaped than mine would ever be. "Brett Duncan," he said, shaking my hand. "I sense a fellow assistant."

"Taylor Henning," I said, smiling. "You sensed right."

Brett took a sip of his alarming-looking chartreuse cocktail. "And what would Taylor like to drink?"

"What's good after a mai tai? I always forget those rules." *To my great regret,* I almost added, thinking about the time I'd reversed the liquor/beer order and ended up vomiting outside Chi Psi, wearing my shoes on my hands.

Brett flagged down a passing waiter carrying a tray of chicken skewers and ordered a Grey Goose gimlet straight up with a lime. The waiter nodded and walked away.

"Friend of mine," Brett confided with a wink. "It pays to come to a lot of these things."

I raised my eyebrows. Considering how easily he'd won me over, I figured Brett Duncan was friends with a lot of people. The waiter returned with my drink in record time, and Brett steered me over to a red leather banquette, where he leaned back comfortably and told me that he was the assistant to development at an independent production company on the Paramount lot. "We're very arty," he confided. He grew up in Kentucky, he was a Brown graduate, and his current pop-culture obsession was the Floridian plumber who sang bluegrass versions of Journey songs on *American Idol*. I laughed and let him talk; he was charming. Every third person who squeezed past us set off a wave of "What's up, man?" and "Let's do drinks," which only served to prove my initial hypothesis correct: Brett was a bright, beautiful social butterfly.

He told me, once he'd learned where I worked, that Iris had the best taste in the business. "So what scripts is she looking at?"

"Unfortunately, I wouldn't really know," I said, gazing into my gimlet.

"Ah," Brett said, mimicking me by contemplating his very green cocktail. "So you're second assistant."

"How'd you guess? My sarcasm or the circles under my eyes?"

"I've been there, honey. And there were times I wished I were selling shoes at Nordstrom. But," he said, placing his empty glass on the tray of another passing waiter, "it's still a job. And in the immortal words of you-know-who, you have to *make it work*. Are you on a tracking board?" he asked, narrowing his blue eyes.

Behind him, someone was setting up a limbo bar under one of the coconut trees. Surely no one was going to use that, I thought. I mean, really, were we on the set of *Cocktail*? Was Tom Cruise going to pop up behind the bar with a big goofy grin and a couple of martini shakers in his hands?

"A what?" I asked, tearing my eyes away from the limbo preparations.

"A tracking board."

I shook my head, picturing some kind of dry erase board with . . . well, with I didn't know what on it.

"It's a message board," he said, waving to someone across the room. "For development people. It's where everyone gets bitchy on which scripts have just come out, which ones are good, and which ones are a total waste of time. It essentially tells people exactly how to think, and it can ruin writers in an instant. But for us, they're great. My tracking board has a drinks thing once a month at Tiki Lounge, and we get *very* sloppy."

"So how do I get on one?" I asked, realizing that Kylie had to be on one of these. I thought of just yesterday, when Kylie had slipped into Iris's office for a tête-à-tête on some war drama I'd never heard her mention before. Was this Kylie's secret weapon?

"I'll work on it, darling," Brett said, seeing my desperation.

I raised my gimlet and toasted him gratefully because, in addition to being a social butterfly, he was also the kind of person who'd be happy to help a sad-sack second assistant out. Quinn's clothes clearly didn't fool Brett—he knew I was in over my head.

Across the room, I spotted a dark-haired girl I recognized from Metronome. She wasn't on our floor, so I didn't know her name, but I recognized her Joan Crawford figure—she was all shoulders and bust—and the handbag she always carried, which I now recognized as Fendi. I gave a little involuntary shudder; she was a friend of Kylie's. The chances that she'd notice me and rat me out to Kylie were slim, but still.

"What's the shiver for, doll?"

"That girl works at my office," I said, pointing as subtly as I could. "And she's as mean as all the others, I'm sure."

"Oh, her? That's Andrea. She's all right. She's not the sharpest knife in the drawer, but honestly, with that look, who cares? Do you know her? No? Well, if you ever meet her, just compliment her on her hair. She's extremely proud of it. You'd think she'd starred in a Pantene commercial or something."

"Thanks for the tip," I said, watching Andrea begin to shake her narrow hips. Her famous hair was in a messy updo, but I'd actually noticed it before and thought the very same thing.

"Look." Brett gazed into my face over the rim of his martini glass. "My last little friend like you had a nervy b and moved home to Wisconsin to eat cheese all day long while wearing sweatpants and watching reruns of *Judge Judy*. But you—you look stronger than that. You've got a mean glint in your eye, I can see it. So what do you say? Are you going to let this town drive you batshit crazy too? Or are you going to make it? And more important," he went on, "do you want a new gay boyfriend or what? Because I'm pretty sure I can help you."

I threw back my head and laughed. He linked his arm through mine and I grabbed two drinks off the tray of a passing waiter and gave one to each of us.

"To us!" I cried.

"To us," he agreed.

We tossed our drinks back, and then he reached for my hand. "Now let's go to the real party. You're never going to meet anyone important down here."

"Except you, of course," I said.

He giggled. "Except me."

He pulled me through the crowd, across the sand, and past the impromptu limbo game that had just begun. A steel-drum band next to the volcano began to play "Stir It Up." The first contestant was a bronzed woman in a micromini that would have made Amy Winehouse proud.

"I don't know when beavers became the new accessory," Brett hissed as we passed.

Upstairs, a hulking bouncer who was a dead ringer for Refrigerator Perry tried to stop us from walking in, but Brett waved him off.

"She's with me, Ruben," he said as he led me into a dimly lit lounge.

I'd left Hawaiian limbo land for a Moroccan opium den, it seemed. The lights were dim and red, and all around people lounged barefoot on low, velvet sofas or sat on fat pillows around candlelit tables. Jewel-colored mosaic tile decorated the floor and the grottolike walls.

"Better, huh?" Brett asked as he led me inside. "Come on, my friends are in back."

As we walked through the room, I spotted someone reclining on a sofa whom I knew but couldn't quite place. He had brown, slightly wavy hair, and he was handsome in that wholesome, boy-next-door way. He was wearing a gray ribbed sweater and talking animatedly to a girl who also looked vaguely familiar. I couldn't remember his name, but I gave a small wave anyway, just to be friendly.

"How do you know James McAvoy?" Brett whispered.

I almost choked on the last of my drink. As I took a closer look around, I realized that everyone was familiar to me not because I knew them but because they were *famous*. There were actors, television personalities, reality TV stars—if you can call them stars, that is—and models I'd seen in countless *Vogue* ads. It was a paparazzo's dream.

Finally, we reached a table where another familiar handsome-but-not-too-handsome face greeted me.

"Taylor?" said Brett. "Tobey. Tobey, Taylor. She works with Iris Whitaker at Metronome."

I smiled, momentarily terrified as I locked eyes with Spiderman. "Hi," I said and left it at that. Tobey Maguire was sitting next to Jessica Biel, who was calling across the room for Justin Timberlake.

I leaned over to Brett as surreptitiously as I could. "These people are your friends?" I asked.

"Just ask them about them. It's their favorite subject," Brett whispered, and he pulled out a chair for me to sit down.

"I think I can handle that," I whispered back. Maybe it was six years too late, but I felt like I was finally heading to the prom—in the cool kids' limo.

CHAPTER THIRTEEN

Here's what I want to know," Peter Lasky, the charismatic but temperamental head of Metronome, barked into the phone line. He always sounded authoritative, but when he was angry—like right now—his voice made you feel like you ought to apologize just for existing. Even though he was talking to Iris, not me, I wanted to take off my headset and duck under my desk.

He took a deep breath, probably to gather volume, and then continued. "I want to know why six months ago you told me that this movie was going be our *Atonement*, and now the Muslim Anti-Defamation League or whoever it is wants my balls cut off. I mean, I'm trying to enjoy a golf game here, and my fucking cell is ringing off the hook!"

"Now Peter, let's not get carried away," Iris began calmly.

"Don't talk to me like you talk to your teenage daughter, Iris! This is supposed to be our Oscar film, goddamn it!"

I winced and pulled the headset away from my ear for a

second. Sometimes being on Iris's calls made me wonder if my dream career was such a dream after all. I mean, what if one day I got to be as powerful as Iris, and once a week I got my ear shrieked off by someone who was more powerful than I was and who called me from a golf course because he was too important to spend any time in his office?

"We're working on it, Peter," Iris said soothingly. "I'm looking at several candidates for a rewrite as we speak—"

"Ah Christ, some asshole's playing into me, I have to go," Peter said. "Are you fucking blind? I'm on this hole!" he screamed, and then the line went dead. Somewhere on the course at Hillcrest in Beverly Hills, Peter Lasky was taking out his rage about *Camus's Nightmare* on an unsuspecting fellow golfer.

I put down my headset. At least that was over until next week. I glanced down at the still relatively neat surface of my desk. There were some scripts, a few back issues of *Variety*, and, of course, my Good and Bad lists for the last few days. I'd actually done a decent job lately. I was getting the hang of call-rolling, I knew the numbers to Iris's favorite restaurants by heart, and I'd memorized the schedule of her regular weekly meetings like it was a holy text.

GOOD THINGS

Brett Duncan, my new gay boyfriend.
Discussion with Jessica Biel about astrology; she says all
    Tauruses are crazy!
Quinn's clothes.
My iPhone. (I drew a lot of hearts after this one.)
Finally learned rhyme: liquor before beer, never fear; beer
    before liquor, never sicker.

Did not break copier because made Julissa make copies.
Do not feel like firing is imminent.

BAD THINGS
Cabbage still smells like sewer.
Kylie still bitch on wheels.
Kylie still bitch on wheels.
Kylie still bitch on wheels.

The funny thing was, even though there were really only two things under the Bad column, they seemed to outweigh the Good. At least Kylie was off gossiping with Cici and Amanda right now. With her gone, the air in the room felt easier to breathe. And it wasn't just because every time she left, I blew out that awful candle of hers.

Just then my beloved phone buzzed. It was another text from Quinn, and this one was even more cryptic than the last:

Lesson #4: Lunch is a battleground. Good allies are key.

I would have written back right then—something really eloquent, like "Huh??"—but I figured I ought to attend to my work duties first. I knocked politely on Iris's door. "I have those scripts from Endeavor you wanted," I said.

The midafternoon sun slanted through the office window at an angle that made me squint as I approached Iris's desk. It lit the jungle of plants along the window, turning them a brilliant jade green, and fringed the edges of Iris's hair, which was swept off her face with a pair of gold-tipped wooden hair sticks.

"Here you go," I said, sliding the scripts onto Iris's black lacquer desk, in between her open *New York Times* and a stack of daily *Variety*s.

Iris screwed up her face, opened her mouth, and then delivered a room-quaking sneeze. "Goddamn Santa Anas," she muttered, pulling a clutch of tissues from the box on her desk. "Every October." Her eyes were uncharacteristically puffy and wet.

"What does that mean?" I asked at the risk of sounding stupid. "I mean, I know they're winds, but why does everyone hate them so much?"

Iris laughed. "I forget sometimes how new you are here." She dabbed at her nose. "We love to complain about the Santa Anas in L.A. They're second only to traffic." She balled up the tissue and tossed it in the waste bin by her feet. "They come from the east, and we hate them because they push dust and pollen and mold and all sorts of horrible things right into our faces, making us look like this." She pointed at her red eyes and nose. "But I can see they don't bother *you*."

"Maybe next year?" I said hopefully.

"Better hope not," Iris chuckled.

I took another little step closer toward her desk. "So I've been doing some reading," I ventured, "and I think I may have found the perfect person to rewrite *Camus*."

Iris opened a box of Claritin on her desk. "Why I decided to buy that movie I'll never know," she said, pushing another tablet through the foil.

"Well, I read this guy's spec last night and I was really impressed. His name is Steven Udesky."

Thank you, Brett Duncan, I thought to myself. The day after we met at the movie premiere, he'd e-mailed me a password to Story Tracker, Hollywood's most exclusive tracking board, with a note: *Here's a little prezzie for my favorite Cleveland girl! Remember, no Judge Judy! XXXOOO.*

Story Tracker was an entirely new world. Thanks to its bulletin boards, I no longer felt like a kid at the back of the class with a dunce cap on her head—I finally knew what people were talking about. I could read that a CE at Warner Bros. had loved a *Legally Blonde*–esque comedy, and I could watch the fluctuating fortunes of a screenwriter named Adam Johnson, whose tender and ironic portrait of a divorcing couple was adored by half of the people on the boards and lambasted as stinking tripe by the other half. I couldn't get my hands on every script I wanted to read, but at least Story Tracker let me know what was out there, and if I happened to be on the phone with an assistant to an agent who repped a lot of writers, all I had to do was ask.

That was how I'd found the script for *Echo Park*, which Iris was now staring at, sniffling. "Kylie already told me about this," she said. "Just a couple days ago. Haven't read it yet, but she said it was worth looking at."

"Oh," I said, deflated. "Well, that's good."

Kylie strode confidently into the room at that very moment, as if trying to prove the saying "speak of the devil." She wore a floaty, poppy-colored minidress that showed off her toned calves, and she seemed incredibly pleased about something.

"Here's the breakdown from production on the fall slate," she said, breezing past me as if I weren't there. She slid a thick black dossier onto Iris's desk. "I had them rush it for you."

Iris opened it and scanned the first page, her gray green eyes flicking back and forth as she leaned her chin into her hand. "Great," she said, looking up. "Thanks, Kylie."

"And you told me to remind you about writing the speech for your achievement award at the Association for Women in Entertainment luncheon next week. And you're all set for six-thirty tonight with Drew Barrymore at Mozza," she added, smiling beatifically. Then she turned to me, as if she'd just noticed me. "You did get the table, right, Taylor?" she cooed.

"I was just going to do that," I said quietly, clenching my right hand into a fist.

"Well, you should probably call right now," Kylie said chirpily. "You know how hard it is to get Nancy after three. *C'est impossible!*"

I glanced at Iris, but she was absorbed in the dossier. I slunk out of her office, imagining Kylie as Drew Barrymore in *Scream*—you know, where she gets dragged out of her house and then attacked with a machete.

While I reserved Iris's favorite table, Kylie teetered over to my desk. "The window!" she hissed.

I resisted the urge to roll my eyes. "And is the window table available?"

When I hung up, Kylie perched her tiny, bony butt on the edge of my desk. "I think it's great that you're so interested in the creative aspects of this job, Taylor," she said, playing with her silver Raymond Weil watch, "but you really shouldn't be pitching scripts. Not when you have other stuff to do." She nodded in an earnest, concerned way, as if she had just delivered this speech out of the goodness of her heart.

I counted to five as she took a deep breath. "I'll keep that in mind."

"Goody." Kylie stood and sauntered back over to her desk.

"Oh, and I just sent you an e-mail about Iris's lunch meetings for the rest of the week. Just so you don't forget."

I gritted my teeth, ignoring her, and tried to look busy as I opened up the *New York Times* crossword puzzle. It had been a habit since college; I always did the puzzle when I was feeling down. It made me feel good to feel a little clever (which was why I never did the Saturday puzzle—too depressing). But before I could be calmed by the orderly black-and-white grid and predictably cryptic clues, an IM pinged on my screen.

Auteur85: hey stranger

Auteur85: how's the biz?

I cringed. Brandon. He was probably at his desk at the production company, drinking black coffee, a salmon-colored copy of the *Observer* at his elbow.

JournalGirl07: Fine. How are you?

I straightened up in my chair and made it a point to type with correct punctuation, which at least made me feel superior.

Auteur85: good, same ol same ol.

Auteur85: u hate yr life yet? ready to come back?

I stared at the screen, my fingers poised over the keyboard. Brandon was a dick, this was clear. But if he were worthy of an honest response, what would I even say? My life here was a constant, uphill battle, but I wasn't ready to pack it in yet, was I? I tapped the keyboard lightly with my fingertips, not typing anything yet.

And then I signed off. Did I mention that I'm good with conflict?

◈

"Oh. My. God. He told you they were Vince Vaughn's pants?" Kylie was nearly doubled over in laughter at the story Andrea was telling her. I hadn't really been listening because I was going through Iris's expenses, organizing them into weekly reports, but I'd heard enough to gather that, after the Bond premiere where I'd seen her, Andrea had gone to Villa, where she'd been accosted by a tattooed makeup artist. Hoping to impress her, apparently, he told lies that ranged from the sexual (he claimed to have had a threesome with Cameron Diaz and Lucy Liu—how very Charlie's Angels) to the sartorial (though he was only five feet seven, he swore on his pet poodle's grave that he was wearing what had been, until very recently, Vince Vaughn's favorite pair of leather pants).

Of course Kylie and Andrea weren't letting me in on the fun at all, but I didn't mind that much; unlike some people, *I* was getting work done.

"Of course you gave him your number," Kylie cackled.

"Not even!" Andrea shook her head and laughed. As she did, its shimmery chestnut-colored waves caught the light.

And that's when I remembered what Brett Duncan said about Andrea. Summoning my courage, I cleared my throat.

"I love your hair," I said to Andrea, smiling brightly. It was true—she did have very nice, very lustrous brown hair. It fell in soft waves around her shoulders and perfectly framed her slightly mannish features. "I know that might seem like a weird thing to say, seeing as how we haven't been introduced yet"— here I shot a glance at Kylie—"but really, it always looks amazing. What's your secret? Products, or just good genes?" It came out sounding a little more gushy than I meant it to, but a wide smile immediately lit up Andrea's dark-eyed face.

"Both!" she said happily. "Bumble and Bumble helps, but really, I have my mother to thank. You should see her hair. It's down to her waist."

"Very Frida Kahlo," I offered.

"Totally," Andrea agreed. "Of course my mother doesn't have a unibrow."

"Well if she did, I'd know where to send her," I said. "My roommate's a genius with waxing. Actually in this case I think she'd call it 'brow design.'"

Andrea laughed again, and I felt a flush of pride.

"By the way, I'm Taylor," I said. "The Robin to Kylie's Batman. Or something like that."

"Andrea," she said, smiling and patting her curls. She glanced down at her watch. "Ooh," she exclaimed, "it's time for lunch already."

Oh my God, I thought. *Lunch is a battleground.* I smiled brightly. "Actually, I was about to head to the commissary myself."

"Great!" Andrea exclaimed, flipping her hair again, a little proudly this time. "You should totally come with us."

I smiled victoriously and reached for my purse, but Kylie beat me to it.

She stood and slung her LV-monogrammed bag over her shoulder. "Actually, Taylor, you need to stay and man the phones," she pronounced. Her tone was pure-blooded bitch.

Just then Iris came sliding out of her office on her way to her own lunch date with the head of marketing. I saw my chance.

"Oh Kylie," I said sweetly, "I'm starving. Couldn't you mind the phones for me, just this once?"

Iris peered at Kylie quizzically, waiting for her response. With

Iris right there, Kylie couldn't possibly refuse. "Of course," she said through gritted teeth.

But as they say, if looks could kill, yours truly would have been sent to the morgue faster than you can say *ER*.

❧

The Metronome commissary was a large, sparsely decorated room with brilliant white walls and floor-to-ceiling windows on its sunny east side. It was one o'clock, the peak dining hour, so most of the shiny chrome tables were occupied by Metronome staffers talking shop. Sitting in here alone, as I'd done on many occasions before, I'd heard about Kate Winslet's donut obsession, Pete Doherty's poor hygiene habits, and our very own Tom Scheffer's body dysmorphia. It had been an education of sorts.

The salad bar took up much of the space in the center of the room and, as usual, there were half a dozen willowy girls diving into the lettuce. You'd think they'd be tempted by the saffron risotto or the glistening flanks of the rotisserie chicken—certainly *I* always was—but no, this was L.A., where everyone was on a diet. So they piled their plates high with mesclun greens, which they supplemented with a few shreds of carrot, a handful of cherry tomatoes, and maybe a slice of beet or two. There were cookies at the far end of the salad bar, but so far I'd never seen a single female eat one.

Andrea was one of the salad girls, of course, though she actually went so far as to put a hard-boiled egg on top of her greens, six grams of fat be damned. In honor of our blossoming friendship, I forsook the pizza station and followed her lead down the trays of vegetables. I learned that we both like balsamic vinaigrette, but that didn't make me think we were sisters or something.

We set our trays down at a table by the wide, plate glass windows that looked out over Metronome's grand front entrance. Andrea ran off to get a Diet Coke, and I tucked myself into my plate of rabbit food. Through the windowpane, the rays of strong sunshine felt blessedly warm on my face, and I closed my eyes for a moment, basking in the glow. Even though L.A.'s warm weather had appeared on my Pros/Cons lists before leaving the East Coast (Cons: Leaving Brandon; Pros: Leaving Brandon), I'd hardly spent any time outside since I'd moved.

I heard a tray being plunked down across from me and opened my eyes. Cici was staring at me curiously. But the fact that she'd chosen to sit across from me was at least encouraging.

"Sorry, I haven't been getting out much," I explained sheepishly. Great. My lunchtime debut, and I was sunbathing in the middle of the commissary like some cave-dwelling freak.

"I totally get it." Cici nodded, smiling, to my surprise, like she really did. "Gould's been making me stay late pretty much every night recently. I have *not* been getting my vitamin D."

Andrea returned with her soda, and then Amanda appeared too. If she seemed surprised to see me sitting with the cool girls, she didn't show it. She offered me a friendly smile, as if our interactions usually went like this. It made her seem a little delusional, if not downright two-faced, but really, I wasn't in the mood to complain.

"So," Amanda began, looking around at each of us as if calling a boardroom session to order. "What do you all—"

But she was interrupted by Wyman, who plopped into the empty seat next to me, his cheeks flushed pink. "Oh my God you guys," he said, pushing his thick glasses up on his nose with—for once—an unstudied air. "You'll never believe what just went down."

I smiled slightly. Gossipy Wyman, I decided, was a refreshing change from Film Snob Wyman.

Not waiting for the girls to play twenty-one questions, Wyman spilled. "You know how Melinda Darling has been looking kind of chunky recently?"

Amanda and Cici nodded, as if this was a normal lunchtime topic of discussion. It probably was. "Yeah, and seems to think those silk charmeuse blouses are helping her case," Cici cackled.

"She's not carb-loading—she's preggers!" Wyman exclaimed, slapping the table for emphasis.

"No!" Andrea cried.

I kept my head bent a little, chewing my mesclun, and made a mental note to throw away anything silk charmeuse until I'd overcome the urge to eat pizza, cookies, and everything remotely tasty in the commissary.

Wyman continued to fill us in on Melinda's pregnancy. I learned it was her first child, and she'd already named it Friday, regardless of the sex. Her husband's last name was Rubenstein, which meant that in a matter of months there would be a child named Friday Darling Rubenstein entering the world. Remarkably, no one seemed to care about the poor child's ridiculous name at all.

Amanda removed a spoon from between her pouty red lips and pronounced, "I'll bet my Light & Fit she doesn't come back to work after she pops out that kid." She gave her shiny black bob a toss.

Wyman clapped his hands and concurred. "Obviously. Her husband makes serious bank at Paramount."

"So how long do you think it'll be?" Cici said softly, looking around the commissary as if afraid someone might hear.

It dawned on me that the assistants, shallow as they might be, weren't fascinated by the fluctuations in Melinda Darling's weight for its own sake. They were interested because her pregnancy meant she'd probably leave Metronome.

"I think she's due in three or four months," Wyman provided, keeping his voice low too.

"I bet you they move up Joey Abel," Andrea whispered. Seeing the blank look on my face, she leaned toward me. "You know, the CE who looks like Harry Potter."

I nodded, instantly knowing who she was talking about. He had unruly dark hair and round, wire-rimmed glasses. All that was missing was the lightning scar on his forehead.

Joey Abel, I also knew, hadn't been CE for more than a year. If he were to move up in rank, an entry-level creative executive position would be open.

We all scanned each other's faces, an unspoken understanding passing between us. In a few months, the job every assistant dreamed of would be available, and all of us could be in the running.

Cici broke the silence first. She tossed her head and raised her Diet Coke. "Here's to Melinda's baby!"

"Long live Friday Darling!" I cried, getting into it. Everyone raised their glasses and laughed.

It felt good, laughing along with Kylie's friends while Kylie was stuck answering phones and sending whiny IMs to her tennis-player boyfriend. But this lunch was bigger than getting back at Kylie. There was something to aim for now. If I could turn things around in a week, who knew what I could accomplish before Friday Darling made her debut?

And did I mention I was wearing Zac Posen?

CHAPTER FOURTEEN

The Santa Anas blew dry, hot air over the West Hollywood basin, frying the chaparral up in Griffith Park and above the Malibu coast. Inside a ballroom at the Beverly Hilton, though, it was absolutely freezing. I pulled one of Quinn's Vince cashmere cardigans around my bare shoulders and wrapped my hands up in a napkin. I'd thought the sleeveless sheath dress from Catherine Malandrino would be perfect for the luncheon, but clearly I should have stuck with my old wool suit.

Iris, in a tailored white suit, was seated at the head table, because the Association for Women in Entertainment had named her Woman of the Year for her clear-eyed vision and outstanding contribution to the film industry. She was very blasé about it all, though; she had drawers full of awards like this.

"What's wrong with you?" Kylie asked, frowning slightly as she delicately spooned some cold cucumber soup to her mouth.

Apparently my teeth had been chattering a little. "Just a bit chilly, I guess." I shrugged.

"It's good for the metabolism," Kylie commented, dabbing at her mouth politely with the lilac linen napkin. A waiter leaned over her and refilled her crystal goblet with bottled Voss water, looking at her like he was starving and she was a steak.

I'd been looking forward to the luncheon, both for a change of scenery and for a chance to wear this slate blue dress, which, if I do say so myself, made my eyes pop. But so far the event had been underwhelming. For one thing, the room was just your basic gussied-up conference room (*not* the International Ballroom, where they host the Golden Globes), with cream-colored walls, cream linen tablecloths, and cream padded chairs. The only real color in the room was provided by the flower arrangements, lurid explosions of lilies and birds-of-paradise that made Iris's eyes water from the pollen. The other problem—and this was the larger one, I admit—was that Kylie and I were seated together, sandwiched between two older women, wearing mink stoles and sipping Bloody Marys, who had absolutely no interest in talking to us.

This meant that I had to scramble around for polite conversation as we worked our way through the fish course. I settled on the topic of her handsome, tennis-playing boyfriend, since he had nothing to do with Metronome and would, in theory, be easy enough to talk about.

"So how are things going with Luke?" I ventured.

Kylie stiffened a little. "Couldn't be better," she said archly, playing with her fork. "How about you? Any dates recently?" Her green eyes scanned mine curiously.

"No," I said honestly. After the disaster with Mark Lyder, I'd been too afraid to go out with anyone else—not that there'd been that many opportunities—and had nursed a secret superstition that another date might cost me my job. But I wasn't about to voice my weird fears to Kylie, especially because the whole Kylie-trying-to-get-me-fired thing was a supremely awkward topic. I said instead, "Everyone I meet here seems to know everybody else. I'd feel weird dating someone, knowing they were . . . I don't know. Always looking over my shoulder, I guess." I leaned back as the enamored waiter refilled Kylie's water *again*. "Is that weird?"

"No, not at all," Kylie sighed, and she actually seemed to mean it. She brushed a long, buttery curl over her shoulder. "In this industry, it's hard to know which relationships are real and which ones aren't. That's why it's so great to have a boyfriend who's doing something totally different with his life."

I speared and ate a little piece of asparagus thoughtfully. (I was starving, but of course I had to keep table manners in mind.) How weird it was to be having what seemed like a normal conversation with Kylie. It almost seemed like she was confiding in me. "So you'll never date, like, a director?" I prompted.

Kylie violently shook her head. "They're fun to flirt with, but you don't want to *date* any of them," she said. "And agents are worse." She shuddered as she knifed her fish. To her left, the older woman in the dramatic fur stole (she'd told us she was a costume designer before turning away to ignore us completely) blathered on about Cate Blanchett, who apparently had a designer's eye for fabric and line. Her companion gazed into the lilies as if she were being hypnotized by an extremely boring shaman.

"On one hand, agents are everywhere, and they can be helpful, but . . . ," Kylie pointed her fork at me, "if something goes wrong, they can talk shit about you to everyone. Have a bad breakup?" She snapped her fingers. "All of Endeavor knows your favorite sex position." A frown came over her pretty features, and I wondered momentarily whether she'd been burned by an agent before. But then she laughed gaily. "For agents, my policy is look but don't touch!"

I thought again about Mark Lyder and how eager he'd been to tattle on me after I'd rejected him. Kylie's policy wasn't exactly revolutionary, but it was probably a good rule of thumb.

"My advice?" Kylie said, swallowing. "Find a guy who worships you. Instead of himself. There aren't a lot out there, especially in L.A., but there are a few. You just have to really look." Kylie dabbed her Chanel-glossed lips with her napkin and put down her fork. After five bites, she was done with lunch. And frankly that was more than I'd ever seen her eat before.

I contemplated Kylie's counsel as I delicately buttered a roll. At least in relationships, she seemed to have her priorities straight. Not many girls as ambitious and calculating as Kylie would date a guy who taught tantrumy Angelenos how to hit a yellow ball across a net. Maybe she wasn't as dreadful as she'd always seemed. Or maybe she was being nicer to me because after my week of victories, she was finally starting to see me as a worthy adversary.

My thoughts were interrupted by my iPhone.

Dress looks good on you
But the cardigan so doesn't go

I sat up straighter, looking around the room for Quinn. A gigantic Asian-inflected branch-and-twig-and-lily centerpiece blocked my view of Iris's table. Keeping the phone on my lap, I typed:

Are you here? Can't see you

A moment later, Quinn responded:

Lesson #5: Enlist a faithful assistant.

Kylie glanced at my phone pointedly. "What are you doing? The speeches are about to start."

"It's nothing," I said, angling my hands further under the table.

Meet me in the ladies room. 5 minutes.

⁊

"I can't believe what you're doing to that dress," Quinn scoffed as she smoothed her long auburn hair in the gilded vanity mirror. "Couldn't you go out and get a cute little shrug or something?"

I sighed and reluctantly slid the cardigan off my goose-bumped arms. I thought about turning on the hand dryer for some warm air, but that seemed déclassé. "What are you doing here?" I asked. "Aren't you supposed to be in school?"

"Columbus Day," Quinn sighed, turning around. She wore a baby blue satin wrap top over black tuxedo pants, and a diamond necklace in the shape of a Chinese symbol. I wondered what it meant. *Spoiled? Too Good for You?* Then I scolded myself. Quinn might not be the nicest girl around, but she was making herself extremely useful.

"My friends are all at the beach, but my mom has to go and get herself honored by a bunch of dried-up old ladies. It's so unfair." She toyed with the petals of a potted orchid and gave me a quick appraisal with her cold blue eyes. "So at least you look better."

"I feel better," I said honestly. "I'm starting to get things under control."

Quinn fingered the Chinese symbol on her necklace. "So then maybe you don't need me anymore." Her voice was cool and calculating.

"No, no, I do, I really do," I said quickly. "What did you mean about enlisting an assistant?"

"You need someone who's got your back at all times. Someone who helps you out."

"You mean like that guy who carries JLo's umbrella?"

Quinn rolled her ice blue eyes and didn't even bother to dignify my remark. "Did you notice the tall brunette girl who was with me at Pinkberry? That's Lucinda. She's my number two. You're looking for someone who'll be loyal to you and do what you say. Also she'll have to tell you what people are saying about you. It's like rule number one. I should have given that one to you first."

"What if I don't want to know what people are saying?"

Quinn picked up a bottle of spray cologne from the silver amenities tray on the counter. "It's about knowing the brutal truth at all times," she said, spraying perfume into the air. "That way, no one can hurt you or surprise you. You take away their power. Think about it: nobody ever wants to hear anything bad about themselves. But don't you ever lie awake in bed at night wondering what the worst is? Doesn't it make you afraid?"

I sat down on one of the pink satin chairs in the powder area. I didn't know if these Manolos were Quinn's or one of her friend's, but they were not as comfortable as I would have liked. "I guess it could be a little scary."

"Like, nobody except for me is going to tell you that you sort of look terrible right now. But doesn't it feel good to know that I'm always going to tell you the truth?"

I plucked at a stray thread on the seat cushion and glanced at my reflection in the big gilded mirror. I looked cold and tired. "Fine, then. I hear what people are saying about me. Big deal."

Quinn smiled. "And I guess there's kind of a companion lesson to that one too. A lesson number six. That's not so brutal. If you want to hear it." Quinn pushed a row of gold bangles up her tanned arm.

I pursed my lips and made a funny face at myself in the mirror. "Fine," I said.

"Always know more than your enemies. Get inside info whenever possible. Like on my mom, for example. You should totally be using me to learn how to suck up to her."

I very nearly smacked myself on the forehead when she said that. Why hadn't I thought of that? I should have been pumping Quinn for info on Iris weeks ago. It was like ninth grade, when it took me months to realize that everyone was just looking up the answers in the back of the geometry book, whereas I was figuring out everything for myself like a good little nerd. Granted, that was what I was supposed to be doing, but cheating was so much *easier*.

I gazed up at Quinn towering over me. "I was thinking of getting her some flowers. To congratulate her for the award."

Quinn held up her hand and shook her head. "She hates flowers, duh, she has allergies. Here's what you do. She loves these chocolate bars that you can only get in France."

I held out my arms helplessly. "Well, unless you've got a ticket to Paris in your little Chloe bag—"

"France *and* at the French deli in the Farmer's Market," Quinn

cut me off. "My mom goes crazy for them." She propelled herself off the counter and walked past me toward the door. "Which
is where getting the *assistant* helps," she said.

"Right!" I exclaimed, clapping my hands together. That
would be easy, actually: Julissa. She was covering Iris's phones
right now.

I walked over to the amenities tray and spritzed a little hair-
spray onto my updo while I dialed. Julissa picked up on the first
ring. I told her about the bars and gave her the name, supplied by
Quinn. When I clicked off, Quinn was staring at me. "I'll ask her
to be my official assistant later," I explained.

"Okay." She nodded, seemingly satisfied. "And one other thing
I've been meaning to teach you." She came back from the doorway
and stood directly in front of me. "The ultimate deathstare."

"The deathstare?"

"It's crucial, so pay attention. Okay. First, you sort of squint
your eyes. Like this." Quinn narrowed her blue eyes until they
were slits. "Almost like they're watering up. And then, you do
the mouth." She raised her top lip a half-inch and curled it slightly.
"And then you just stare that person down and hold for at least
five seconds. Like this."

I was shocked that such a simple expression could make
someone look so cruel. Honestly, I would have done just about
anything to make her stop staring at me.

"Now you try," Quinn commanded.

I tried to squint my eyes into mean little slits. I frowned too,
just for good measure, and then I raised my upper lip in my best
imitation of a ferocious snarl.

Quinn guffawed. "Give me your iPhone," she said, reaching
for my purse.

When I handed it to her, she held it up to her face, deathstared into the camera, and snapped a picture. "There," she said, handing the phone back. "Just practice that in the mirror."

I gazed at the picture. It was very intimidating. "Thanks."

"You'll get the hang of it," she muttered, walking to the door. It was the closest thing to a pep talk she'd ever given me.

I went to follow her, but Quinn stopped and held up her hand. "Count to a hundred," she said. With that she turned on her heel and waltzed out.

"Are those Anne-Sarine bars?" Iris turned the purple and gold foil-wrapped bars, tied together with red ribbon, over in her hand. "Oh, Taylor. These are my favorite."

Kylie glanced up from her computer. "What's that?" she asked, her eyes darting suspiciously from Iris to me and back again. She'd been surprisingly nice to me since the luncheon, but I had a feeling that after this, that would no longer be the case.

"You like them?" I asked innocently. "They're my favorite. I got addicted to them the last time I was in Paris." Not true, but whatever. Kylie tensed up defensively, as if she owned France. "When my roommate told me you could get them at the Farmer's Market, I totally flipped! I could eat them all day long."

Iris held the bars and beamed at me. "I really appreciate this, Taylor," she said warmly.

"Well, congratulations again," I said, smiling back. "I've got to go catch up on some agent e-mails, but enjoy!"

Kylie was staring at me in disbelief. I could get used to seeing her face like that.

I found pert, elfin-faced Julissa at the Xerox machine, copying scripts. "Did everything work out?" she asked eagerly. "Those were the right kind, right?"

I peeled a ten and a twenty out of my wallet and handed them to Julissa. "It worked out great."

"Oh no, that's too much," Julissa said, eyeing the bills.

"Take it," I urged. "It's not like anyone's paying you around here, right?"

Julissa smiled and gingerly took the money. Behind her the copier spit out page after page of what some were hoping would be the next Seth Rogen flick.

"So, Julissa, I have a question for you," I said, leaning casually against the fax machine. "Sort of a proposition. How'd you like to be my personal script reader?"

Julissa gave a little squeal. "Seriously?"

"Yeah, there's no way I can handle them all. Just read the ones I give you and let me know if they're good enough to pass on to Iris."

I thought she was going to fling her arms around my neck, but then she composed herself and turned to the copier, plucking out the first few copies of the script. "Thank you," she said, blushing and looking down at the pages.

"Oh, and one more thing," I paused. "You're coming out with me tonight. That is, if you're free."

"Are you hanging out with Jessica Biel?" Julissa asked breathlessly. In the kitchen the morning after the premiere I'd told her about my astrology conversation with Ms. Timberlake.

"No. It'll be with my friend Brett. To El Guapo."

"Awesome. I love the Guapo!"

As Julissa skipped down the hall, I couldn't help feeling a little bit guilty. This girl didn't even have a desk of her own, and she was one of only three interns in the office. How was she going to read all these scripts?

But then again, wasn't that what assistants were for?

CHAPTER FIFTEEN

So how do you think I'm going to get out of this?" I asked, looking down at my rubber nurse's dress, white fishnet tights, and red satin fuck-me pumps.

"Lots and lots of baby powder." Magnolia adjusted her cleavage to its maximum plumpness inside her skimpy French maid outfit. "You *did* Purell that, by the way, right?"

"Yes," I said, elbowing her in the ribs. I'd gotten my little get-up from Wardrobe (no doubt it was left over from the Brett Ratner movie the studio had done a few years back). When Magnolia asked me who I was supposed to be, I told her Florence Nightingale on Cinemax. She said she was Jennifer Anniston in that one housecleaning scene in *Friends with Money*, but really, she looked a little sluttier than that and she knew it.

Ah yes, Halloween. Back in Cleveland, we celebrated by decorating our houses with spiderwebs and black lights, wearing costumes from the drugstore. In college, it was all about witty, ironic costumes; my senior year I'd gone as a Desperate Housewife, complete with an apron and a bloody knife. The residents of L.A., however, apparently viewed the holiday as an excuse to bare as much flesh as humanly possible without showing their reproductive organs. From where I stood in the middle of Heidi Klum's annual costume party at The Green Door, I could count three Officer Naughtys, three Skanky Nurses (plus me, number four), three Hercules, two Greg Louganises, and five Playboy Bunnies. As I sipped my martini, Adam and Eve passed me by, strolling along in fig leaf–decorated G-strings, golden Mystic Tans, and his-and-her six-packs.

Magnolia whistled. "Who is the cutie?"

I thought she was talking about Greg #2, but then I saw her gazing raptly at a man with long straggly hair and a full beard wearing a navy sweatshirt and faded jeans. "You're not talking about the Unabomber, are you?"

"He's cute," Magnolia said defensively.

I'd almost forgotten that Magnolia's taste in men was the same as her taste in dogs: shaggy and smelly.

"I suppose he's got a certain Cisco Adler thing going on," I offered.

Magnolia drained her drink, then handed me her empty glass. "Wish me luck," she said and then sauntered over to him.

The music changed to a remix of a Silversun Pickups song as I took another sip of my martini and scanned the crowd for Brett. Other than our trip to El Guapo, I'd barely seen him recently. I'd had too many scripts to read. Even after pawning some off on Julissa, I still had a stack two feet high on the floor of my living room.

And I wasn't the only one up to my ears in work. Iris was chasing some Gondry script, Tom Scheffer and Peter Lasky were still trying to figure out *Camus's Nightmare*, the assistants were all still gossiping about Melinda Darling's possible departure, and yours truly was trying to keep Iris happy and Kylie off my back. Both of those tasks were getting a little easier every day, though, and as I felt my cocktail beginning to have its effect I was pretty certain that things were all right with the world.

Of course, I *was* standing alone in the middle of a party wearing a latex dress. So I figured I ought to find a friend and do a little mingling. Since Magnolia and the Unabomber were still looking deeply and soulfully into each other's eyes (and since I thought I saw his hand moving toward her butt), I decided I should find the bar.

I pushed my way past some potted palms and two women dressed like Sexy Kittens (really, did they *have* to go there?) and grinned. There was Brett Duncan, leaning against the bar, talking to a white-faced Dracula. Brett was in a medieval doublet and blue stockings that showed off his enviable legs. At his hip, he carried a long sword that looked as if it might actually be dangerous.

"Brett, hey!" I called. "Nice tights! Who are you? I'm slutty Florence Nightingale."

"Romeo! And you can be my Juliet," Brett cried, kissing me on both cheeks. Instead of introducing me to his wan-faced friend, he dragged me to the dance floor. I tried to protest that I needed a drink, but his nicely buffed fingernails were insistent on my arm.

"Perfect timing," Brett whispered in my ear once we'd made it a safe distance from the bar. He nodded toward Dracula, who was now staring dejectedly into a blood-colored cocktail. "That was awk. I haven't seen that guy since I ran out of his apartment.

I'd had too much to drink, and trust me, he looks better with the bloodsucking makeup *on*, as I discovered once my beer goggles wore *off*."

I giggled and grabbed Brett's drink, taking a hearty swig. It was funny to think of Brett being so skanky. Although I supposed I wasn't in a position to talk, given my current outfit.

"Listen," Brett continued, twirling me as a Duffy track blared over the speakers. "You have to come up with me to my aunt's house in Sonoma for a weekend, for a little wine tasting. The fall is all about the merlot, and it's the perfect place for some L.A. detox. I won't take no for an answer!"

"Of course!" I agreed, even though it sounded like my presence was not optional. It was funny, though. A few months ago, a quiet "detox" weekend away from Hollywood was all I could have wanted. Now the idea of leaving L.A., even for a weekend, made my body quake a little. What would happen when I was gone?

"Hey Sexy Nurse," slurred a voice from somewhere behind me. "I've got, uh, something *swollen* down below. I think you should look at it!" Then whoever it was guffawed and fell over with a crash. I turned to look and saw a surprisingly cute guy, dressed up as an astronaut, sprawled on the dance floor a few feet away.

"I love you," he called from his prone position. "Will you marry me?"

"Sure," I laughed and kept dancing, tossing my hair in what I hoped was a sexy-nurse kind of way and trying not to topple over on my hooker heels. I was at a fabulous party with my fabulous gay boyfriend wearing a fabulously slutty costume. Did life get any better than this?

Just then my eyes were drawn, almost instinctually, up toward the VIP banquettes. They landed on a familiar figure. She was wearing a green velvet medieval-style dress with an empire waist and a low-cut neck that revealed ample golden cleavage, a tiny gold crown nestled in her blond waves. Kylie. Dressed as a princess or a queen. She looked gorgeous in her costume, classy and chic, whereas I looked like someone you could rent by the hour.

Beside her was Troy Vaughn, a funnyman actor whose opening weekends always grossed in the forty-million range and who reportedly wanted to make the transition to directing—as did every actor in this town, regardless of his or her talent. He whispered something in Kylie's ear, and she threw her head back, laughing. I instantly felt jealous. No matter where I went, who I was with, or what I wore, was Kylie always going to one-up me?

But then a very strange thing happened: Kylie glanced down, spotted me, and smiled. She gave me what could only be described as a friendly wave.

Next to me Brett gasped. "Do my eyes deceive me, or is the ice queen melting?"

The new Britney song came on, the one Brett had IMed me about yesterday. (*I don't care what people say about Britney's new single, it makes me want to limbo!*) The dance beat was loud and insistent and thumped wildly through my now-buzzed frame.

I shrugged, shaking my pleather-clad hips. It had taken weeks of mean-girl lessons, some outright trickery, and even a few deathstares. But whether or not Kylie Arthur genuinely liked me, Brett was right—the ice was starting to thaw.

CHAPTER SIXTEEN

Dear Michael,
Everything is going really well here in L.A.—I'm getting
the hang of my job, looking for good projects, you know—
and . . .

Here I paused, looking up from Magnolia's lumpy brown sofa
toward the water stain on the ceiling (it was shaped like Florida).
Oddly enough, I didn't really know what else to say. I hadn't
written Michael Deming since things had gotten so busy at work,
and I was starting to think it was kind of a stupid idea in the first
place. I was contemplating chucking the letter entirely when
Magnolia burst into the living room, her eyes nearly popping out
of her head.

"Guess who I saw at Buddha Ball?"

Buddha Ball was the latest L.A. fitness obsession. It involved
a sword, a medicine ball, and some yoga poses, and proponents
swore it burned a thousand calories an hour. It also cost thirty

dollars a class, but Magnolia didn't have to pay because she waxed the instructor. Magnolia's parents had actually been early adopters of Buddha Ball when it first hit the scene in the late 1990s—along with that awful wave of Tae Bo—and even though it had become sickeningly trendy, Mags was sticking with it for its health benefits.

"Who?"

She flopped down on the couch next to me, and immediately Cabbage and Lucius—a new mutt, who looked like a spaniel of some sort—came and jumped on her lap, bringing with them their powerful doggy breath and a small cloud of flying fur.

"Well, if that's how you feel about it, I won't tell you," she said, burying her sweaty face into Lucius's brown and white–spotted head. When she looked up again, there was a small clump of his fur sticking to her cheek.

"No really, come on," I said in a slightly more animated voice. I actually was sort of curious.

"Oh look, they're kissing," she said, pointing to the two dogs, who were indeed now licking each other's faces. Then she turned to me. "I'm totally not going to tell you until you stop lying around on the couch. Go into your room, put on some real clothes, and meet me back here in half an hour. It's Sunday evening, and you haven't been out of the house all weekend, which is completely and totally pathetic. As Cesar Millan, the Dog Whisperer, says, all dogs need walks!" She clapped her hands together and said, "Go on, girl! Go fetch a decent outfit!"

"I'm not a dog," I mumbled, but I got up off the couch and did what she told me to anyway.

We went to a little bar called Valentines because a) it was close to our apartment and b) Magnolia got free drinks because she waxed one of the bartenders. (Seriously, who *didn't* she wax? Was there anyone in all of L.A. with a little, um, hair left?) It was a cute place, though, with cozy little red vinyl booths and lots of black-and-white photographs of old Hollywood on the walls. It was the kind of bar where the arty kids hung out and traded zines or compared tattoos or did whatever it is that arty kids do. It occurred to me that if I'd wanted to, *I* could have become an arty kid. I had the film degree to prove it. But then I'd hate the me that wanted to work her way up at a Hollywood studio, the me that put together her outfits the night before and was actually starting to enjoy it.

As usual, the bartender was checking out Magnolia, but she mainly had eyes for her bloody bishop. ("My Sunday drink," she called it.)

"All right," she said after she'd had a few nourishing sips. "Are you feeling perky yet? Do you deserve to know who I saw?"

Magnolia usually took a long time to get to her point, but this was ridiculous. By now I'd been waiting an hour to hear the news. "I'm totally perky," I insisted, raising my gimlet.

"Okay then," she said. She leaned in close to my face and whispered, "Holden MacIntee!"

Well, color me impressed—that was some real star power.

"You cannot believe how hot he is. I mean, the *Vanity Fair* cover does him no justice at all. His eyes are this amazing sea green, you know, like the ocean off Hawaii or something. And his arms are like these beautiful golden sculptures and he can hold tree pose for ages. And I swear he gives off these phero-mones that like, make you woozy. I could have *licked* him."

I think Magnolia would have gone on for another fifteen minutes, but she stopped to eat a bite of celery and noticed that my eyes had totally glazed over.

"Oh, am I boring you?" she said, only slightly indignantly. "Ms. Second Assistant to Iris Whitaker? Well, I do have a point. But you have to be nice to me to hear it."

I sighed theatrically. "I'll buy this round."

"But it's free!" she cried.

I smiled and shrugged. "Well, I guess you're just going to have to tell me then."

Luckily Magnolia was too excitable—and too good-natured—to keep her secret any longer.

She put an olive on the end of her finger, just like a little kid, and pointed it at me. "The best part is that he and you have the same taste."

"How so?"

"His favorite movie is *Journal Girl*!"

I laughed out loud. "You're joking."

"No, he's totally obsessed with it. At the beginning of each class, the teacher makes us do a 'confessional' of what's on everyone's mind, so we can purify ourselves before class starts. We all go around in a circle, letting go of our worries and what's keeping us stressed. Like, I said that I just didn't know how to help this Great Dane I'm walking who's terrified of my tennis shoes."

"And?" I demanded, poking her.

"And then Holden said that he had this movie *Journal Girl* on his mind because he'd been watching it that afternoon when his DVD player broke. He said it was his favorite movie, and now it was stuck inside his Sony. And I just thought, Oh my God, isn't that weird? Like, what are the odds? He's watched it like twenty

times or something." She ate the olive off the tip of her finger
and dove into her drink for another one.

I sipped my drink, not exactly sure what to do with this information—it wasn't like I could just call him up and tell him how
much we had in common. But somehow, it felt nice to know
someone out there had the same blind devotion to Michael
Deming I did.

"Wow, Mags," I said, patting her on the shoulder. "Good de-
tective work!"

"It was nothing," she said, but she looked proud.

Just then my iPhone buzzed. (I'd finally put it on vibrate, because that Timbaland song had started to drive me crazy.) It was
an e-mail from Kylie.

Hey! Hope you had fun at the party this weekend—you
looked hot! So, sorry for the late notice, but Iris needs you
to go up to her Malibu house tomorrow to let in some
couch that's being delivered. 7:30. So early, I know! Good
luck and I'll see you in the morning.

The address was typed neatly below and, I was amazed and
pleased to discover, there was no smiley face to mock me. So
maybe the wave at the Halloween party wasn't just a fluke. Kylie
had dropped the fake act and was acting like a normal human
being, albeit one whose job was to order me around.

I downed the rest of my drink in a single gulp. "I have to go,
Mags," I said. "I just found out how early I have to get up."

Magnolia frowned. "Kylie?" she asked.

I nodded and stood up. "But not like that. She was actually
nice about it."

Magnolia twisted her long legs around on her stool. "Sit," she commanded me, just like I was one of her mutts. "Tonight *I'm* in charge," she said. "And I'm going to make you have some stinking fun for a change." And with that she signaled the bartender for another round.

CHAPTER SEVENTEEN

Move! *Move!*" I yelled through my windshield, but the white Celica in front of me didn't budge.

Of course I could yell all I wanted, but I'd still be stuck on the I-10 Freeway with the rest of the city, at a complete standstill, while two uniformed deliverymen stood in front of Iris's empty house, a couch resting on the sidewalk behind them, ringing the doorbell and finding no one to let them in.

It was 8:15. I had overslept, and it was Magnolia's fault.

It's ugly out there this morning, the DJ on 97.5 FM said. *Back-up on 101, and a three-car fender-bender on the 10 making everyone just a little bit late this morning.*

"Oh really?" I hissed. I punched the tape button (my car was too old to have a CD player, thank you very much), and the DJ was replaced by the mellow, depressive voice of Leonard Cohen.

Here's what had happened. I was awakened by a scratching sound on my door. I could have ignored it and gone back to sleep, but then came the whining. And finally, the yelping. The dogs.

I sat up and rubbed my slightly sore and fuzzy head. (It was the gimlets.) Where was Magnolia? The dogs would never expect me to pay attention to them if she were home—I mean, they were ugly, but they weren't completely stupid. Gingerly I eased myself out of bed and opened the door, and the dogs fell over themselves in excitement. Or perhaps desperation: poor Lucius was practically crossing his legs in an "I really have to pee" posture.

I looked at the clock and then I about fell over myself. 7:40. 7:40!! I'd set my alarm for 6:00, so I'd have time to shower, grab a coffee at the hippie café around the corner, and make my way leisurely to Malibu. I reached for the clock: yes, I'd set it for 6:00 . . . *p.m.* Oh my God, I was dumber than a bag of hammers.

So that's why I was currently freaking out, stuck behind the granny in the Celica, not being at *all* calmed by Leonard Cohen. It was a beautiful clear morning, and I could see the tiny planes flying over the Hollywood range out of the Burbank airport. I wished I were on one of them. I didn't know who I was more mad at, myself or Magnolia. If she hadn't made me drink all those gimlets last night I might have been sober enough to tell the difference between a.m. and p.m.

"Move!" I shrieked again.

The Celica inched forward—hey, maybe granny could hear me!—and then my BlackBerry buzzed with an e-mail.

Taylor—please see me when you get in. Iris.

My knuckles turned white as I gripped the steering wheel.

☙

Needless to say, when I got to Iris's, neither the deliverymen nor the couch were anywhere to be found. A crow called derisively from a jacaranda near the garage, and I could have sworn it was laughing at me. By this point, I was probably going to be late for work too. In desperation, I grabbed my phone and texted Quinn. The crow continued his nasty chatter as I backed out of the driveway.

Quinn's response came when I was inching my way to the office, this time stuck behind a little Mazda with flames painted on its sides and a dude with a mullet behind the wheel. (I'd checked his plates, thinking he must be from Alabama or something, but no, he was a Californian. Some people are just impervious to L.A. style, I guess.)

Lesson #7: No matter what, it's *never* your fault.

Easy for you to say, I thought. I was pretty sure Quinn was good at bending the truth, but I'd always been honest, sometimes painfully so. Like when my fifth-grade teacher asked the class who'd barfed in the garbage can after the Salisbury steak lunch— you'd think I would have been able to keep my hand down. But no. I raised it right up there.

When I finally got to work, I dumped my bag on my Aeron chair with a sigh. Kylie sat at her desk, composedly typing an e-mail. Her wavy hair was pulled gracefully back off her face, and she looked as fresh and rested as if she'd just come back from the spa at Canyon Ranch. "I think Iris wants to see you," she said evenly.

"Taylor?" Iris called from her desk. "Could you come in here please?"

I shuffled through the doorway, brushing against one of Iris's miniature orange trees. An orange no bigger than a clementine fell off its branch and rolled away. I was about to duck into the midst of all that plant matter to find it, but Iris said quietly, "Leave it. And close the door behind you."

Those were words you never really wanted to hear, but I did as I was asked. I was already preparing my apology, which was going to be as genuine and eloquent as I could make it. It would also involve an element of self-defense, though. I wasn't going to deny that I'd screwed up, but I'd only overslept; it's not like I dropped a call from Steven Spielberg or told Harvey Weinstein he could stand to put in a few hours on the treadmill. I mean really, who *hasn't* overslept something or another? My father was late to his own wedding, thanks to an ill-timed nap.

Iris's newly brightened hair fell in reddish gold waves to her shoulders; she pushed it back and then crossed her hands on her black lacquer desk. I lowered myself into the leather chair by her desk, the one I'd sat in my very first day and that kept me at eye level with her chest. I sat up as straight as I could, wishing Iris would just get rid of this stupid thing. Sure it was a Mies van der Rohe–inspired design, but it made everyone who sat in it feel like a munchkin.

Iris cleared her throat.

"Iris, I'm so—" I began.

"When I ask one of you," she said, leaning toward me, "to be at my home for a delivery, you must know that I am asking because it is important. I don't relish sending my assistants on pointless errands. You have better things to do with your time." Her voice was calm. "But sometimes I am *forced* to ask you to perform what seems like a menial or trivial task, and I expect you to do it. When it doesn't get done, it is a definite problem." She blinked her ocean blue eyes at me. "Do you have anything to say for yourself?"

If I'd felt three feet tall before, I felt about one foot tall now. The worst part of it was, I hated to let Iris down. Her disappointment in me was way worse than her anger. I felt like a little kid, chastised by my favorite teacher.

"Taylor?" Iris prodded.

I nodded mutely. I could feel the apology building in me, and maybe even a tear or two. We'd been getting along so well—it wasn't fair! I wanted to reach across the desk and grab her hand and promise to never disappoint her again.

"I . . . I . . . ," I stammered. Iris raised her eyebrows, waiting somewhat impatiently. And then it hit me: *It's never your fault.* Iris had *two* houses in Malibu, didn't she? There was the one she was selling and the new one she'd just bought. I'd gone to the one she was selling. "Actually, I *did* get to the house on time," I said. "But I went to the wrong one. And for that I am truly sorry."

Iris sat up straighter in her chair. "The wrong house?"

I nodded very earnestly. "I went to the one in Colony, not the one on Carbon Beach." I held my breath.

"I see." Understanding dawned on Iris's pretty features. "Kylie?" Iris called, peering through the plants that separated her from her assistants. "Can you come in here please?"

Kylie opened the door with a pleasantly vacant expression, as if she had no idea what was going on. She cocked a bony hip inside her patterned shirtdress. "Yes?"

"I'd like you to tell me the address you told Taylor to go to last night," Iris said in a commanding voice.

Kylie's eyes flicked to me—a little guiltily, I thought—then back to Iris. "Um, oh God, at this point, I don't really remember. I think it was the new one."

"I sent you an e-mail with the address," Iris said, growing more impatient. "Didn't you forward it to Taylor?"

Kylie pawed the carpet with the toe of her boot. "No, but Taylor knows both addresses. They're in the assistant's manual," she said defensively. "I'm sure I told her the new house, though. I mean, why would you have a couch delivered to the house you were selling?"

As Kylie scrambled, I couldn't believe my luck. *She had sent me the wrong address.* And I was sure she'd done it on purpose. Kylie hadn't turned over a new leaf after all, but who cared? She'd been caught, and I was reaping the benefits.

Iris sighed, as if Kylie were a difficult child. "The next time you decide to pass a job off on *her*," she said, pointing to me, "please make sure you give her the correct information. Do you understand?"

I looked from Iris to Kylie. Did that mean that Iris had asked *Kylie* to go to Malibu?

Kylie stared at the thick, white Berber carpet. "Yes."

"I e-mailed you, Kylie," Iris continued, "and asked *you* specifically to go to my house, because I wanted Taylor to be in the Steven Pritchard notes meeting this morning."

I felt my cheeks flush with pride and happiness. Iris had wanted *me* to go to a meeting!

"All right, that's it," Iris said, leaning back and twisting her hair into a clip. "You can go."

Kylie turned on her heel and stalked out, staring at the ground.

I could barely contain my glee. Kylie had gotten told off, *and* she had completely caved the second she was called out on her behavior. And Iris was still looking at where Kylie had been with an expression of deep annoyance on her face.

"So how was the meeting?" I asked. I thought I should try to smooth over the awkwardness.

Iris grimaced slightly. "Postponed. I need you to reschedule it. Oh, and call Diva on Melrose. Tell them we need the B&B Italia sofa delivered for Saturday. And get me New York, please." She smiled wearily and turned toward her computer. "It's time I got on with my day."

"Of course," I said, turning to go.

"Taylor."

She turned around.

"I apologize," Iris said, shaking her head. "It's really unfortunate you went all the way up there for nothing."

"It's okay," I replied. On my way out, I had to force myself not to grin.

☙

"Oh my God, did you hear?"

Julissa marched into the kitchen, where I was sucking down a Red Bull. She was wearing a cute little jumper dress I recognized from Gap, Fall 2007 (I had tried it on back in Middletown, but it made my thighs look terrible), and an eager, almost scandalized smile.

Boy, that got around fast, I thought. *Newsflash: sycophantic first assistant finally gets her comeuppance.*

"About Melinda Darling!" Julissa hissed.

I rolled my eyes. "Friday Darling Rubenstein, I know. It's absolutely insane."

"No, not *that,*" Julissa said, tossing a bunch of scripts I'd asked her to read onto the counter. "She's not coming back after she has the baby. She just announced it."

I perked right up. It could have been the Red Bull, but more likely it was Julissa's news. "So Metronome's going to be needing a new CE," I mused.

"Totally," Julissa exclaimed. "And you *know* it's going to be one of the assistants. All they have to do is package a movie or discover a great screenwriter or something, and they'll get the promotion. And Iris gets to make the final decision about who gets it, so you're already a step ahead of Wyman or whoever. Wouldn't it be great if you got to be a CE and I got hired as an assistant? I'd actually get a paycheck!" She was practically bouncing up and down.

I smiled gently. "In a perfect world," I said. Meanwhile I was thinking, Yeah, right—I'm the newest hire and Julissa is a total spaz. What, really, were the chances?

"Melinda'll be gone in two weeks. You should see it out there. Wyman and Amanda are already in a fight. It's like *Game on.*" She giggled. "Oh, and I did those scripts last night. Coverage is clipped to the front." She waved and skittered away down the hall.

I got another Red Bull out of the fridge and popped the top. I'd always prided myself on having high but reasonable expectations about life, and usually I'd been justified. I wasn't valedictorian, but I was salutatorian (which was better, really, because I didn't have to give a speech); I didn't get into Princeton, but I did go to Wesleyan; and I hadn't driven down the Sunset Strip with the wind blowing through my hair, but I had at least learned how to *find* the damn street in my car. To hope for a promotion to CE after only a few months of work seemed pretty unreasonable to me, and I told myself to put it out of my mind. I pretty much had too, until I went into the copier room and saw the Holden Mac-Intee *Vanity Fair* perched on top of a pile of scripts, including *Psycho Killer Pigs,* in the recycling bin.

Holden MacIntee, I whispered. *Journal Girl.* Michael Deming.

Everything became clear in an instant. All I had to do was pitch Holden a movie with Michael. Hot Hollywood stud, meet your reclusive idol. Reclusive idol, meet critical acclaim.

And Taylor, meet your new job title: creative executive.

Okay, Holden had a multimillion-dollar asking price, and Deming lived in a log cabin . . . so maybe it wasn't going to be a breeze. But suddenly it seemed like a promotion wasn't so far out of reach.

CHAPTER EIGHTEEN

Hi, is Bob Glazer there please? It's regarding Holden Mac-Intee. This is Taylor Henning," I added, just in case the assistant on the other line didn't recognize my voice after three days of messages. I felt a little ridiculous, but as my mother always said, "Persistence removes resistance!" As a kid, I'd pictured resistance as a laundry stain.

"Oh . . . hi," he said limply. "I don't think I can get him right now."

"Are you sure?" I chirped, tapping my pencil on my desk. "I'll hold."

The assistant sighed. "Let me see if I can get him," he muttered and put me on hold.

I stared at the clock on the wall. Kylie had blown out her candle and left for the day while I was still here, pestering this poor assistant with my pushiness. Not surprisingly, getting a meeting with Holden MacIntee was proving to be as impossible as getting a table at Sushi Roku on a Saturday night.

"Bob Glazer," a voice suddenly said in my ear.

"Hi, Bob, this is Taylor. I'm calling from Metronome," I said, eagerly leaping into my spiel, "and I was wondering if there's any chance that I can—"

"*Who* are you?" Bob asked, as if I were a small child who had wrestled the phone away from her parents.

"Taylor Henning. From Metronome."

"And you're a *creative exec?*" he asked.

"No, actually," I said reluctantly, "I'm an assistant, but I may have a project to discuss with Holden." It would have helped if I'd dropped Iris's name, but since I couldn't risk this getting back to her, I kept my mouth shut.

"Sorry, he's committed through 2010," he said. "And we don't deal with assistants." Then he hung up.

I threw down my headset on top of my list of Good Things and Bad Things. (*Good Things: my brilliant movie idea; lost three pounds by following lead of salad-bar girls. Bad Things: possibly allergic to Kylie's aromatherapy candle; Cabbage peed on my favorite bra when I left it drying in the bathroom.*) Zero for three, I thought. Now that I'd run through the Holy Trinity of Hollywood gate-keepers—agent, publicist, and manager—I was out of ideas as to how to reach Holden MacIntee. What was I supposed to do? I briefly wondered how the paparazzi always knew how to find their prey. Should I hang out at Winston's and hope he showed up? Should I figure out where he lived and then stake out his house? God, I thought, I was starting to sound like a stalker. And not a nice, harmless, epistolary one either.

I glanced at my IM buddy list and saw that Brett was still at work, too—he was often my partner in late-night drudgery. We'd chat on IM and, when things got really bad, pick up the phone (who else would sing me an ABBA song in totally off-key falsetto?).

JournalGirl07: Hey, I need your help

Bduncadonk: Anything for you Miss Thing!

JournalGirl07: Thx. Need to reach Holden MacIntee. Already tried the holy trinity.

Bduncadonk: I heart you but . . . you're screwed. Drinks later?

JournalGirl07: Sigh. Yeah.

I watched the cursor blip back and forth, feeling helpless. But then I had a thought.

There was still my sixteen-year-old secret weapon. Maybe Quinn knew him. Hell, it wouldn't surprise me if she'd dated him. I took out my iPhone and dialed her as I turned off my computer and readied myself to leave the office.

"What?" Quinn asked when she picked up.

"How do you get a celebrity to talk to you?" I walked past the magenta and violet pulsing walls toward the front door. Honestly, if I had to look at those all day, I think I'd go insane. Or start reading *Us Weekly* all day long, which would *really* send me to the loony bin.

Quinn laughed a short barking laugh. "Depends on who it is."

I hesitated. "Holden MacIntee."

"Are you high?"

I could just imagine the look on Quinn's face: the rolling eyes, the raised brows, the pursed, incredulous mouth. "I don't have a crush on him, I just need to talk to him. About work."

I proceeded to explain the Melinda Darling situation, and how her departure meant that I needed to pitch Holden a Deming project.

Quinn interrupted my story. "Friday Darling?" she crowed.

"Focus!" I cried. "Focus."

Quinn stopped laughing, and her habitual coolness returned. "What makes you so sure he's into this director?"

"My roommate. She saw him at Buddha Ball," I said, zipping down the stairs so I wouldn't lose reception in the elevator. I noticed that on one of the walls, someone had written *My job makes me feel like my head is going to explode.* I smiled, feeling a certain kinship with the anonymous scrawler.

It sounded like Quinn was banging the phone against something hard. "Duh," she said when she came back on. "Take the class. But don't stalk, you know? Never pretend you don't know who someone is, either, because that's totally lame. Just be cool. Do you think you can manage that?"

I rolled my eyes and pushed out the door into the L.A. evening.

"And hey, even if he's not there, your triceps will thank you."

Ouch. If I didn't owe her everything, I'd give that girl a piece of my mind. "Toodle-oo!" I cried into the phone, just to annoy her a little.

She made a hissing noise and hung up.

⟨☙⟩

"Have you done Buddha Ball before?" The woman behind the check-in desk had short, platinum hair, a tattoo of a Japanese symbol on her popping bicep, and a no-bullshit expression.

"Definitely not," I said, smiling in a way that I hoped was ingratiating.

The pale green waiting room was lined with merch, for those who liked to shop after they exercised: shelves of jade Buddhas, aromatherapy candles, handmade soaps, and cute little T-shirts. On the walls, someone had hung posters of extremely limber men and women in yoga poses that looked, to a neophyte like me, slightly terrifying. Were they going to expect me to be able to put my feet behind my ears? I certainly hoped not.

The woman checked off a box on a clipboard. "Any martial arts training?"

I shook my head, feeling somewhat concerned.

The woman checked another box. "How about boot camp experience?"

"You mean the army or a gym class?"

The woman gave me a funny look then handed me a thin white towel. "Thirty dollars, plus two for the towel. Take off your shoes and socks before you go in, and you'll need to sign this release."

She handed me a clipboard with a page of small print on it. The words "bodily harm," "severe injury," and "death" leapt out at me. Was I ready to sign my life away for a shot at a promotion? I thought about this for a little while as the peroxided blonde tapped her fingers impatiently on the desk. I picked up the pen. Yes, I was.

I removed my shoes and socks and tiptoed into the exercise room, wishing Magnolia were here for a little moral—or physical—support. Too bad she'd developed a bad bout of what she called groomer's elbow.

"First I had to walk a totally psychopathic sheepdog, poor thing, and then I had the world's hairiest man," she'd moaned from her place on the couch. "I mean, I was like, is your uncle a yeti or an orangutan, because it's obviously one or the other." She'd been holding a bag of frozen peas to her right arm while

Cabbage and Lucius milled around on the floor, whining. "I'm thinking of asking for worker's comp," she sighed.

I looked around me at my fellow Buddha Ballers. According to Quinn's guidelines (*Actors have better faces than they do bodies; for porn stars, it's the other way around*), I would be risking life and limb with three actors, two stars of adult films, and a handful of hyperfit, very tanned women who'd obviously made a career out of going to gym classes and tanning beds. There was no Holden MacIntee, however. I crossed my fingers in the hope that he was just late.

Sitting cross-legged on the shiny wooden floor, his back to the long mirrored wall, sat our instructor, a whippet-thin man wearing nylon runner's shorts and a lilac tank top. He seemed to be either meditating or asleep. I took a mat from the pile, feeling a growing sense of dread. It was one thing to face serious bodily harm if Holden were alongside me—but to do so for nothing? Not a chance. I set the mat back down and was getting ready to duck out the door when the instructor opened his eyes. "All right, class," he said, flopping his knees up and down. "My name is Ted. I'll be leading you on your journey tonight."

"Hi, Ted," the class said in unison.

"Excuse me, you there, in the back," Ted called out to me. "Aren't you staying?"

I slowly turned around. "Actually, I just realized that I—"

"Please. Join us. Better yet, come up front. With me." He beckoned to me with his wiry arm.

"Come up there?"

"Yes, please. As Yogi Shankativi said, it is often best to meet reluctance with a direct challenge." Then he pressed his hands together in prayer position.

I wasn't really sure what Ted—or Yogi whoever—meant by that, but I could hardly disobey a direct order. I picked my purple mat back up and went to join Ted near the front of the room. One of the porn stars snickered. She wore a shirt that said SILICONE FREE, which was very clearly false advertising. I shot a little deathstare in her general direction.

Ted smiled beatifically at all of us and announced that it was time for the confessional. "This is when we release negative energy before our practice," he intoned, his voice turning soothing and singsong.

The confessional was how Magnolia had learned that *Journal Girl* was Holden's favorite movie. What I learned, however, was far less useful to me. I got one tale of woe after another: a blown audition, a demanding boss, a negative reading from a psychic, a colonic gone awry. It was like group therapy, except that everyone was in spandex.

Finally it was my turn. "Why are you here?" Ted asked, turning his wide, earnest eyes to me. "What negative emotions do you want to neutralize?"

Obviously I couldn't admit the real reason, because I'd offend Ted and I'd look like a stalker. I thought about it for a moment. "Fear," I said. (And this was true—I was very much afraid that I would snap a tendon in class.) "And, um, maybe a little anger."

Ted nodded encouragingly and so I went on. "My roommate is turning our apartment into the West Hollywood ASPCA, I hate my coworker, and I feel like I'm stupid for even coming here." All of which was true.

"Perfect," Ted said gently. "I hope that felt freeing to you. You unburdened your soul just now, and maybe you feel just a little bit lighter."

I nodded vigorously. I didn't feel lighter, but maybe I would after an hour in this sweatbox. And a little white lie wouldn't kill me.

"I believe," Ted continued, "that today the class will follow your lead in addition to mine." He held up his hand, stopping my protests before they were even out of my mouth. "If you don't think you belong here, then this is how you learn that you do," he said. His voice wavered between meditative and commanding. "If everyone's following your example, then you'll see how important your presence here really is." He picked up a medicine ball stamped with the image of a fat Buddha and handed it to me. "Now, let's start in Warrior Three. But the ball stays in your hand the entire time. Go ahead, go."

I held the heavy ball in my hands with my head hung down. "I don't know Warrior Three," I whispered.

Ted nodded. "Everyone, grab your medicine balls and show this young lady what to do."

I watched as the actors and porn stars and fitness obsessives each lifted their left leg, bent forward at the waist, and held the ball out in front of their faces. Okay, I thought, I can do this. Fixing my right foot firmly on the mat, I tried to follow their lead. I wobbled, my arms wavered, and there was a white-hot stab of pain in my hamstring.

"Aaaahh!" I yelled.

"There you go," Ted said, starting to meander around the room. "Everyone follow her lead. Everyone say, 'Aaaahh!'"

"Aaahhh!"

"Hold it, hold it, keep holding," Ted encouraged.

Obviously he wasn't some caring, hippie-ish exercise instructor at all; he was a total sadist. How could Magnolia have taken this class? Why had I ever listened to Quinn? Was it possible for someone's arms to fall off from holding a medicine ball for too long? Was my heart going to explode? These and other questions were swirling around in my head at a dizzying rate. Then I toppled over onto my face.

"Excellent," Ted whispered in my ear. "The first step toward grace is surrender."

Hidden under my crumpled body, I gave Ted the finger.

CHAPTER NINETEEN

Okay," I said, paintbrush in hand as I contemplated the plain white cotton onesie before me on the table. "What do I put on it? 'Thanks for quitting'?"

Julissa giggled. "Definitely," she said.

We were standing in the immense, sunlight-filled family room in Peter Lasky's Bel Air estate, each of us halfway through a third mimosa and feeling a little buzzed from the early-afternoon Dom Pérignon. Through the large French doors, which were open to the fine November day, I could see most of the Metronome development and production staff mingling on the lawn as they were serenaded by a small chamber orchestra.

Melinda Darling sure got a fancy baby shower/farewell party. But it pays to know the right people, as they say—or perhaps, more accurately, it pays to be *related* to them. As it turned out, Melinda was the niece of our volatile studio head, Peter Lasky (no wonder she'd never had to work her way up from assistant!), and he had spared no expense in helping her celebrate her big day.

"Are you done with the yellow?" a gaunt platinum blonde in pearls asked me.

I realized that a crowd had begun to form around the onesie table.

"And where are the fabric markers?" asked her red-faced, jowly companion in a deep baritone. "Honey, how do I do this?"

"Just make a smiley-face," the blonde hissed.

Good idea, I thought. I took my onesie, dabbed a couple of eyes and a big grinning mouth on it, wrote "Happy Baby!" underneath, and grabbed Julissa's arm. "Let's go look at the gifts," I whispered.

The marble foyer of the house contained enough presents for a hundred babies. There were boxes wrapped in pink paper and magenta bows and gift bags with the heads of stuffed animals peering out. There were also dozens of gifts apparently too large or too oddly shaped to wrap: a sparkly purple tricycle, a medieval castle complete with catapult and moat, a five-foot-tall stuffed giraffe, and a teak crib that looked like it had been hand-carved by Mayan artisans or something.

"My God, some people must have spent thousands of dollars," I muttered. What had I gotten ol' Friday Darling? A blanket from Target with a kitten on it, that's what. Twenty bucks and she could love it or hate it—I'd certainly never be the wiser.

Julissa fingered the giraffe's ear in awe. "Thank God I'm an intern," she said. "I can just get drunk and not feel guilty about it." She took a sip of her mimosa for emphasis.

We wandered back into the family room, heading for the chocolate-covered strawberries.

"Hey, look at that." Julissa drew me over to one of the French doors.

Kylie and Iris were walking across the lawn together, deep in conversation. Intense conversation. Ever since the Malibu incident, Iris had been careful to avoid both of us, like a parent trying not to show favoritism between two warring children. But she was hunched over a little, bringing herself closer to Kylie's level, intently listening. After a moment, she tipped her head back and laughed.

Julissa squinted. "Kylie's kissing ass, as usual."

My nemesis looked positively radiant in an empire-waist gold dress and a messy but perfect updo. "Oh my God," I said. "She's not kissing ass, she's *pitching*." While I was standing there watching, half-hidden behind the gauzy curtains, Kylie was probably cinching her promotion. Damn Holden MacIntee and his stupid, lazy, can't-make-it-to-Buddha-Ball ass!

Kylie was still talking, waving around her champagne flute for emphasis.

"You know," Julissa said, "we're not the only ones spying."

I scanned the lawn. It was true. Amanda, a pink cocktail in her hand to match her pink sheath dress, was stalking Iris and Kylie with her eyes. Over by the pool, Cici talked to Tom Scheffer while staring daggers at Kylie—rather blatantly, if you asked me. Wyman was subtler in his ogling, but that was only because he was wearing a giant pair of Ray-Bans.

I finished my mimosa with a sinking feeling. "I think I need to eat. You want anything?"

Julissa shook her head. "Nah. I'm going to go snoop upstairs."

On my way to the food tent, which had been set up on the emerald green lawn overlooking the marble-lined pool, I fired off a text to Quinn. *Kylie pitching your mother. Must be taken down!*

Quinn would help, I was sure of it. I tried to let that cheer me up. Ditto for the buffet. Though I'd gotten out of the habit of drowning my sorrows in a pint of ice cream, I felt justified in attempting to alleviate my new anxiety at the buffet table. Also, since I'd kept going to Buddha Ball (despite Holden's continued absence), I figured I'd earned myself the right to binge a little. It was almost Thanksgiving, and since I wouldn't be going home to Cleveland or celebrating the holiday in any other way (my mother had threatened to send me a ham, but I told her that Magnolia and I had agreed to go out for sushi that day), I could certainly stuff myself on free gourmet food at a baby shower.

I plucked an ivory Limoges dinner plate from the stack and regarded my options. I could feel my stomach rumbling as I contemplated the heaps of raw and grilled vegetables, the mountain of miniburgers, the pâté swan, the plates of French cheeses, the four-foot-long poached salmon, and the hills of fruit salad.

"Would you like me to explain the difference between the beluga and the osetra?" asked a server, pointing to two glistening mounds of tiny black eggs.

I was about to say that when it came to caviar, I was on a not-need-to-know basis, when someone sidled up beside me. I recognized the lily perfume even before I turned to see Kylie.

"I'd *loooove* some beluga," Kylie said, holding out her plate. "No explanation necessary," she added, winking at Mr. Toque. Then she pretended to spot me for the first time. "Oh hi. Cool party, huh?"

"Yep," I murmured, spearing a paper-thin slice of smoked salmon.

The server placed some toast points around the beluga. "Gorgeous," she breathed. "Thank you *so much*." Kylie smiled at me as she scooped some caviar onto a toast point. "Are you doing okay?" Her voice had lowered in pitch, and she sounded genuinely concerned.

I squeezed a wedge of lemon onto my salmon. "Sure. Why?"

"Just because you and I haven't been getting along."

I stared at her blankly.

"I mean, not that I'm lying awake at night worrying about it or anything," Kylie said, taking a delicate bite, "but it seems kind of unnecessary, don't you think?" She popped the rest of the toast point in her mouth and chewed.

"Well," she said, not waiting for an answer, "I guess I just wanted to clear the air a little. Because for the next few days, I'm going to be kind of busy. I just packaged a movie."

I sucked in my breath. There was a part of me that had anticipated this. But just because you're expecting bad news doesn't mean you like hearing it. I put my plate down on an empty table.

"Well, it's almost there," she continued, as if I'd asked. "We're just waiting for Troy Vaughn to sign on, but it's *so* close. I found this amazing script on one of the tracking boards, and Troy just really took to it. It's going to be his directorial debut. Oh my God—he is so funny! The first time we went out for drinks, I was just cracking up. He just sent me the funniest text, actually."

I bit my lip, fighting back anger, expletives, hunger, and maybe even tears. I thought back to Halloween, when I'd spotted Kylie with Troy Vaughn. She'd had her plan in motion even then. The smile, the nice wave, that brief period of seeming humanity—Kylie had never warmed to me, not even for a second. She just didn't care to fight with me because, in her mind, she'd already won.

"So, I just told Iris that it's almost a go, and, well, she didn't come right out and *say* it, but it sounds like if it all works out, the promotion's mine." Kylie sighed, as if the weight of her own achievement were too much even for her. "Can you believe it?"

"Congratulations," I said grimly.

Kylie acted as if I hadn't spoken at all. "I guess before everything sort of . . . changes, I just wanted to clear the air." She popped her last toast point into her mouth. "I mean, it's not like we're going to stop working together, even if, you know, we're not in the same office."

I looked down at my hands and realized that I'd shredded one of the cocktail napkins into tiny, confetti-like bits. Clearing the air? Is that what she was calling this chat? Because if you ask me, she was rubbing my nose in it.

"Wow, I am *stuffed*!" Kylie put down her plate on the tray of a passing waitress and picked up her champagne. "Oh hi, Iris!" she called over my shoulder.

I turned to see Iris filling a plate with fruit salad.

"How's my team doing?" she asked cheerfully as she picked around for the ripest strawberries.

"Great," Kylie exclaimed. "But I'm out of champagne!"

"Better go get some," I chirped, and mercifully she smiled, told me that was a great idea, and left.

I plucked a mini quiche from a platter and chucked it into my mouth, barely chewing. A line had formed at the end of the buffet table, which I was probably guilty of holding up, considering I'd been standing in the same place for ten minutes. Not that I cared—these Metronome folks could just step around me.

"Are you having a good time, Taylor?" Iris asked. Her voice was low but not gentle. It sounded almost strained.

"Kylie just told me about the Troy Vaughn movie," I blurted.

"Kylie might be getting a little ahead of herself," Iris said slowly, moving down to the salmon. "But I will say that she's done a great job. And that's exactly what *everyone* should be doing right now." She smiled at me, letting her words sink in. "You know I think you have terrific instincts, Taylor. And whatever happens, you'll continue to be an asset to me and to Metronome."

I looked down at my toes in their hand-me-down designer sandals. "Well, thank you," I managed to say. "Will you please excuse me? I think I need to find the powder room."

Iris smiled wanly and turned back to the buffet. As I walked toward the house, feeling terrible, I saw Julissa bearing down on me with a wild look on her little freckled face.

"Kylie's got something," she said, grabbing my hand. "A project. Something she's been working on in secret for weeks. It just broke."

I kept walking. "I know. She just told me."

"She *did*? Oh my God, what'd she say?"

I just shook my head. I didn't want to talk about it.

"Your phone," Julissa said.

I looked up at her dully. "Huh?"

"I can hear your phone vibrating in your purse," she said, pointing.

I scrambled among the loose lipsticks and eye shadows rolling around in the satin-lined bottom of the bag.

Malibu Country Mart, half an hour, the text said.

"I've got to go," I said. "Go ask Kylie about her movie. She'll tell you more than you ever wanted to know."

CHAPTER TWENTY

It was almost twilight when I turned off the Pacific Coast Highway into the Malibu Country Mart and parked in front of the Ron Herman shop. For all its high-end boutiques (Lisa Kline, the Madison Gallery) and big-ticket restaurants (Nobu Malibu), the Mart was essentially a strip mall, albeit the most upscale strip mall in the world. It was a little like Malibu itself: on the surface, a rough-and-tumble stretch of beach and chaparral-covered hills, nothing especially grand or beautiful. But hidden in those hills and squeezed into postage stamp–sized lots on the beach were some of the most valuable pieces of property in the world. You just had to step inside them.

I found Quinn on a bench in front of L'Occitane, wearing a purple cashmere sweater coat and an enormous pair of white sunglasses. Several shopping bags from Planet Blue sat at her feet, and she held an enormous Coffee Bean cup.

"You're late," she said loudly, moving some of her shopping bags so I could sit.

"I know. The PCH was insane."

I sat down and pulled my black pashmina closer around my shoulders. "I'm in trouble," I said.

"No shit. You're wearing a pashmina," Quinn scoffed.

"What are you *supposed* to wear with a strapless dress?" I asked, annoyed.

"I was only kidding," Quinn said, taking a noisy sip of her coffee. "So what's this Kylie emergency? I don't love the face-to-faces, so this better be good."

"Kylie's gonna get the promotion," I said shrilly, and I could almost feel tears welling up. "She lined up some movie with Troy Vaughn. And your mom knows about it, and it sounds like it's happening. So there it goes. Right through my fingers." I swallowed. "I mean, it's not like I thought *I* was going to get it or anything, but I just don't want *her* to, you know?"

Quinn was silent for a moment. "Okay," she finally said. "I get it." She reached into her distressed leather bag for a Kleenex, which she handed to me.

"I'm not crying," I said indignantly.

"Well, you look like you might. But listen up. I've got a solution for you, and it's called *hit her where it hurts*." She paused dramatically. "We steal her boyfriend."

"What?" I laughed, partly out of shock and partly out of the impossibility of it.

"I'm dead serious," said Quinn, frowning at me. "You break them up."

"But even if I could do that," I said slowly, "how's that going to get me a promotion?"

"Look." Quinn pulled the glasses off. Her blue eyes were almost navy in the diminishing sunlight. "You know what happens when girls get dumped. They get *fat*. They *cry*. They *crack*. And it goes double for a girl like Kylie, because she so totally doesn't expect it. If she gets broken up with, it'll be all she can think about." Quinn deposited the glasses in her bag and took out a little pot of MAC gloss, which she dabbed on her lips. "It's like when Joanna Beers and Kevin Collins, this superhot boy from Cathedral, broke up. She quit cheerleading and went for a varsity letter in bingeing at In-N-Out. Same'll happen to Kylie. She'll be so out of it, she'll make a mistake. That movie'll get fucked up *real* fast, I promise."

I played with the fringe on my pashmina thoughtfully. I had to admit it made sense, though it was also a) evil and b) twisted.

"Once, I did it to someone at exam time," Quinn said softly. She stared straight ahead, and I watched her proud profile. "I didn't want this girl to get an A on the history final. She was the only person who did better in the class than me." She sipped her drink pensively. "Plus I'd heard about some nasty rumors she'd spread about me. So I hooked up with this guy who she was sort of hooking up with—not dating, exactly, but a guy I knew she liked." The wind blew Quinn's hair across her face and she brushed it away. "And it worked. Big-time."

My sixteen-year-old savior was, I had to admit, something of a monster. "I can't do it," I said.

"Why not?"

I watched a paper bag scuttle across the asphalt. A woman who looked like she kept a lifetime supply of Botox in her enormous Dooney & Bourke satchel walked by with her two labradoodles. "Because that's evil."

Quinn slapped my knee. "Hello? Don't think for a minute that she wouldn't do this to you."

She had a point. But logistically I couldn't see how it would work. "I mean I don't even think I physically can," I said. "He's apparently drop-dead gorgeous."

"He's a *guy*," Quinn sighed. The salty ocean breeze whipped her lustrous red hair around her face, and it momentarily softened her features. "Getting a guy to hook up with you is about as hard as falling out of bed. Or *into* bed, I should say. What does he do?" She took out her iPhone and started checking her e-mail.

"Teaches tennis."

"Perfect. Sign up for lessons." She popped the phone back in her bag, aimed her empty coffee cup at a garbage can, and tossed it in. "Two points."

A gold Lexus hybrid convertible pulled up and idled outside of Starbucks. Really, was there any car they *didn't* make hybrid anymore?

"But I already know how to play tennis, and anyway, how am I just supposed to—"

Quinn stood up and pivoted around to face me. "Taylor," she asked, a strong note of impatience in her voice, "since we started this, when have I steered you wrong?" The setting sun threw a blood red rash into the sky above the Pacific, framing the edges of her coat and hair with rosy light.

"You haven't," I admitted. And it was true. Quinn had been amazing, and I couldn't imagine how I was ever going to repay her.

"Right. So do what you want. But just remember what Kylie would do." She picked up her colorful shopping bags. "The exact same thing." She walked away into the lot, leaving me alone on the bench. In the distance, the Pacific stretched out toward the horizon, and I sat quietly, watching the explosion of light above the water. I'd quickly learned that here in L.A., no one above the age of twenty actually went to the beach. But now I wondered why. Why live so close to the ocean and not take a dip?

Slowly I slid my iPhone out of my purse. I Googled and dialed. When you thought about it, it really was so simple.

"Hi," I said when a woman picked up. "Is this the Beverly Hills Tennis Center? I just wanted to make an appointment."

CHAPTER TWENTY-ONE

The next morning, I rubbed a little Neutrogena sunblock into my face and some Dr. Hauschka SPF 20 lip balm onto my lips, grabbed my old Prince racquet out of my trunk, and made my way into the Tennis Center. At eight o'clock on a Sunday morning, half of the ten green courts were deserted, and on at least one of them the players were obviously still recuperating from the previous night's indulgence.

The morning fog had yet to lift, and a cool breeze blew against my bare legs. My bare, very white legs. I'd slathered on the Bain de Soleil Deep Dark Self-tanner last night, but apparently it had done little to take down the glare. And then there was my outfit. I'd imagined walking onto the court in a cute little tennis dress, à la Maria Sharapova, but sadly there was no athletic gear in Quinn's bag of hand-me-downs, and I hadn't had time to go shopping. So it was a pair of old Nike running shorts and a Black Dog Martha's Vineyard shirt that I'd found balled up in my underwear drawer for me. (If Quinn could see me, she'd gag. But

a) she didn't play tennis and b) she told me she never got out of bed before ten on a weekend.)

In other words, there was very little hope of me seducing Mr. Kylie Arthur, aka Mr. Tennis Hottie, aka Luke Hansen, today. But the lesson itself was a step in the right direction. Today I'd aim to be funny and charming, and the next time I came in, I'd add the cute and the sexy. As best as I possibly could, of course.

He wasn't hard to spot. He had tousled light brown hair that was sort of bleached gold at the ends—from the sun, of course, not from hairdresser-to-the-stars Ken Paves or whomever—and his skin was bronze against his tennis whites. He was tall, and his legs were long and muscular.

I took a deep breath, reminded myself to forget years of tennis lessons (and to stop staring), and stepped onto the court. He turned around.

"Taylor?" He walked over to me, his strong hand extended. "Hi, I'm Luke."

In the rush of trying to find something to wear and my wrong turn on Santa Monica, I'd never stopped to think about the most nerve-wracking part of this plan: Luke himself.

Now that he was right in front of me, I could see that his smile was a little crooked, and his ears stuck out slightly. Actually, he wasn't classically good-looking at all, and for a moment I was surprised Kylie would even go for him in the first place. But there was something decidedly striking about him, and suddenly my whole body felt as taut as the strings on my racquet.

"So, they told me you're a beginner," he said in a friendly voice, tossing a ball up into the air and then catching it.

"Pretty much." My palms were starting to sweat, even though

it really wasn't that warm out. Maybe sucking at tennis wouldn't be so hard after all. "I've taken lessons before, though."

"I can tell. That racquet of yours is pretty serious," he pointed out.

I'd figured he'd notice my 1200 power-level Prince Ozone—a gift from my parents for my last year on the team in high school—and so I had my lie ready. "It's my roommate's," I chirped. "Is it a really good one or something?"

Luke smiled. He didn't have perfectly straight teeth, and actually mine were whiter than his, thanks to Crest Whitestrips—an attempt to negate the effects of a lifetime of Diet Coke consumed over the last few months. Still, I felt dazzled, as if I were watching a Colgate commercial. "It's pretty nice," he said. "Why don't we hit a few? I'll get a look at some of your strokes, and we'll take it from there."

He hopped the net and dashed to the other side. "We'll start with forehands," he called, drawing back his racquet. "You ready?"

I nodded again, and he sent a ball flying over the net. Before I could stop myself, I hit the ball in the center of my racquet and sent it whizzing past him into the advantage court, where it just kissed the baseline.

Luke gazed back from the ball to me, taken aback. "You sure you're just a beginner?"

"Wow!" I said. "Must be beginner's luck."

"Uh-huh," he said in a teasing voice. "Let's try a few more."

For a second I thought he might be onto me—maybe women tried to fake cluelessness in front of him all the time. But he just grabbed another ball from his pocket and sent it flying over the net.

A few courts over from us, four fortysomething women wearing pristine white dresses played a doubles match. The melodic *thwap-thwap* of tennis balls hitting the rackets' sweet spots lulled me into a familiar rhythm.

As we hit more ground strokes and then volleys, I made sure to throw in as many mistakes as I could remember: clumsy footwork, bad follow-through, open-faced racquet. Luke stopped and gently corrected me each time until, during a backhand volley, he ran around the net to check my grip.

"Oh yeah, here we go," he said, placing his hand on my wrist. "The eastern is here," he said, gently moving my wrist over. His hands were warm and firm. "There. Feel that?"

I held my breath and hoped he would keep adjusting my grip. The sun was starting to reach its highest point in the sky, and my body felt warm all over.

"And then when you hit, it's like this," he said, snapping my wrist back and forth. "Feel that?"

You have no idea, I thought. I was suddenly reminded of weekday afternoons in high school, waiting for the boys' team to finish practicing so the girls could take the courts. We'd sit on the benches, quietly doing our homework until we got bored and instead decided to distract the boys and make them double-fault. It always worked. Now if only I could remember my distraction techniques.

"So it's like a stop sign when you hit," he said, holding my arm out in front of me. "Like you're just stopping the ball." His hand curled around my bicep.

"Why aren't you an actor?" I blurted out.

He blushed. "Excuse me?"

"I said—oh, I'm sorry. I just meant . . . you're just so . . . I don't know . . . it seems like everybody here is, but you really seem like you'd have good stage presence." So much for funny and charming, I thought. Good one, Henning.

Luke took a step away from me, looked down at the green surface of the court, and ran his hands through his hair. It was then that I realized that I had embarrassed him.

"Thanks, but believe me, *Pirates of Penzance* in junior high was enough for me. And for my parents." He grinned wryly. "Luckily I had something else to fall back on."

"Well, you're very good at what you do," I said. I wanted to pay him a compliment he'd enjoy—and also it was true. It was easy to see how patient he'd be with true beginners.

"Thanks," he said. He spun his racquet on the tip of its head. "What do you do?"

This lie too I had prepared in advance. Today I was Magnolia, and Magnolia was me. "I own a dog-sitting business. And I do a little personal grooming on the side."

Luke raised his eyebrows and smiled. "That's interesting. I thought you were going to say something in entertainment."

I gave him my best blank stare. "What do you mean? Was it my acting comment? I'm sorry about that."

"Really, it's okay. I guess living here, after a while, you start to jump to conclusions," he explained. "It's funny. I moved out here thinking L.A. would be just what you see on TV. Fake boobs, fake blondes, dudes with hair implants wearing silk shirts. I mean, coming from Virginia, that's what you expect. But most of the people I've met here are great. Maybe it's because they're all from somewhere else," he said. He pushed his Oakleys on top of his head and looked at me with his intense blue eyes. "Even the ones I know in entertainment, some of them are pretty solid, you know?"

"Um, have you spent time with any agents lately?" I challenged. "Because they would probably steal your dog, turn it into steaks, and then invite you over for a barbecue." I stabbed my racquet onto the court for emphasis.

Luke laughed, and my heart thumped hard against my chest. "Okay, they're not all sane. But my girlfriend is, and she works at a studio."

I flipped my bangs out of my eyes. Less than two minutes into the conversation, and he'd already brought up Kylie. Not a good sign.

"She's not interested in that Hollywood stuff," he went on, pinching the strings of his racquet. "I mean, she just wants to make really great movies. I never thought I'd meet someone so . . . I don't know, cool, I guess. Just really cool."

From the dreamy smile on his face, I learned everything I needed to know. Kylie had Luke good and whipped, and even in the cute little tennis dress that I was going to immediately go buy, I was going to have a hard time catching his eye. I wondered what sort of evil spell she'd cast over him that would make him so blind to her deviousness. And where she kept her evil-spell book.

"Well, that's sweet," I said limply. "I'm sure she feels lucky too."

I swatted a stray ball across the net in defeat. The injustice of it all was really too much. There was no way that Kylie had any idea how lucky she was. Luke was sweet, modest, and freakily normal. I could imagine him barbecuing in the backyard with my dad, and then challenging my mom to a game of badminton.

Which meant that he and Kylie couldn't have been more wrong for each other. Except for the fact that sweet, modest guys always seemed to fall for the mean girls. It was practically one of the Ten Commandments of Dating.

"So what about you?" he asked, watching the ball I'd hit roll away into a corner of the hard courts. A tanned, fit-looking dad helped his son hit it back to us. "You have a boyfriend?"

Luke had put his sunglasses on, so I couldn't look him in the eye. "No, not right now. It's hard to meet normal guys out here." I thought of Mark Lyder with a small shiver.

"Yeah," he said noncommittally. "I'm sure." Then he looked at me and smiled, a crooked but encouraging one. "Let's try that new and improved grip, okay? You're going to see a big difference, I promise."

He jogged away to the far side of the net, giving me another glimpse of his toned calves. As I stood waiting for him to serve, I felt a nagging sense of defeat. I had not been charming or funny, and I certainly hadn't been sexy. I tugged on my raggedy old shorts and held my racquet like the beginner he thought I was. At least he bought my lies, I told myself. I may be a bad seductress, but I'm not a horrible actress.

"And what about the movie stars?" I called out to Luke. "They're not solid! I heard Catherine Zeta-Jones uses a face mask made out of kitten placentas and that Owen Wilson refuses to put on clothes before six p.m.!"

Luke sent a yellow ball flying toward me. "You're funny, Taylor," he said.

I smiled a little tiny smile. He thought I was funny. Next time I just had to add the charm and sex appeal. One down, two to go.

CHAPTER TWENTY-TWO

Oh, hey you! How was Vegas?"

I watched Kylie make her entrance into the office, which was by now choreographed to perfection: BlackBerry glued to her ear, rapturous smile on her face, enormous Kooba bag flung to the ground as she slid into her chair and swiveled toward the window. All while pretending I wasn't sitting four feet away.

"Oh my God, you are *so gross*," Kylie said loudly to the window. "No!" she shrieked. "*No!* Shut *up! Shut up!*"

My right knee began to jerk uncontrollably under my desk. I wrapped my fingers around a pencil, considered breaking it, and then instead wrote, under Bad Things: *Kylie on BlackBerry sounds like cross between Valley girl and squealing piglet.*

"Oh my God, Troy," she gasped after a long peal of laughter. "You are too funny."

Ever since the baby shower, Kylie had unleashed a new and surprisingly effective tactic: *act as if you've already won.* Iris had so far refrained from making any kind of announcement, but as far as Kylie was concerned, she was already promoted. From nine-thirty on Monday morning, when Kylie walked into the office declaring, "Of course we can discuss final cut!" into her phone, to now, Tuesday afternoon, as she shrieked with syco-phantic giggles, Kylie played the part of Metronome's newest junior creative exec. She spoke to Troy's agent about rewrites and plot points and deal memos. She went to meetings with junior production executives across the lot. She spent her lunches having meetings in the green leather booths at the Grill.

And not once did she acknowledge me, verbally or otherwise. Though the other assistants continued to drop by her desk to trade gossip, it was as if I were so trivial, so unimportant, that I had frankly ceased to exist.

I pretended to type an e-mail while I listened to Kylie finish her call. "We are *totally* doing karaoke this weekend," she announced giddily. "And you are so singing Bon Jovi, it's not even funny."

I gritted my teeth and drew a little picture of Kylie's face and then put a big X through it. If Luke could see his girlfriend now! I had another lesson with him tomorrow, and there was a part of me that wondered why I'd made it. Luke was clearly in love with this skinny phony in her Celine dress, and so, as deluded as the poor guy was, my hopes of seducing him were faint at best. But I'd enjoyed my lesson on Sunday, and there were worse ways to spend an hour than getting some exercise on the court. At least I could work on my serve.

"I'll talk to you later," Kylie cooed into her BlackBerry. "You are sooo bad."

I got up and went to the kitchen, where I found Julissa on a step stool, one hand thrust into the upper cabinets. While the rest of Metronome was glossy and chic, the kitchen, like all the rooms our hotshot clients never saw, was desperately in need of an upgrade. The checkered floor reminded me of my high school cafeteria, and the hinges on all the cabinets creaked. There wasn't even an ice machine.

"Do you know who keeps hiding the candy?" she asked, groping around blindly in the disorganized cabinet.

"I think it's Lisa Amorosi. She's trying to stay on Tom's diet. You know, with those sludge-colored smoothies he's always drinking in staff meetings? Now she's having them too."

"Gross," Julissa said. Then she hollered, "Yes!" and produced a basket of Hershey's Christmas Kisses and minibags of M&M's.

"I can't take it anymore in there," I sighed. "I'm going to do something desperate."

"You mean Ms. Michael Eisner?" Julissa rolled her eyes toward Kylie's desk. "Well, you won't have to listen to it long. They're making the announcement on Friday," she said casually and proceeded to rip open a brown packet of M&M's with her teeth.

"What?" I dropped the Diet Coke I'd been reaching for in surprise. It rolled across the floor and nestled in the dark space under the cabinets.

"That's what I heard." Julissa popped a handful of candy into her mouth. "Troy and his people sign their contracts tomorrow at some big lunch meeting, and then Iris is going to make it official."

"Shit." I picked up the can and popped the top, even though I knew it would probably spray me. And it did: Diet Coke drops rained onto my cute little Marni cardigan. "Shit again," I hissed. But really, who cared? It was black. And it was the least of my problems.

"So when you get promoted to first assistant, they'll need to fill *your* spot, so"— Julissa fidgeted in front of me, grinning and chewing her M&M's—"could you put in a good word for me?"

"Yeah, of course," I said, dabbing at my sweater with a paper towel. I tried to keep the dejection from my voice, but it was impossible.

"You all right?" Julissa asked. "Do you want an M&M?"

"God no," I sighed. "I want to go lie down in the nap room."

Julissa shook her head, looking very serious. "You know what they say about that—it doesn't look professional."

I drank down most of the soda and tossed what was left into the sink. "I was the one to tell you that, you know."

Three months ago, I would have been thrilled at the prospect of being promoted to first assistant. But the problem with that now, of course, was that it meant that Kylie would become a CE. Hello, domino effect: Kylie would have even more pull with Iris and the rest of the execs. She'd use her new power to shoot down my ideas in meetings, and she'd try her best to turn the other execs against me. She'd have her own assistant—one she'd have to share with another junior CE, but still—and she'd make sure the assistant hated me too. So pretty soon no one at Metronome would hear anything nice about me. And even if I managed to overcome Kylie's ill will to finally become an exec one day, Kylie would always be just one step ahead of me—and more than happy to remind me of it.

"Taylor?" Julissa asked, waving her hand in front of my face. "Hello?"

"I have to get back to work," I mumbled and left her there, her plump little cheeks full of M&M's, just like a hamster's.

When I got back to my desk, Kylie stood in her beige cashmere coat, gathering up some memos and scripts.

"I'm off to Ingenuity for a meeting," she announced without looking at me.

It was amazing: a day and a half without a word from her, and now she was acting like I was there simply to record her comings and goings. Kylie leaned down and blew out her vanilla votive.

"Have a good one," I muttered, obviously not meaning it.

With her nose firmly tilted toward the sky, Kylie shook her head to herself, as if my childish behavior were just oh-so-amusing. She stalked out of the office.

I sat motionless in my chair. I knew as well as anyone that life wasn't fair, but this was just *too* unfair. *I* was the one who spent all night reading scripts while Kylie went off to Socialista or wherever it was she went. *I* was the one who actually helped Iris do her job while Kylie merely pretended to. *I* came in earlier than she did, and *I* stayed later. I didn't know how Kylie had managed to package this deal of hers, but it certainly didn't come from working that hard. She was smart, but she was also beautiful and had the confidence that only comes with being told your entire life that the world is your oyster.

Just do your best and you'll beat the rest. That's what my dad always used to say to me—on the tennis court, in math class, whatever. But I'd never been more convinced it wasn't true.

I stabbed my pencil into my Bad Things list (*Dana totally harassing me to read script; still can't keep Weinsteins straight*) and broke the tip.

From across the room, I heard a soft little chime from Kylie's computer. An IM from Luke, no doubt. Maybe I just wanted to drive the knife deeper into my gut, but I couldn't help but wonder what sweet, loving things he was writing her.

I looked guiltily around the office. Iris was in a meeting with Peter Lasky—probably being yelled at, as usual—and wouldn't be back until after lunch. Glancing out toward the hallway to make sure no one was about to walk by, I slowly crossed the four feet to Kylie's desk. An IM from Netboy had flashed onto the screen.

Just finished my 11:30. How's your day going?

Luke's photo appeared to the left of it. My stomach did a little flipflop, even just seeing him in a thumbnail jpeg. Then a second IM popped up.

You there?

Impulsively I bent over her keyboard. *Good—how are you?* I wrote, my heart now joining my stomach in gymnastics. I hit Send.

A few seconds later, he sent a response.

Want to see u. What's your plan tonight?

Oh, this was a really bad idea. Why had I written back? There was no way he wouldn't find out. Just then another IM popped up across the screen.

Hey gorgeous. Can't wait for tonight. Chateau at 7?

This one also had a photo. A smug half-smile, intense dark eyes, preciously tousled hair.

It was Mark Lyder.

Maybe this time we get a room???

Really, I almost sank to my knees from shock. *Mark Lyder and Kylie.* She was cheating on Luke, the supposed love of her life.

And then it all fell into place. Mark was Kylie's Ingenuity connection. He was the one who had gotten her to Troy Vaughn. *He* was her industry contact. And—oh my God—she was *sleeping* with him, which was exactly what she told me not to do at Iris's benefit. So much for her policy of "look but don't touch"!

She wasn't just a liar. She was a hypocrite. And no wonder she'd been so surprised when Mark had asked me to Koi.

I was about to shut off Kylie's computer and pretend I'd never seen any of this when I heard Quinn's voice in all its raspy teen glory. *She'd do it to you.*

It was almost too easy.

I wrote Mark first.

Absolutely! See you there!

I hit Send.

And then I clicked on Luke's message.

Meet me at Chateau Marmont at 7:30.

And then I hit Sleep on the computer and got up. Nobody had seen me. It was as if it had never happened.

You just did something bad, a small but distinct voice inside me said as I eased back into my seat. Really really bad.

An unbidden, uncontrollable smile spread across my face. All I could think was, Quinn would be proud.

CHAPTER TWENTY-THREE

Where's Kylie? Is she sick?" Iris craned her neck to glance at Kylie's empty desk. "Have you heard from her, Taylor?" She stood in the center of the room with her hands on her hips and her brow furrowed in annoyance. (An expression, incidentally, that Tom Scheffer could no longer make, thanks to a recent high dosage of BOTOX.)

I shook my head. I'd been guiltily averting my eyes from Kylie's dark computer monitor since I'd gotten in this morning, an hour and a half ago. Kylie liked to sleep in, but she was always in the office by nine-thirty. And if she was going to be late, she'd call or send a text. So the silence, and her empty chair, were eerie.

"Please give her a call," Iris said. Her exasperated look softened. "Something might have happened."

Oh yes, I thought, I'm pretty sure something happened.

As I dialed Kylie's cell, I was acutely aware of Iris staring at the top of my head. I was on the third digit when Iris put out her hand to stop me.

"Wait," she said.

I looked up to see Kylie trudge into the office holding a venti Starbucks and staring at the ground, as if she knew that two pairs of eyes were boring into her skull. "Sorry I'm late," she mumbled. With her back to us, she unbuttoned her sweater coat to reveal a tent dress in a dark blue jersey knit. Normally, I knew, she would have belted it, but today it fluttered out around the waist unflatteringly. Her hair sat in two big clumps in the back, as if it had just left the pillow.

"Are you sick?" Iris asked, obviously concerned.

"I'm fine," she said vaguely, over her shoulder.

Iris gave me a questioning look, and I shrugged.

We watched her light one of her vanilla votives and slowly fold herself into her chair. When she finally swiveled to face us, I literally gasped and then covered it with a very fake-sounding cough.

Kylie looked as if she had spent the night crying or drinking—maybe both. Her eyes were red and swollen, with pink puffy bags beneath them that she had tried—and failed—to cover with concealer. Her normally golden complexion was blotchy and uneven. Her lips, too, seemed swollen, and they looked pale and strange without the usual berry tint. The fluorescent light of the office made her look older, harder.

I'd wanted to take Kylie down. But I'd never imagined that I could deliver a knockout punch.

"Are you sure you're all right?" Iris asked gently. She took a Kleenex from her enormous Balenciaga bag and extended it toward Kylie. Even though Iris was the seventh most powerful player in Hollywood, she was still a mother, and she had the Kleenex, the Band-Aids, the aspirin, the dental floss, and the iodine wipes in her purse to prove it.

"Oh, yeah, I'm fine." Kylie waved off the tissue and pretended to busy herself with starting her computer. "Just had some bad sushi last night."

Iris tossed the Kleenex into the trash. "If you're not feeling well," she said, "then maybe you should take the day and rest. You have that meeting tomorrow with Troy—"

"I'll be fine," Kylie said, sniffling. "Really."

"All right then." Iris shrugged, as if to say *I give up.* "Then someone just get me New York," she said, and walked into the jungle of her office.

Kylie refused to look at me as I made the call, pretending to be busy scrolling through her e-mail. When I hung up, I knew I had to say something. "What happened?" I asked softly.

Focused on the screen, Kylie blinked her green eyes rapidly. "Nothing."

I got out of my chair and went to stand before her. "Kylie. I know we're not friends or anything, but something's clearly wrong." Even as I said this, I felt dread coming over me like a wave. I really didn't want to know the details of my deceit.

Kylie's mouth began to tremble, but still she wouldn't look at me. "It's over," she whispered. "It's all over."

"What happened?" I asked gently.

"He just showed up out of nowhere," she wailed. She held her head in her hands, rubbing her temples. "It was like he *knew* or something. I don't know how. But he did."

"Who showed up? Where?"

"Luke," Kylie explained, looking at me with glazed, unseeing eyes. "He came to the Chateau. I was there with another guy. Nothing was even happening, but"—her face was about to crumple into a sob and she stopped herself—"we were kissing."

She wiped her eyes with the back of her hand. "And Luke just *punched* him right in the face." One solitary tear spilled out of her left eye and dropped miserably down her cheek. "In front of everyone. And he looked right at me and said that he *never* wanted to see me again. *Ever.*" She sniffed loudly. "And that I had shown him who I *really* was," she said, her voice breaking. She pulled some Kleenex out of the box on her desk.

Luke—sweet, laid-back, I'm-just-a-boy-from-Virginia Luke— had punched Mark Lyder? At the Chateau Marmont? My plan had played out more perfectly than I could have imagined. And yet . . . I didn't really feel like gloating.

"And now he won't talk to me," Kylie continued, wiping her eyes. "He won't pick up his phone. He won't answer my e-mails." She sniffled into her Kleenex. "I mean, that can't be it, you know? He can't just *dump* me like that."

"But you were seeing someone else," I said. My voice was quiet but forceful. I felt bad for her, but I felt worse for Luke. What a nasty shock he'd had, coming across his beloved tonsil-diving with another man.

This time when Kylie spoke, her voice was flinty. "I told you, it didn't mean anything. Mark was just helping me. We got carried away, but it didn't mean anything."

"Mark *Lyder*?" I feigned surprise, and the words felt fake in my mouth, but Kylie flushed guiltily.

"Look, you know as well as I do that you don't get ahead around here by taking good messages and hoping someone notices," she said. "I didn't do anything wrong, Taylor. It was just what I had to do. So just get off your fucking high horse. It's nothing you wouldn't have done."

"No," I said. "I would never have done that, Kylie."

Kylie bolted to her feet and ran out the door. I heard the ladies' room door slam.

I stared at Kylie's empty chair, the wad of Kleenex she'd left on her desk. The wreckage of Kylie.

Kylie wasn't just a mess, the way Quinn promised she'd be: she was a complete and utter disaster. Twelve hours later, Kylie was already off the deep end.

And yes, I felt guilty for my part in this. But I told myself that in a way, this had nothing to do with me. Luke would have found out eventually. Kylie would have gotten caught. And if I really wanted to get philosophical about it, Kylie had brought this on herself. As my dad liked to say, you get what you deserve.

I thought Quinn deserved an update. I took out my iPhone, scrolled down to Quinn's e-mail, and began to type.

Kylie dumped
Having meltdown
Can we say Britney?

CHAPTER TWENTY-FOUR

A few hours later, I stored my gray suede Stuart Weitzman boots in the tinsel-decorated locker outside the Buddha Ball classroom and breathed in the familiar smell of jasmine incense and dried sweat. I'd grown to love Buddha Ball, even though I was still one of the worst students in class. (A woman named Kelly—porn name Nevada Blue—was the best; she could hold one-legged king pigeon pose for ages, which is the kind of thing that only professional contortionists should do.)

"Hey, Magda." The tattooed blonde behind the check-in desk dropped her scowl and waved—last week we had finally bonded over our shared hatred of Pinkberry—and I threw open the door.

As usual, Ted was in his nylon running shorts, in deep meditation at the front of the room. Kelly, in pink Lycra, was up in front (she liked to show off), and the guy I'd come to call the proctologist was behind her (he always looked a little displeased, the way someone who spent their days dealing with people's butts probably would). I smiled at Joanna, an actress whose biggest credit was a TV commercial for a chat line (555-SEXY) and waved to Arthur, a popular voice-over man who was rolling in dough (the orange Lamborghini parked out front was his). The room seemed more crowded tonight, probably due to people's upcoming holiday trips to Hawaii and Bali.

"Hey, Taylor," said Zena, arching her tanned back into cat pose. "Your calves are looking great."

I glanced down at my legs, which were looking more toned these days, though they were still horribly pale. "Thanks," I said, grabbing a mat.

"You could use a tan though," she said, sinking into cow pose.

I grinned. "You don't need to tell me."

"Oh, and don't look now, but guess who's here?" Zena asked, cutting her eyes toward the back of the room.

I glanced over. And then I blinked, just to make sure I wasn't imagining things. On a mat in the corner of the room, bent over his straight legs as everyone in the class pretended not to stare, was Holden MacIntee.

I'd completely given up on ever running into him, and now there he was, in a faded Powerade T-shirt and a pair of red running shorts. I needed a strategy, stat. I ducked toward the back of the room and reached into my bag for the iPhone, trying not to be too obvious—Ted went ballistic over handheld devices.

HOLDEN IN CLASS! HOW TO WORK IT?

A moment later, Quinn's reply popped up.

Lesson #1: Fake it till you make it.

I sighed and turned off the phone. A total rerun! Where was my brilliant *new* advice when I needed it?

I tiptoed back to my mat and Buddha Ball, picked them up, and tried, as quietly as I could, to maneuver my way to a spot near Holden. (If Ted opened his eyes and saw me, he'd probably make me lead class with him again, an experience I did not want to repeat.) Zena winked at me, and I winked right back. No doubt she thought I was going to hit on him. But I wasn't interested in Holden *that* way. As tempting as he was, far more tempting was the chance to become a CE. Iris would be making the announcement any day now.

Luckily, there was plenty of space on either side of him. Summoning all the nonchalance I could, I plopped my mat down in his celebrity force field and sat down.

I took a deep breath and went for it. "So I don't know if I'm up to this tonight," I said oh-so-casually as I stretched a hamstring. "Last week they had to scrape me off the floor with a spatula."

Holden turned his smoldering eyes toward me and smiled. "I haven't been here in weeks. I'm going to get killed."

"You look like you can handle it," I teased, leaning over to copy his stretch.

"Well, Ted likes me, so at least he shows me a little mercy," he replied. The lashes around his bright green eyes were as long as a girl's, but there was nothing else feminine about Holden.

"You're lucky—Ted sort of likes to pick on me. The first time I ever came here, he made me stand up beside him, and whenever I shrieked in pain, he made the rest of the class copy me." I popped up into a quick downward-facing dog to stretch my calves and looked over at him. He was just as handsome upside down.

Holden laughed quietly so Ted wouldn't hear. "He did that to me too. I think it's a sign of affection. Or at least that's what I tell myself. And I try to believe it." He smiled at me, and I smiled back at him from my pose, and then there was nothing I could think of to say.

I bit my lip and came down into child's pose with my forehead on my mat. Then it came to me.

"Well it's like they say, 'I believe in believing,'" I said, praying he would recognize the quote.

He leaned in closer to me. "What?"

I blushed. "'I believe in believing.' You said that thing about Ted, and it just made me think. It's a line from—"

"*Journal Girl*," Holden exclaimed.

I rearranged my face into what I hoped looked like an expression of shock. "You recognized that?"

He nodded vigorously. "It's one of my favorite movies."

Bingo. I kept the shocked look. "Really? That's so weird. It's my *favorite* movie."

Holden crossed his legs and bent over, grunting a little as he stretched. "Don't tell anyone I can quote it, though," he whispered conspiratorially.

I raised my eyebrows and tried to put a flirty lilt into my voice. "Why, because it's girly?"

Holden, still bent over, turned his head and grinned at me. "Well, it's not the most masculine movie out there, I'll give you that. But I love *all* Deming's movies, the independent ones especially. That guy's a genius."

"I know. He's kind of the reason I got into development at Metronome." Nice segue, I thought to myself, even though at the mention of Metronome, Holden's eyes had gone a little glazed.

Fake it till you make it, I told myself and crossed my fingers. "This is totally on the DL," I said, leaning toward him. "But we're already in talks with him on a script. And I think you'd be great for it."

He sat up straight and stared at me.

At the front of the room, Ted cleared his throat, and we turned forward like naughty schoolchildren. "All right, people," Ted said. "Let's get started. Silence, please. We begin in lotus, and we clear our psyches."

Everyone sat up straight and prepared to listen to each other's sob stories. Shit, I thought, there goes my chance. But maybe I could bring it up while clearing my psyche: *Gee, Ted, I'm just worried I won't be able to concentrate on my lateral adductors tonight because I'm thinking about this phenomenal project I've got in the works.* . . . This little bit of play-acting was unnecessary, however, because Holden was not so easily distracted.

"What's the project?" he whispered.

I realized that I had no idea what to say—I had faked it about as much as I could. Then I thought about my purse, sitting there in the back of the room, with Dana's script inside it.

"It's in my bag," I whispered back, nodding toward the rear of the classroom. "It's called *The Evolution of Evan.* It's by a young writer we just found who's fantastic. We think she's going to pop."

Of course, none of this was true, but wasn't this what Brett had talked about all those weeks ago? *Hype. One person thinks something is good, and the rest of the town wants to buy it.*

"Cool," he said. "Can I read it? I'm going to New York tomorrow, so, you know, it'd be good to read it on the plane."

My stomach plummeted down toward my mat. I stammered

for a second and then regained my cool. "Sure," I said. "I'll give it to you right after class. You can be in touch, let me know what you think."

"Great," Holden said, looking pleased. "What's your name, by the way?"

"Taylor," I said, reaching over to shake his hand and hoping Ted wouldn't notice. "Taylor Henning."

Taylor Henning, who is also hoping against hope that that spastic little Dana McCafferty pulled off a decent revision, one might add. It was really too bad I'd never gotten around to reading it.

"People, we're listening to Kelly talk about her body image," Ted scolded from the front of the room. "Can we tune in, please?"

As I turned to listen to Kelly clear her psyche (she was feeling anxious about her eighteen-ounce weight gain and blamed it on a change in the Whole Foods yogurt formula), I wanted to jump up on my mat and do a spontaneous headstand. This was turning out to be the best day of my life.

CHAPTER TWENTY-FIVE

At eight the next evening, when the other Metronome assistants were probably prepping for a big Thursday night out (Cici donning Manolos for Socialista, Wyman polishing up his nerd glasses for a Godard festival downtown), I was in the Tennis Center parking lot, holding back a moan of pain as I stretched my legs and felt the result of the extra fifty lunges Ted had made me and Holden do for talking in class the night before.

The pain, of course, was a small price to pay for what was possibly the most exciting thing to ever happen to me. I still couldn't believe how perfectly it had all gone. I'd been confident, persuasive, and spontaneous: a pitch-perfect performance, if I do say so myself. The only hard part—and really, it was excruciating—was waiting to get another copy of Dana's script. The stress practically gave me hives, and Magnolia finally had to calm me down by force-feeding me half a box of Samoas Girl Scout Cookies and half a bottle of cheap chardonnay. The minute I'd gotten to work, I'd called Dana and asked her to e-mail me another copy, and as it printed out, I chewed one thumbnail down to the quick. I read it with my heart in my mouth. And miracle of miracles, Dana's script was a massive improvement on the original. The story was more complex, the characters sharper, the stakes higher, and the dialogue more polished—all my suggestions, I noted with a certain pride. As I sipped my double Americano, I felt a swelling of happiness—there was every chance that Holden might actually *like* this script.

But just to help things along, I planted a seed on the tracking boards. All I had to write was the title, followed by *Heard this script is great. Unrepped writer?* By the end of the day, ten threads trailed it, and everyone was wondering where they could find this "hot new writer." On my speed dial, I thought giddily.

And the even better part? I'd managed to get a breakfast meeting at the Four Seasons with Michael Deming's agent. It hadn't been easy to find him. For one thing, I had to make all the calls when Kylie wasn't around (luckily she was spending a lot of time in the ladies' room and the unprofessional nap room), and for another, no one I spoke to seemed to know. "Deming's been gone for years," one assistant had said snidely. "Who cares who his agent is?" But finally an assistant at William Morris told me what I wanted to hear. "Yeah, we have him," she'd whispered. "But please don't tell anyone."

All I needed to say was that I had a possible project with Holden MacIntee, and in less time than it took to order a double Americano, I had a breakfast meeting with Arnie Brotman.

"Shall I send over the script?" I asked.

"Of *course*," the girl said and hung up.

Victory was almost mine—I could taste it.

I finished my stretches and walked toward the tennis complex, which was lit by humming fluorescent lights and was nearly empty. Apparently the rest of the world had something better to do. I spotted Luke on Court Three. He picked up a ball from a basket by his feet, tossed it into the air, arched his body toward it, and with an explosive swing, sent it hurtling into the service box. I watched him do this a dozen more times. It looked more like stress relief than tennis practice.

"Wow," I said brightly, stepping onto the court as another ace zipped by. "Just don't try that on me."

Luke turned toward me, and his face brightened a little. "Hey. I thought you'd forgotten about me."

I smiled and pulled the hem of my new little black tennis dress down (it was only Nike, but it was darling—more Audrey Hepburn than Billie Jean King, that's for sure). Luke was even cuter than I remembered, and even in the fading light, his eyes were so blue and intense that I blushed and had to turn away.

"Forget about you?" I asked. I unzipped my sporty little jacket and tossed it on a bench. "Never."

I gave my hips a little extra swish as I took my place on the court, just because I was feeling good and I could sense him watching me. Yes, the dress had been a smart investment. Not that I wanted something to come of our lesson, I told myself. Or I didn't think I did. After all, Quinn's advice had already worked.

"You look nice," Luke said softly.

I turned and smiled. He almost looked a little nervous, and there were faint dark circles under his eyes. Involuntarily I glanced down at his knuckles to see if I could tell where he'd punched Mark, but there was nothing.

"Thanks," I said and touched my hair, which I'd pulled back into a shiny ponytail.

He hit me a forehand, and I moved to slam it back to him. But then I pulled back midswing and dropped my arm so I'd miss. "Oops!" I said cheerfully.

"Try another one," he said encouragingly. "Here you go."

This one I allowed myself to hit, but I made sure it landed out of bounds. On the next one, I permitted myself to knock it into the deuce court, and he handily returned it.

"Nice job," he said, following through on his swing. He kept the balls coming, and I still tried to miss a lot of them, but soon enough we had settled into a nice easy volley.

The familiar exercise allowed my mind to drift to Kylie. Things were going downhill for her fast. This morning she'd arrived at work showered, wearing a silver and red wrap dress (nice, if a little schoolmarmish compared to her regular attire) and carrying what looked like a new bag. But her face was even puffier, and the way she guzzled down bottle after bottle of Evian, I realized that she was either profoundly hungover or possibly still somewhat drunk. Needless to say, she didn't acknowledge me at all. She just lit her candle and put her head down on her desk.

When she got back from her big lunch meeting, it didn't take a genius to figure out that her signing meeting with Troy Vaughn hadn't gone well. This was only confirmed when Kylie tipped four Advil into her shaky palm and washed them down with regular—not sugar-free—Red Bull.

"How'd it go?" I'd asked.

"Great," Kylie had said thickly, without looking at me.

Then Iris had walked in. "Kylie? In my office please. And can you shut the door?"

Kylie emerged ten minutes later, looking smaller and paler

than she had when she went in. Her delicate hands were trembling. She walked to her desk with as much dignity as she could display, grabbed her bag, and left.

I blew out her candle for her. I felt bad, I really did. But I couldn't help but be relieved. There was no way that Iris was going to promote Kylie tomorrow anymore, which meant that a) she couldn't lord it over me and b) I had a better chance to make a play for it myself.

A ball hurtled toward me down the center line of the court, and I was so wrapped up in thinking about Kylie that I let fly with my power swing on instinct. I whacked the ball straight down the line, past Luke's Nikes.

"Hey!" he yelled. "And you say you haven't been practicing?"

"Um, it's that beginner's luck again?" I called back. "And, of course, because you're a great teacher."

Luke grinned. It was kind of a lame answer, but he seemed to buy it. "How about a water break?" he said.

Side by side we walked toward the vending machine. I swung my racquet back and forth to hide my sudden case of nerves. Something about Luke made me want to turn cartwheels down the walkway. Of course, cartwheels were something I shouldn't do for many reasons, not least of which was my little black dress. Its short length and formfitting cut left little to the imagination. Thank heaven for the little built-in shorts. Not to mention the Clinique self-tanner I'd used—an upgrade from the Neutrogena—which had given my legs a natural-looking glow. Even Zena, my porn star friend from Buddha Ball, would be proud.

"Admit it, you're not a beginner," he said.

A sudden wave of panic rolled through me. Was there any way he'd figured out who I was? Had he described me to Kylie before their breakup, or had she said something to him about me? I swallowed and tried to keep my face blank and innocent. "What makes you say that?"

"Beginners are just plain bad. You're bad most of the time, but then you turn around and swing like Venus Williams."

I laughed, relieved. "Oh, so I'm sending you mixed signals," I said. Ugh, terrible pun.

Luke smiled and ducked his head. "Maybe." He slid a dollar's worth of quarters into the vending machine. A bottle of Poland Spring tumbled out, and he grabbed it and handed it to me; then he bought one for himself.

"Actually I have a confession," I said, taking a drink. "I went to tennis camp in seventh grade. But I thought I'd lie and pass off any good shots as natural ability. It's more dramatic that way, don't you think?"

He laughed. "When you said you had a confession to make, I thought you were going to give me a heart attack."

"A heart attack!" I exclaimed. "You must be much older than I thought you were."

We turned and walked back toward the courts. I took the sport cap off my water bottle—I can't drink from one without getting it all over myself—and tossed it into the trash.

"I'm not that much older than you," he said. "I don't think."

"Okay, quick," I said. Feeling bold, I put my hand on his tanned forearm. "First crush. First *movie star* crush."

Luke thought about this. "That girl from *Say Anything* . . . , when she was in that white dress." He smiled. "I have a thing for brunettes."

My hand dropped from his arm in surprise. "Ah. So your girlfriend must be one," I said.

Luke's face darkened. "No, she wasn't. I mean, she's not." He paused as he kicked a loose pebble by the court fence. "She's not really my girlfriend anymore."

"Oh!" I said, sounding startled. "I'm sorry."

"Yeah," he said quietly, twisting the cap off his water bottle. He shrugged. "Me too."

We kept walking, and there was a long pause that was sort of uncomfortable. But I didn't feel like we were strangers—we were people who just hadn't quite figured out how to be friends yet. I ran my racquet along the chain-link fence of one of the courts, just to break the silence.

"She was cheating on me," Luke finally said. He kept his eyes on his bottle.

"Oh no," I whispered. I thought about putting my hand on his arm again but stopped myself. I didn't want him to think I was hitting on him—right then I just wanted to comfort him.

"With some slick agent type." When he looked up, his eyes had gone glassy, as if he were replaying the scene of Kylie with Mark Lyder in his mind. "I guess she was more into the Hollywood scene than I thought."

"I'm so sorry," I said. "Do you want to talk about it?" Instead of going back to the court, I led us to a wooden bench overlooking the grounds. I sat down and patted the seat beside me. Down on hole nine of the golf course, a gardener was mowing the already-perfect green.

He shrugged and collapsed onto the bench. "At least I know now who she really is. So that's a good thing," he said. He was trying to sound optimistic but was not doing a very good job of it. He took a long drink of water.

I set my bottle on the bench between us and turned to him. "I hope you don't mind," I blurted, "but it sounds to me like she just wasn't good enough for you."

Luke looked up at me, surprised.

I knocked my racquet against my knee because I was nervous and because I wanted him to believe what I was saying. "You need to be with someone who doesn't care about that stuff," I said. "Someone who's real. Someone who knows a good thing when she sees it." I stopped myself. How obvious was I? I'd meant only to make him feel better, but then I'd basically just told him that I thought he should be with *me*. "Sorry, that's just what I think," I whispered.

He continued to study me, as if I knew some secret that he could decipher by staring at me with those blue laser beams of his. I found it hard to look at him, and so I looked down at my legs. I picked at the hem of my cute dress. What did I want? I closed my eyes for a second. I had to admit it. I wanted Luke.

Beside me, he cleared his throat. "Look, I hope this isn't weird or inappropriate or anything. But would you want to have dinner sometime? Like tomorrow maybe?"

I felt all the blood in my body rise up to the surface of my skin. I was glad it was getting dark, because I could tell that my cheeks were scarlet. I took a sip of water to calm myself. "I'd love to," I said.

CHAPTER TWENTY-SIX

Just make sure you know what you're getting into," warned Arnie Brotman, as he neatly folded a slice of bacon into his mouth. "Deming's a genius, but he's also a little nuts." Brotman made the international sign for crazy next to his head.

I took a sip of coffee and tried to look away from Brotman's open, chewing mouth. Deming's agent was stocky and compact, with a shaved head that was slightly pointed at the top. I could see how he'd gotten the nickname the Silver Bullet, back when he had several A-list clients. It was mostly the shape of his body, but it was also his no-nonsense, cut-to-the-chase manner. Arnie wasn't a bullshitter, which set him apart from pretty much all the other agents I'd met. But he, too, had had a meltdown, albeit one that didn't send him off to Grizzly Adams land like Deming. As I'd learned from a little Internet research, he'd had a year-long coke binge in 2000 (at the advanced age of thirty-seven), which cost him pretty much all of his high-profile clients. He was clean and sober now, but not exactly humbled. He still looked like a powerful player, there among the theatrical red and gold décor of the Gardens restaurant at The Four Seasons. Beneath the brightly colored (and frankly ugly) contemporary paintings on two of the walls, executives in their power suits checked their BlackBerries and brokered multimillion-dollar deals over their Belgian waffles.

"I know he's a handful," I said carefully, "but there has to be *some* project that would entice him to come back." Thus far in our meeting, Arnie had been friendly enough, but far from encouraging. I was beginning to feel a little less sure of myself.

"Look, I'll be honest with you," he said, cutting into his Dungeness crab cake Benedict with the side of his fork. "I'm not sure he *wants* to come back. From everything he says about Hollywood, it'd take a hell of a lot for him to get behind a camera again, especially for a studio. You know the story of his last movie. Nightmare." Arnie shuddered. "He never shuts up about it."

I swirled my orange juice around in my glass. Deming's one and only major studio movie had been plagued with problems from the get-go, from unforeseen budget cuts to unreasonable demands from the studio bigwigs. (The latter thought they should have a say in the movie's plot and editing; Deming felt they should write him a blank check and go about their business.) When they finally locked picture, it was with the bigwigs' cut, not the one that Deming had wanted, and of course Deming threw a fit. The bigwigs were so sick of him by then that they sent it to just forty theaters its opening weekend and hardly marketed it at all, with the result being that it was a total box office disaster.

"Well, that's not going to happen with us, Arnie," I assured him, picking at the strawberries in my fruit plate. "He'll get to call the shots here. And with a talented, budding star who happens to worship him."

"It's still kind of a long shot, kid," Brotman said as he delivered a forkful of crab cake into his mouth. "I mean, the guy's almost a conspiracy freak. Just warning you."

"Look," I said firmly. I leaned forward and put my fork down on my plate so that Arnie would know I was all business. "I'm guessing Deming's the most talented client you have at the moment. Right?"

Arnie Brotman slowed his chewing and then sort of shook his head around in a gesture that could have meant yes, no, or maybe. My heart was beating hard—I was shaking down an agent!—but at the same time I felt strangely calm. I knew what I was doing, and it felt good.

I looked him right in his beady brown eyes. "So doesn't it bother you that he's just sitting up there on an island, birdwatching or whatever he does? When he could be making great movies again? *And* making *you* a nice commission? Have you seen the fan pages on the Internet? Do you know that the original posters for *Journal Girl* sell for thousands? I mean, Deming is a huge deal. He affected a lot of people. Don't you feel some responsibility to get him back out there?"

Arnie dotted his lips with his snow white linen napkin. I had his full attention now.

"Look, I just want him to be working again," I went on. I knew I was close—I just had to keep talking until I could get Arnie to nod yes. "And if he wants to work with us, we've got all the elements here. A good script, a great star, and a studio that will do everything to keep him happy. So what are we waiting for? Let's get him on the phone today and pitch him the script."

Arnie shook his head. "Nope. Doesn't work that way."

"What do you mean?" I asked. I glanced over at the nearest table, where a starlet was playing with her egg-white omelet and gazing into the eyes of a man wearing the silky shirt and predatory look of a would-be manager. I was starting to get impatient.

He tore off a piece of croissant. "You gotta go up there. Pitch him in *person.* He won't do any business on the phone, doesn't trust it. He wants to get a 'read' on you in the flesh." He chewed and swallowed. "Now you know why the guy doesn't work any-more. You know where he lives? It's practically Alaska."

I sighed. I knew this, didn't I? I'd been sending postcards up there for years. Of course, I didn't know *exactly* how remote it was. But if the U.S. Postal Service could get there, surely it wasn't that hard. "Have you visited him?" I asked carefully.

"Once." Arnie pierced a slab of melon. "And that was enough."

"If I go up there, what do you think my odds are?" I asked.

Arnie squinted until his eyes nearly disappeared as he idly tapped his knife on a croissant. "Pretty good," he said after a while. But his voice seemed a little hesitant. "Who knows? I mean, he's no Howard Hughes—he does cut his fingernails at least—but he also makes Stanley Kubrick look normal. But I'll tell you this." He took a sip of coffee, then put it down in its saucer with a clack. "I looked at the script last night. And I think it's as close to something he'd do as anything else I've seen. So go up there, stroke his ego a little bit, make sure he knows who Holden MacIntee is, and I think you've got a shot." He wiped his mouth and got up. "And now I gotta go. I got another breakfast at L'Ermitage." He checked his thick gold watch. "But good luck, kid." He tossed his napkin on his seat. "And for a rookie, you're not a bad ball-buster."

I crossed my arms across my chest as I watched the Silver Bullet wend his way out of the restaurant. I figured it was time to invest in a pair of hiking boots and a compass. If anyone was going to get to Michael Deming, it was going to be me.

◌

"Iris is looking for you," Kylie said in an imperious tone when I walked into the office. "And I think she mentioned she has some dry cleaning that needs to be picked up."

From the way she delivered this information to her computer screen, it was clear that Kylie was herself again. Her hair, drawn up into a chignon, was once again silky and straight. A flower-patterned silk blouse and a cute little pencil skirt had replaced the tent dresses and the wrinkled capri pants. And her superiority complex seemed firmly, resolutely back in place.

I put my bag on my desk with an irritated thump. I booted up my computer and instantly a barrage of IMs from Brett Duncan lit up my screen.

Bduncadonk: where you been, girl?!

Bduncadonk: u didn't rsvp to my Goog invite

Bduncadonk: u better be ready to slug some vino this wknd!

I rubbed my temple furiously. The Sonoma trip. He'd sent me a Google calendar invite with all the details, but I'd totally forgotten about it.

Just then Iris called out from inside her office. "Taylor? Are you out there?"

Kylie smiled smugly as she played with a pearl drop earring. She was so confident, so composed—it was as if her meltdown had never happened. It was as if . . . it was as if she knew she was getting promoted.

Maybe somehow it was happening after all. Maybe Iris wanted to tell me herself, before she made the general announcement.

"There you are." Iris appeared in the doorway, an exuberant look on her face. "Where have you been?" she asked, almost out of breath.

"I had a breakfast. With Michael Deming's agent," I said. "I was just going to tell you all about it—"

"Is this about Holden MacIntee?" Iris interrupted. "I got a call from Bob Glazer this morning." Iris folded her arms. "Apparently you pitched Holden MacIntee a script that we don't own and that nobody here has even read."

Uh-oh. I clutched the edge of my desk—suddenly I needed to sit down. Out of the corner of my eye, I saw Kylie sit up straighter, eager, no doubt, for what she hoped would be a real fireworks show.

"Um, actually I can explain that—," I began.

"Apparently Holden loved it."

My hand tightened even more on my desk. I sort of wobbled a bit, then steadied myself. "What?"

"He loved it," Iris repeated. "And he wants to *do* it. Holden called Bob this morning from New York to tell him. Provided of course that Deming is on board. So, is it true?"

Behind Iris, Kylie's eyes were still wide, but the smug smile had vanished. Now she just looked shocked.

"Didn't you tell Holden that you had a commitment from Deming already?" Iris asked.

I couldn't help it—I sank into my chair, which squeaked a little in protest. "Oh . . . yes. Yes. I did."

Iris was so focused on me she wasn't even blinking. "So it's all done?"

I was about to tell her the truth when Quinn's words flew into my head. *Act like you know everything, even when you don't.* The project *was* done—almost. All I needed to do was just see him in person and pitch the project. Of course he'd say yes.

"He's in," I said confidently, sitting straighter in my chair. "I just need to go up there and meet with him and have him sign the contracts. But otherwise we're all set."

Iris nodded, and I watched as a radiant smile slowly bloomed across her thin, handsome face. "Then congratulations, Taylor. You just got the promotion."

At first I didn't think I'd heard her right, but Kylie's horrified expression confirmed it—Iris had just promoted me!

"Oh my God, really?" I gasped. I wanted to seem cool and collected, but it was impossible; I could hardly breathe. I felt the tears rising up behind my eyes but I blinked them away.

"Really," said Iris, reaching into her pocket for a tissue and holding it out to me. "This was quite an accomplishment."

I waved it away, smiling gratefully. I wouldn't cry—not today! I wanted to dance on my desk and turn a cartwheel down the hall; I wanted to run to the commissary and eat every cookie on the cookie cart; I wanted to kick off my kitten heels and throw them into the air; I wanted to take Kylie's votive candle and fling it out the window. But of course I did none of these things. I simply grinned like an idiot as Iris shook my hand.

"Oh, and this writer," Iris remembered. "Who is she?"

"Dana McCafferty," I said, beaming. Maybe I should send myself a bouquet of flowers, I thought. Maybe I should finally get those highlights I'd been thinking about forever. Or maybe I should go out and spend two thousand dollars on a celebratory dress. "She sent in a spec to us, but nobody would read it."

In my peripheral vision, I could see Kylie stiffen.

Iris shook her head in wonder. "Well, call her up and tell her we're buying her script. And print me out a copy, please. Oh, and Taylor," she said, stopping on the way into her office. "You'll move into your new office on Monday."

"Thank you, Iris," I said.

My new office! I was almost too happy to breathe.

Six feet away, Kylie was typing an e-mail as if none of this had just happened. I cleared my throat to see if she'd look at me, but she kept her eyes on her computer. It was as if I were already gone.

Well, fine—if that's the way she wanted to play it, let her. She'd lost and I'd won, but I didn't need to gloat. I just needed a little breath of fresh air. I got up from my desk and hooked my purse over my shoulder. As I walked down the pulsing, multicolored hallway to reception, past the open office doors of the other CEs, I felt the tears welling up again. I'd actually done it—I was going to be one of them.

I stepped outside the office into the crisp, sunny December morning. The palmettos lining the walkway moved slightly in the breeze. There was a marble bench a ways up ahead, book-ended by planters full of jade green succulents. For the first time in all these weeks, I allowed myself to sit down on it. As of Monday, my days of worrying about answering a ringing phone for somebody else were over. I'd never have to make another spirulina smoothie. From now on, someone else would photocopy things for *me*. Peter Lasky pulled up in a Porsche convertible and I swear he almost smiled at me. In the distance I could hear the rise and fall of a tour guide's voice as he explained to his group of wide-eyed visitors the wonders of movie magic.

I could sit out here all day long if I wanted to. This was my home now. I wasn't going anywhere. Finally, after months, I could relax.

After a few more happy, solitary moments, I got out my iPhone.

"Hello?" said a tiny voice.

"Dana? This is Taylor Henning from Metronome." I closed my eyes. "We want to buy your script. We're going to make your movie."

The shrieking that followed was so loud and high pitched that I had to hold the phone from my ear.

"Really? *Really? REALLY?*" Dana asked.

"Yes, Dana," I said, and this time I really did cry a little. "Really."

CHAPTER TWENTY-SEVEN

Damn, girl," cooed the Calypso salesgirl when I breezed out of the fitting room and examined myself in the three-way mirror. "If you *don't* get that, it'll be a crime against humanity."

The other salesgirls gathered around me as I gazed at myself from several sides at once. The girl was right, even if she *was* working on commission. The lavender silk dress wasn't cute, it was seriously hot. I hardly recognized myself. My arms were toned from Buddha Ball, my hair was falling softly around my shoulders, and even my butt was more JLo than "oh no."

"I'll take it," I said definitively. "And whichever earrings go with it."

I normally avoided the shops on Sunset Plaza, but in two hours I'd be gazing into the big baby blues of Mr. Tennis, Luke Hansen, and I thought he ought to have something nice to look at as well. And it would be a gift to me too—a victory gift. As I walked back into the fitting room, I didn't know what to be more excited about—the promotion this morning, my first date with

Luke in less than two hours, or my trip to see Michael Deming tomorrow. Really, never in a million years would I have anticipated so many good things happening at once. It was like *The Secret* had exploded in my face.

I was halfway out of the dress when my iPhone buzzed with a text. It was Brett.

> Where'd you disappear to yesterday? Hope you're packing.
> Just bring a cute dress and your liver—we leave at 7 a.m.
> I'll bring the coffee!

Shit. I still hadn't told him about Michael Deming, my promotion, or the fact that I would *not* be heading to Sonoma tomorrow morning. *Got promoted,* I wrote back hastily, feeling a little guilty but knowing he'd get over it. *Can't make it this weekend. Sorry!*

I had just hit Send when my phone rang again. I rolled my eyes. I loved Brett and all, but did he have to be so clingy?

But instead of another text from Brett, Quinn's face flashed on the screen. I hadn't spoken to her in days, and truth be told, I'd almost forgotten about my sixteen-year-old former mentor. I hadn't even called her about the promotion.

"Congratulations," Quinn said when I picked up. Her tone was only a little warmer than usual. "I heard the good news."

I grinned as I finished working my way out of the dress. It was good to hear Quinn so impressed for once. "Thanks. I meant to call you, but—"

"Hey, can you meet me at the Chateau in fifteen minutes?" Quinn interrupted.

That wasn't much warning, but what should I expect from a

spoiled teenager? I glanced at my watch. It was six-thirty, and I had to be at Koi at eight. And why did Quinn suddenly want to be seen with me, at Chateau Marmont no less? "Um, I don't think I can," I said breezily, sliding into my jeans.

"I really need to talk to you," Quinn demanded. "So can you just come here?"

The salesgirl's hand suddenly darted through the crack in the curtain. It held the perfect pair of silver drop earrings, which I took from her eagerly.

"What about Sunday?" I asked. "My Sunday is looking much better." I pulled my top on and stepped out into the store, shaking my head. I admit that I'd certainly called Quinn in a crisis, but I'd never actually demanded that she meet me anywhere. All I ever asked for was a little advice, sent my way in a timely text.

"Seriously, Taylor," Quinn said, her tone growing much cooler.

"Fine, I'll be there. But I only have a few minutes." I hung up without waiting for Quinn's answer and then handed the Calypso girl my credit card.

☙

Fifteen minutes later—and three hundred and fifteen dollars lighter—I walked into the lobby lounge of Chateau Marmont and tried to look like I knew where I was going. The room was dim, with large crushed-velvet couches and chairs, high arched windows, and an unmistakable old-world glamour. Ever since I'd moved to L.A., I'd wondered what it was like, perched as it was, high above the Strip. It looked like a Gothic fortress from the outside, and I—like any movie buff worth her salt—knew its legendary past, as well as its occasionally notorious present. (For example, it was where James Dean first read the script for *Rebel*

Without a Cause; it was also where a certain Hollywood starlet stayed after her drunk-driving arrest.)

I turned into the twinkling garden, where a holiday cocktail party was in full swing. People huddled under heating lamps, drinking wine and talking over Jay-Z on the speakers. Availing myself of a flute of champagne off a waiter's passing tray, I stepped down into the party. Rashida Jones and Molly Sims were chatting by a large potted palm. Orlando Bloom held court at a table full of young and giggling women. Stephen Dorff walked past me with an Amazonian supermodel wearing a Santa hat clinging to his arm.

Ah yes, I thought, Christmas in L.A.

Finally I spotted Quinn behind the DJ turntables, a cigarette in one hand and a glass of champagne in the other. She wore a sleeveless burgundy dress with tiers of ruffles on the skirt and a silver tiara in her auburn hair. An Olsen twin—not sure which one; I could never tell them apart—and a buff, scruffy-haired DJ who looked extremely familiar stood on either side of her, looking full of holiday spirit.

"Hey," Quinn said when she looked up and saw me. She stepped away from her little crowd. "Thanks for coming. And congratulations again," she said, holding up her champagne flute. "Here's hoping Kylie's on suicide watch."

She took a healthy sip, and I followed her lead. "So does your mom know you're here?"

Quinn rolled her eyes. "What do *you* care?"

I shrugged. She had a point. What did I care? Quinn's relationship with Iris was definitely not my problem. I guzzled the rest of my champagne, which was already starting to give me a little buzz. "Well, thanks, Quinn. Seriously. I couldn't have done it without you."

Quinn put up her hand. "I didn't ask you here to congratulate you."

I smiled. Of course not. Did I really think Quinn was capable of such niceness? Um, *no.* "Well, what is it? You need a ride somewhere or something?" I said this just to annoy her, and it seemed to work.

Quinn rolled her eyes. "Aren't you forgetting something? Our deal?"

I gazed around at the party. Over by a cluster of chairs, I saw Kate Hudson getting an impromptu foot massage from a friend in a purple sequined top. Leaning against one of the colonnades with a very blasé look on his face was Shia LaBeouf. And wasn't that Nicky Hilton in the corner, talking on her cell phone? None of these people owed something to a teenager, and for a moment, I felt a wave of indignation.

"Remember I told you I'd figure it out? Well, now I know what I want," Quinn continued. "Get my mom out of town for the weekend."

I laughed. "*What?* Are you kidding me? Look around you— it's already Friday night."

Quinn shook her head as she sipped. "As long as she's gone by tomorrow afternoon, it doesn't matter."

I snagged another glass of champagne and tossed a big sip back. "What for?" I challenged.

Quinn's stare was blistering. "You really think I'm going to tell *you* that?"

This was really too much. I hiked my bag up on my shoulder and made as if to walk away. "Quinn, this is ridiculous. What sort of insane reason am I supposed to come up with that would get your mom on a flight in twelve hours?"

"Uh, *none* of this is my problem," she said, putting her glass down on a table. "Figure it out. I don't know." She took a long, meditative drag on her Marlboro. "You know, it would be a shame if all that work was for nothing."

Her tone of voice—and what she was implying—made me feel like she'd just given me the deathstare. "I beg your pardon?"

Quinn folded her arms. "I'm just saying. You don't do this for me? Then my mom hears *everything*."

This girl was crafty—I had to give her that. I wanted to toss my champagne in her face. But crazy as she was, I'd made a deal with her.

I narrowed my eyes at her and slowly finished the rest of my drink. "Fine," I said. Then I handed her my empty glass and wove through the revelers on my way back to my car.

❦

"Honey? Are you serious? Tomorrow morning?" the travel agent said. "Isn't that late notice?"

"That's how business gets done sometimes," I snapped into my phone as I sped down La Cienega to my apartment. "Iris just told me she has to go to New York. The first flight out tomorrow. As long as it's first class. American if you have it, but we'll take anything." My other line beeped. "Hold on." I clicked over. "Hello?"

"Hi, Taylor, I have Bob Glazer," said the assistant.

"Okay, put him through."

I turned up my West Hollywood street and pointed my garage-door opener at the gate, adrenaline coursing through my body. On my way home from Chateau, as I crawled my way down

Sunset under the lit billboards, it had finally hit me—I could send Iris to New York to meet with Holden MacIntee. He was still there, doing press before going to Europe on Monday, where he would hopscotch between London, Paris, and Berlin for two more weeks. This would be the last opportunity for a face-to-face between studio and star until after the holidays. Iris actually sounded more than game for the trip when I called her from the car and told her Holden had requested a face-to-face.

Now I just needed to tell Holden's people about it.

Bob Glazer picked up the line. "Taylor?" he asked gruffly.

"Bob, hi!" I said, trying to sound cheerful as opposed to desperate.

"What do you want? I'm just about to get out of here."

"Iris wants to have dinner with Holden tomorrow night in New York," I said, pulling into my parking space. "About *Evan.* Before he goes to Europe."

Bob sighed. "All right, fine. I think we can do that."

In my excitement, I very nearly bounced up and down in my seat like a two-year-old. All systems go. Or almost: I still had the travel agent on the other line.

"What do you have for me?" I asked, clicking back over.

"I have her on a 9 a.m. flight that gets into New York tomorrow at 6 p.m. First class. American. Returning nine o'clock Sunday. And the Mandarin could give her a suite with a street view."

"Perfect. Thanks. Gotta go."

Ten minutes later, I'd ordered Iris a car, e-mailed Iris the itinerary, and texted Quinn.

All done. Leaving Sat. morning, returning Sunday night.

Now all I had to do was get ready to meet Luke in the handful of minutes I had left.

I laid my new dress on the bed, closed my bedroom door, and took a frantic, three-minute shower. When I got out, I could hear *The Dog Whisperer*, Magnolia's favorite show, on the TV.

"Hey!" Magnolia called from the kitchen. "I got Poquito Mas!"

"I've got a date!" I yelled and opened my bedroom door. Then I screamed.

Lying on top of my silky lavender Calypso dress was the most disgusting creature I had ever seen. Was it a dog? Or was it some giant sewer rat? It gazed up at me from beneath a shelf of gray, matted hair.

"What the *hell*?"

"Oh, that's Woodstock!" yelled Magnolia, running down the hall. "I just pulled him from the shelter. They were going to put you down, weren't they," she cooed.

"You brought *another* dog here?" I didn't bother to disguise the anger in my voice. "And you let him lie on my fucking *dress*?"

"It's just for a few days. Isn't he cute? He's a Lhasa apso mix. I figure he just needs a quick bath, and he'll be snatched up in seconds."

"We already have two dogs that have not been snatched up," I hissed.

Magnolia stuck out her pretty lips in a pout. "Taylor, they were going to euthanize him—"

"Does this look like a shelter to you?" I yelled. "Because it looks like an *apartment* to me. Though God knows it's now got as many dogs in it as the fucking pound!" I stalked over to the bed and shoved the slobbering mutt off my brand-new dress. "I just *bought* this!" I yelled, holding it up.

"So it has a little hair on it," Magnolia said defensively, scooping up the frightened dog.

"It cost two hundred and ninety bucks! It's not *supposed* to have hair on it!" I shrieked.

Magnolia edged her way to the door. "What's happened to you?" she mumbled. "You've changed."

"What?"

She didn't look at me but I heard her words very clearly. "When did you turn into such an alpha bitch?"

I clenched my fists at my sides. "I don't know, when did you turn into the crazy dog lady who watches Cesar Millan every night and eats only Poquito Mas? What's next—are you going to start knitting dog-hair sweaters or something?"

Magnolia buried her face into Woodstock's disgusting fur. "I'm gonna take him for a walk," she murmured. "Have a good time on your date."

"Whatever."

I flounced into the hallway and held the dress up before the mirror, smoothing its silky folds and brushing away Woodstock's hair. I observed my image and immediately cheered up. The lilac color brought out my eyes and looked great with my new tan. It was going to look absolutely fabulous on me, just like the Calypso girl had said. I took a deep breath. All I had to do was slip it on, put a little makeup on my face, and go have myself an excellent date. Everything was good.

No, everything was *great*.

CHAPTER TWENTY-EIGHT

Welcome to Koi," the valet said as he opened my car door.

I gave myself one more glance in the rearview. I'd put my hair up to show off the new earrings, and the mineral makeup I'd picked up from Sephora made my face glow. (How was it that I had never used bronzer before?) Thanks to Quinn, the past couple of hours had been profoundly unpleasant, but now I felt things once again falling back into place. With a final deep breath, I stepped out of my Civic. I realized, with a smile, that once my new raise kicked in, I might even be able to get a hybrid.

Inside, the bar was even more packed than the last time I'd been there, and I quickly realized I should have suggested somewhere else. I'd been on the other line when Luke had called to set our plans, so I'd just said the first place that popped into my head. It made sense to me why I'd picked it—this was where I'd been on my first L.A. date, such as it was, and I guess my subconscious had brought me back. I didn't even like the place that much.

Luke was nowhere in sight, so I squeezed past a group of girls who were already drunk and squealing at the tops of their lungs and made a beeline for the bar.

"Pomegranate martini," I said to the Barbie bartender. "As soon as possible."

To my left, a guy in a Tommy Bahama shirt and a gold chain smiled at me, looking like he might want to make conversation, but I stopped him cold with a mini-deathstare. He turned away— obviously I was getting better at it.

As I waited for my drink, I couldn't help but replay the fight with Magnolia. I'd had no idea I was signing on to live with Ms. Canine Fucking Rescue, I'll say that much. Who the hell did she think she was? Telling me *I'd* changed? I wasn't the one who was slowly becoming a member of the animal kingdom. And what was I supposed to do, anyway? Apologize for not staying a loser? Was I a better roommate when I was on the couch, stuffing my face with ice cream and wondering if I should go back to Connecticut or even Cleveland?

Maybe Magnolia was jealous. She had a degree from Wesleyan, but she spent her days scooping up dog shit and waxing people's genitals. It wasn't unreasonable to imagine that she resented my success. After all, I'd already accomplished more in a matter of months than I'd thought I would in a year.

The bartender returned with my drink and carefully placed it on the bar. "Fifteen dollars," she said, holding out her hand.

"It's on me," said a male voice.

I assumed it was Tommy Bahama and was about to tell him to get lost when Mark Lyder stepped up beside me. His hair was tousled in that perfect way, and his large dark eyes still looked deceptively friendly, even as they scanned the room, always on the lookout for someone more important to talk to. And of course, his jaw was still dappled with two-day-old stubble. But then there was the small matter of the black eye he was still sporting.

"Congratulations," he said as he dropped his black AmEx on the bar. "Cleveland scored a home run. And then some," he added with a chilly grin. "All the way to junior exec." He raised his beer to salute me. "And Holden MacIntee. That's quite a get."

I sipped my drink, ignoring his salute. "And that's quite a shiner. Did you take up boxing?"

He flashed me an even bigger phony smile, like Tom Cruise on a talk show. "Funny, Cleveland. You know where it came from."

I shrugged. "Yeah, maybe. I hope it was worth it." *You snake,* I wanted to add.

"I could say the same thing to you," he shot back.

Coolly I raised an eyebrow. "I don't know what you're talking about." I turned to watch the door for Luke. Mark Lyder continued to hover in front of me. I couldn't imagine what he wanted. "Are you here for dinner? Or are you trolling for clients? I hear times are tough."

"Wow, Taylor," he said, shaking his head. "Looks like you're in need of another lesson. Never burn bridges. Especially in Hollywood."

I was about to tell him to go eat some edamame and grow some breasts when Luke strolled through the door in a brown suede jacket and a cream-colored button-down shirt. I'd never seen him in anything but tennis whites, and the effect was impressive. He looked nervous—and very, very handsome.

Mark whirled around to see the object of my gaze. "Well,

well," he said, understanding flooding his face. "Now I'm *really* impressed." With one last swallow, he drained his glass and left it on the bar. "Congratulations again, Cleveland," he hissed and then disappeared into the dining room.

I left my drink on the bar and made my way, as quickly as my Jimmy Choo boots would let me, over to Luke. Mark Lyder and Kylie deserved each other—even snakes need mates, right?— and I was in no mood to stay and eat dinner anywhere near him.

As I approached, Luke gave me a broad, warm smile. My heart did a little dance in my chest.

"Sorry I'm late, I had to shower at the club," he said, leaning down to kiss my cheek. "Wow. You look beautiful." He took in the formfitting dress appreciatively.

"Thank you," I said. "You don't look half bad yourself." He was getting ready to take off his coat but I put out my hand to stop him. "You know what? Would you mind very much if we went somewhere else?"

Luke chuckled. He almost seemed relieved. "Not at all. This place not your scene?" He gestured to the drunk girls and the men eyeballing them.

"Not tonight it's not."

"Cool. Then let's go to my neighborhood," he said. "You can follow me in your car."

"Sounds great." I sighed in relief as I followed him to the door. Then I gave another mini-deathstare to a redhead who looked Luke up and down like he was something she wanted to eat. "Where are we headed?"

He smiled. "You like the beach?"

☙

I followed Luke's Wrangler down rough-and-tumble Lincoln Boulevard. I was pretty sure we were headed into Venice, and so far, I wasn't that impressed; I saw a few cruddy-looking restaurants and a handful of guys who looked like they spent more time drinking than they did anything else. But then we turned onto a tree-lined street full of cute little brightly painted bungalows. It was dark and quiet down there, and as Luke's taillights continued on toward the water, I started to smell the salt in the breeze.

He finally parked in front of Hama Sushi, an open-air restaurant just steps from the beach.

"This good?" he asked when I walked up to join him. "Shouldn't be too hard to get a table here. You won't, like, miss the velvet rope or anything?"

I lobbed a flirty little punch at his arm. "This is great."

As much as this was a waste of my gorgeous new dress, I liked being so near the beach. And I was surprised at how relieved I felt to get away from Koi and all the prying eyes—Mark Lyder's in particular.

On one side the restaurant was a big, airy, tent-covered space with a giant projection screen broadcasting a football game on mute.

"Let's sit in here," Luke said, leading me into a more private room to the left. As we walked past the sushi bar, the chefs cheered; someone had made a touchdown or something. "It's nothing fancy, but the *otoro* here is amazing," he said happily, sitting down.

A waitress walked over with a tray of hot towels and, using a pair of tongs, handed us each one.

"Do you know this is the closest I've been to the beach since I moved here?" I asked. It struck me as incredible even as I admitted it.

"I figure why move to L.A. if you're not going to live near the beach?" Luke said, placing his towel on the dish left by the waitress. "Do you surf?"

"Uh, no," I answered. "I mean, I can barely stay up on a skateboard, and sidewalks don't move the way waves do."

"I could teach you that too," he said, eyeing the menu.

"Are you kidding? Sidewalks don't have sharks, either."

He grinned at me, and I felt myself beginning to blush. I didn't want to get all nervous again, but every time I got near him, my brain and my body seemed to stop communicating with each other.

Luke ordered plates of seared albacore, hamachi rolls, seaweed salads, heaps of extra ginger "for the lady" (and here he winked at me) when I mentioned I liked it, and big cups of green tea. "I'm not much of a drinker," he confided. "Too many years of training. I know, I'm a little boring."

I shook my head vehemently. "Are you kidding? Sitting in traffic is boring. The commercials they show before movies are boring. Sunday-night TV is boring. You, Luke Hansen, are not boring."

He reached out across the table and touched my hand, and the little jig my heart did earlier turned into a full-scale tango. "You're not boring either," he said. "You're a hell of a lot of fun." A little trace of a Virginia accent came out when he said that, and any doubts I might have had about how much I liked him flew out the window like a flock of seagulls.

Later, we walked up Abbot Kinney Boulevard, past the lit storefronts of groovy home furnishings stores and clothing shops. I could hear the waves just a few blocks away. There was a stiff ocean breeze, and I rubbed my arms for warmth.

"It's cold down here in your part of town," I said, smiling up at him.

"Here." He took off his jacket and put it tenderly around my shoulders. It was still warm from his body, and I shivered in pleasure. "That better?" he asked, bending down to peer into my face.

"Thanks. It's great."

We passed a man asleep in a doorway wearing what looked to be a pair of antlers on his head. His nose was a bright red ball.

"You got to love L.A. in December," Luke said, but by the slightly sorrowful tone of his voice, I could tell he didn't mean it.

I dropped a dollar into the cup the man had set out on the sidewalk before falling asleep. It was the season for giving. "Are you going home for the holidays?"

"Not this year," he said, shaking his head. "Everyone'll have to have their fruitcake without me."

"You like fruitcake?"

He shook his head again. "Nah, it was just a figure of speech. But I do miss home around now. It snows there sometimes—not often, but we get white Christmases sometimes."

"We have only white Christmases in Cleveland," I said. "It's like a commandment or something: *Thou shalt have a blizzard three days before the holiday so that no one can get their shopping done.* Or maybe you get your shopping done but you run out of wrapping paper, so you have to wrap everything in Kroger bags." I paused. I was on the verge of talking too much, I knew it, but I went on anyway. "Or maybe that was just me. Anyway, growing up my parents would unwrap their presents from the Kroger bags and I'd unwrap mine, and then we'd all go to the park and feed the Canada geese who don't migrate anymore, which we've done every year since I was ten. Then we'd go back home and drink hot chocolate with Baileys in it. Well, that tradition didn't start until I was a little older than ten." I had a sudden longing for my parents, my house, my childhood bedroom, with its shelves of My Little Ponies (elementary school), its splatter-painted walls (junior high), and its half-ripped Cure posters (high school).

I finally stopped myself. The truth was, I wanted to know more about *him*, but it was hard to keep my mouth shut. I tried to think of a question to ask him—about Virginia or his favorite holiday memory or something, but instead I turned to him and said, "So, do you want to teach tennis the rest of your life?"

Luke laughed. "That's kind of a non sequitur, isn't it?" He pointed us up a cobblestone side street. "But to answer your question, yes, I think I do. But not in Beverly Hills. It pays the bills and that's great, but I'd rather teach kids."

"Really?"

Above us the moon appeared, low and round and almost orange. The sound of the waves grew, and I breathed in the salty air. I didn't feel like I was in L.A. at all—or at least not the L.A. I knew.

"Yeah. I mean, don't get me wrong—it can be really fun teaching adults. Most people graduate high school or college and never take risks or learn anything new, so it's cool to be part of that. But a lot of my clients seem to want to learn to play for . . . professional reasons," he said carefully. "I guess tennis comes in handy for networking, that kind of stuff. That's why I'd love to teach kids instead of adults. It'd be cool to run my own tennis academy someday, I think. Kids don't really think about anything else when they play sports. They just do."

"True," I agreed. I'd sought out tennis lessons from Luke for career reasons too. Even though I'd brought my Prince racquet across the country with me, it had sat in my closet for months, untouched.

He steered me up a walkway to a two-story cottage painted mint green and decorated with white Christmas lights. From the bottom floor, I could hear music and voices.

"So my downstairs neighbors are having kind of a holiday thing," he said, kicking nervously at a shrub near the sidewalk. "Want to stop in and say hi? They're really cool. I promise."

I shrugged. Why not? And if he wanted to introduce me to his friends, wasn't that a good sign? "Sure," I said.

The room we stepped into was cozy, lit with flickering votives. Dishes of candy sat on top of piled coffee-table books about surfing and art, and striking black-and-white framed photographs of waves hung on the walls. Galaxie 500 played softly on the stereo. It was a lovely little room, but no one was in it.

"They're probably in the back," Luke said, seeing my questioning look.

He led me down the hall toward a tiny kitchen, which was indeed full of about a dozen people. At the sight of Luke, everyone yelled, "Hey!"

Luke steered me over to a willowy, barefooted brunette in a flower-printed dress and a blond guy with a goatee wearing a Neil Young T-shirt. "Guys, this is Taylor," Luke said. "Taylor, meet Julia and Tom. This is their place."

"Great to meet you!" Julia exclaimed, thrusting a glass into my hand. "Try some. Homemade eggnog. Seriously spiked." She winked. "And if you don't like it, we have plenty of wine."

Tom just grinned at all of us and sipped his beer. "Not an eggnog man," he whispered, but he clinked his bottle against my glass.

I felt surprisingly welcome, considering I was in the center of a room full of strangers. There were jars of home-canned fruit and preserves on shelves and a basket of dried flowers on the counter. It was shabby chic meets Martha Stewart, and it made me feel right at home.

"Julia and Tom make sure I get fed," Luke offered. "She's an amazing cook. And a great photographer."

"And a seriously bad tennis player," Julia added, dumping a bunch of macaroons onto a plate. "Cookie?" She held out a plate to me and I took not one but two. Macaroons were my favorite.

A lanky brown-haired guy in a cowboy-ish button-down sidled up to Luke and clapped him on the shoulder. "Good to see you," he cried. "Is this the lady we've been hearing about?"

Luke went bright red and stared down into his eggnog. "This is Hank," he said softly.

Hank looked chagrined. "Sorry, man, was I not supposed to say that?"

I giggled and took a sip of the eggnog. It was delicious.

Julia jumped in, hoping to ease Luke's embarrassment. "Luke says you're a dog groomer," Julia said.

"Oh no," I said, "I'm—" But I remembered my lie just in time. "I'm a dog *walker* and a *personal* groomer. A groomer for humans, that is." I smiled brightly, as if these were the most normal jobs in the world. "I work at a little place in West Hollywood called Joylie."

And I realized that this just proved what a nice person Luke was—there I'd been, asking him if he wanted to teach tennis for the rest of his life, and he could have turned right around and asked me if I wanted to wax men's *testicles* for the rest of mine. But he hadn't. He was a gentleman.

"And she's a very good tennis player," Luke offered.

"He flatters me," I said, giving him a playful little shove.

"You two are really cute together," Tom whispered into my ear.

I bit my lip and looked down at the floor. As an eggnog-induced warmth crept over me, I felt a strange combination of excitement and sorrow. I was excited because, well, this seemed like it could really be something. But I had lied to him, and I was still lying. So exactly how much of a "something" could this turn out to be?

After another half hour of chatting, Luke pointed upstairs, and I nodded. I wanted to have him to myself.

Luke's apartment was more sparsely furnished, but it was still cozy. The walls were painted a warm gray, lined with book-shelves holding a sloppy array of novels and sheet music. There was a faded, aging sofa beneath a large Basquiat print, and a rug that looked handmade. I counted four different guitars, three acoustic and one electric.

"You must play," I said, like the genius that I was.

He laughed as he lit a couple of candles on the windowsill. "That I do. Want some tea?"

"Sure." I followed him into the roomy kitchen. "This place is great. And your friends are really sweet."

"I know," he said, flipping on his electric kettle. "I'm lucky. It's a pretty good group down there. Tom actually runs Big

Brothers here in Venice—you know, they pair up inner-city kids with older mentors?"

I nodded, thankful he was talking about the charity organization and not the tacky reality TV show.

The kettle began to bubble, and he poured boiling hot water into two mugs. "Actually I guess I'll get my wish soon, teaching kids—Tom's sending some of the kids in his program my way for some lessons." He handed me a mug with a picture of the Santa Monica pier on it.

"That's really sweet of you," I said, meaning it.

He shrugged modestly. "It's all Tom. But I'm happy to do it."

I looked down into my tea thoughtfully. "I guess sometimes you just forget that there's more to this city than entertainment," I mused.

"Of course there is," he said, grinning, and led me back into the living room.

A whole *lot* more, I thought, staring at him through the steam rising from my cup. Suddenly I felt warm all over. Metronome and Kylie and even my trip to see Michael Deming seemed like part of another world, a world completely foreign to this cozy one here by the ocean. Here people ate sushi in flip-flops and talked about sports instead of movies, and girls drank eggnog and hung out in living rooms instead of at Hyde. As I drew a scratchy wool blanket over my legs beside him on the couch, I realized I didn't want to leave.

"Hey." He put his feet on the coffee table and looked at me intently. "This is going to sound a little weird, but this is one of the most fun nights I've had in a long, long time. So thank you, Taylor."

I put my feet up next to his and leaned against him. "You're welcome." I put down my tea. "I was just going to say the same thing."

He leaned over, and I stopped breathing. Softly, his lips brushed mine, and as I ran my hands up his arms, I actually shivered.

In the window, the candles flickered, and I could hear the faint sounds of the party down below. Someone had put "White Christmas" on the stereo, and it sounded like Hank was singing right along.

"We can stop," he whispered a few minutes later as he slid a warm hand over my thigh and under the hem of my Calypso dress. "Just tell me. It's okay."

I had a flight to catch in a few hours. I needed to sleep. I barely knew this guy. I knew all these things, and yet nothing in the world could make me get up off this couch.

"I know," I said, smiling, and tipped my face back up to his.

CHAPTER TWENTY-NINE

Almost twelve hours later, I peered out of the back window of my bright green taxi and into another world. I was only a few miles off the coast of Washington, but I might as well have just landed in Middle Earth. Puget Sound was flat and cold-looking, the color of slate, and above it, huge, fir-covered mountains disappeared into the mist. The winding road my bearded, gnomish driver took us down was deserted.

"Are we getting close?" I asked, yawning.

"Almost there," he said, smiling at me in the rearview mirror. "I'd put on the radio, but I hardly get any stations around here."

Almost there. I'd been telling myself that since four-thirty, when the cab arrived at my apartment to take me to the airport. Then I'd boarded a 6 a.m. flight to Seattle, after which I'd boarded a two-seater seaplane for the forty-five-minute, white-knuckled flight to Orcas Island. (Needless to say, they didn't serve vodka on the prop plane, but if they had, I would have seriously considered breaking my no-drinks-before-three rule.) I had to hand it to Michael Deming—he did a great job of discouraging visitors.

But in a way I didn't mind all the traveling—it had given me hours to think about last night. I drew my parka tighter around me, closed my eyes, and ran through it all once again. It had been, in a word, perfect. Luke was attentive and affectionate—a complete and utter Southern gentleman. At three in the morning, he had walked me to my car and kissed me tenderly, rubbing my arms so I wouldn't get cold.

"I'll call you," he said, and I could tell that he meant it. "I had a great night, Taylor."

"Me too."

I wondered what he was doing right now. I liked to imagine him curled up in his big soft bed, maybe waking up only long enough to wish I were still there. I hadn't mentioned a word about my trip, for obvious reasons.

And that was the sticking point, wasn't it? He thought he was getting to know me, but half of what I'd told him was a lie. I shrugged down deeper in my jacket, shaking my head. I wouldn't think about that just yet. I would just keep replaying our date, and I'd find a way to tell him when I got back.

"Here we are." The driver turned down a narrow, unpaved road. Snow-covered firs blocked out the sun, and banks of snow rose on either side of us. After a bumpy mile or so, we turned into a gravel drive and pulled up behind a Ford pickup truck. The only building in sight was a squat, primitive cabin that looked more like a Hobbit hovel than a house.

"Are you sure this is 4576 Deerhead Road?" I asked, squinting at the ramshackle cabin. It seemed to lean to one side, and the porch appeared to be wider on the left half than it did on the right; the whole place looked like it had been built by people with no grasp of basic geometry.

"Hey, nobody said this was Beverly Hills," the driver cracked as he threw the car into park.

"Here," I said, handing him a fifty. "Just wait."

I stepped out into the damp cold. Michael Deming lived here? This was where all my postcards had been sent? There had to be some kind of mistake. Hollywood geniuses didn't live in dumps like this, no matter how eccentric they were.

After searching in vain for a doorbell, I rapped on the plywood door. I stamped my feet on the porch as I waited, and a little pile of snow that had been balanced on the crooked railing landed on my boot with a soft plop.

After another moment, the door opened, and a small, wiry man with darting brown eyes, a full beard, and a look of suspicion on his face stood before me. It was hard to reconcile this man with the pictures of him on the sets of his films, some of them made less than a decade ago. I mean, this guy looked like he didn't know the meaning of the word "razor." But it was definitely him. "Mr. Deming?" I asked. "I'm Taylor. From Metronome. Your agent told you I was coming?"

Deming nodded. "Yes, welcome," he said softly as he gestured for me to come inside. "Taylor. I like that name. And I'm sure you're hungry. Do you like tuna?" he asked, peering at me with his yellow brown eyes.

"Um, yeah, that's great," I said, wiping the mud off my boots. I lingered near the door for a minute. I guess there was a part of me that thought maybe he'd gone completely off the deep end and was planning on chopping me up into a hundred little pieces and adding me to the tuna salad.

The main room of Deming's house was a combination of kitchen, dining area, and living room—the kind of thing that an L.A. real estate agent would call "loft style" but was really more Laura Ingalls Wilder. In the corner were a couple of doors, which I assumed led to the bedroom and the bathroom. There was no TV in sight, but books lined the walls, and piles of them rose from the floor like stalactites. A pair of binoculars sat next to a plate of sandwiches and a jar of Miracle Whip on the broad kitchen table. The stove was one of those *Little House on the Prairie* contraptions that use logs instead of gas.

It occurred to me then that Michael Deming wasn't just living under the radar. He was living under the poverty line. This made me shrug off my jacket with a new confidence. Deming's dire financial straits were about to make my job a lot easier.

"Please. Sit down," he said gently, pointing to one of the Shaker-style chairs. "And what would you like to drink? Coffee?"

"Yes, thank you," I said. I was feeling more relaxed now. I had a winning lottery ticket in my pocket that I was ready to hand the guy.

"I still make a good cup, if I say so myself," he said as he poured me a mug from the Cuisinart ten-cupper, which seemed to be the only electrical appliance in the house made after 1986. He set it in front of me and then sat down himself. "So, Taylor."

He looked at me very intently, and for a long time he didn't blink. If this was a staring contest, he was welcome to win it; I blinked and looked down at my coffee. Deming cleared his throat. Who knew how long it had been since he'd spoken to another person? It could have been weeks.

"You can see that I live a very different life from my peers. Or rather, my ex-peers," he said with a humble smile. "Believe it or not, I'm very happy here."

"I believe it." I didn't, actually, but it seemed rude to disagree. I mean, really, how happy can one be living alone in a house made of Lincoln Logs? The poor guy didn't even have a dog to keep him company. (I had a few I could loan him, though, if he was interested . . .)

"It suits me. Simple. Quiet." He cut my sandwich into halves with a steak knife and passed it to me. "When I left Los Angeles, I was a very unhappy man. I think I've changed quite a bit since then."

No doubt, I thought. Certainly he looked different—he looked like he could really use a personal grooming appointment with my roommate. But I raised my eyebrows encouragingly. If he wanted to talk, I ought to listen. "How so?" I asked and then took a bite of my sandwich. It wasn't half bad, but then again, I was starving.

"I'm sure you've heard a little bit of what happened to me," he continued as he gazed ruefully into his coffee cup. "It was my fault too, of course." He shook his head, smiling. "I believed what people told me. God, I was an idiot."

I know the feeling, I thought but didn't say. It had taken me a while to see through Kylie's crap.

"I had to take their orders. I had to cast their stars. And then they recut the film until I didn't even recognize it." He shook his head with regret. "Now the only movies I make are of wildlife." His eyes twinkled. "Squirrels and foxes are so much easier to work with than actors."

I laughed. "You have a point. Squirrels don't need personal chefs or bodyguards, and I've never met a vain, insecure fox."

Deming leaned back in his chair and put his hands behind his head and stared at the ceiling for a while. I wondered how long this was going to take. I appreciated a thoughtful decision-making process, but I wanted to get the deal done and then take a nap. I was so tired, my hands were tingling. I looked up to see what Deming was seeing. Cobwebs.

Deming finally cleared his throat. "I guess I'd like to ask you why, knowing all of this, I should make your movie, Taylor. I read it last night. And yes, I can see what you might think I might . . . add to the story. But I guess my question to you is, why me?" He tore his gaze away from the cobwebs and turned his disconcerting eyes to me. "Why would I be your first choice?"

Because I've been writing to you once a week for seven years, and you are responsible for even putting me here in the first place, I wanted to say.

But I couldn't say that. For one thing, the idea that he'd even gotten my letters seemed far-fetched, now that I knew how far from civilization he lived. He probably communicated with people by smoke signals and didgeridoo. And second, I wasn't here as a fan. I was here as a creative executive. And creative executives didn't gush. They pitched.

"You should do this movie because movies are your passion, Mr. Deming," I said confidently, leaning forward in my chair and fixing him with the same frank stare I'd given his agent, the Silver Bullet. "This is what you should be doing. Not hiding your talent away in a cabin. But bringing another poignant, true story to the screen."

He nodded slightly, but I couldn't read his expression. He leaned over and produced a pipe from a small drawer, which he put in his mouth, unlit. A *pipe?* I thought. He was really taking this backwoods thing seriously. Once he agreed to the deal, I was going to have to introduce him to Tom Scheffer's superhealthy, super-L.A. smoothies—those would get him straightened out.

"We'll respect your vision," I went on. I could feel my voice gathering force. I knew I was right, and I wanted him to know it too—he *needed* to do this movie. "We will let you make this movie the way you want to. Everyone involved with this has the highest regard for your talent. And one of the biggest and brightest male stars on the planet wants to work with you."

He stopped nodding and took the pipe out of his mouth. "Who is that?"

"Holden MacIntee. *Vanity Fair* just proclaimed him the new *It* boy."

His brow furrowed in concentration. For a moment I wondered if Deming didn't know who Holden MacIntee was. But no, that was impossible. Two-year-old girls knew who Holden MacIntee was. Yak herders in Siberia knew who Holden MacIntee was.

"He loves your work," I continued. I had pushed aside my sandwich, even though I was starving. "Loves it. He told me this himself. And putting him in this movie guarantees us a huge opening. At least twenty million, depending on the season. And that's conservative."

Deming slowly nodded at me, now with a faint smile on his lips. Outside it had begun to snow, and I could see the little flakes spiraling down through the kitchen window. I thought of L.A., with its year-round sun, its unapologetic glitter, and its gorgeous chaos, from the green hollows of Topanga Canyon to the funky, trashy lanes of Fairfax Avenue to the gaudy lights of Santa Monica pier. I felt a sudden swelling of homesickness. Who didn't love L.A.? It was such a lonely life out here in Bumfuck, Nowhere. There was no way Deming could stand it any longer.

Deming still watched me, nodding, smiling faintly. He was already getting excited, I could tell. He just needed one tiny more push. "And well, aside from that, we'll give you more money than you've ever been paid in your life." I couldn't help looking around at the ramshackle cabin, with its ancient appliances and secondhand furniture. "I guarantee it."

There was a short pause as Deming studied me. He sure wasn't much of a talker.

"Well, thank you for coming," he said, getting up. "I'll be in touch."

"You know, I'd be happy to quote you a figure right now," I said. "I mean, I'm pretty sure I'm authorized to do that."

He smiled and waved me off. "That's not necessary. I'll be in touch."

As he walked me across the faded woven rug, I thought about telling him about the letters. *It's me,* I wanted to say. *The girl who's been hounding you!* The girl who's your biggest, craziest fan. But it just wouldn't seem professional. And besides, I could always tell him over dinner sometime when I visited the set. He would really get a kick out of it then.

"Thanks again, Mr. Deming," I said at the door. I pressed a business card into his hand.

"No, no," he said. "Thank you." He put the pipe back in his mouth and I swear, his eyes were almost twinkling. Maybe he was thinking about all the remodeling he could do. The cabin could be a nice place, really, if someone poured about a hundred grand into it. Then he shut the door.

"Just take me back to the airport, please," I told the driver.

My hand was in my purse before I even had my seat belt on. Miracle of miracles, my iPhone got service out here. I scrolled down to Quinn's e-mail.

THINK I JUST MADE MY FIRST DEAL!

I held the phone in my hand, waiting for Quinn's normally speedy response, but there was no answer. Odd, I thought, slipping it back into my purse. But then again, our little arrangement was over.

As the cab crunched back down the bumpy, snow-covered road, I leaned back against the soft vinyl and quickly fell into an easy, contented sleep.

CHAPTER THIRTY

Her furniture will be moved out, unless of course you like it." Amanda offered me a forced smile as she unlocked the door to what had once been Melinda Darling's office.

I stepped inside and couldn't help releasing a small sigh of satisfaction. There were red lacquered bookshelves along one wall and a low gray suede couch with sheepskin pillows. I raised the blinds, and the winter sun came streaming in, illuminating everything like a klieg light. "It looks fine. But yes, I think I would prefer white," I said, placing my bag on the sleek Lucite desk. *My* Lucite desk.

"Your schedule's on the computer," Amanda went on, tucking her black chin-length hair behind a delicate ear. "And let me know about artwork and plants, though it might be a little bit tough to get everything done before Christmas break." She shifted her weight from one stacked-heel leather boot to another. "Is there anything else?"

"Yes," I said. "I'd love some cappuccino." I didn't even want it that much, but I couldn't help it—the thrill of having someone else get one for me was just too much.

Amanda looked almost surprised. But wasn't this part of her job too? "No problem," she said after a beat. "I'll let you get settled."

She closed the door softly behind her. In all my excitement about the promotion, I'd never stopped to think about who would become *my* assistant. I felt a little sorry for Amanda—she'd felt so superior to me my first day, when I broke the copier with the Paul Haggis script, and now she was forced to fetch me my caffeine. Well, at least I didn't have Wyman. I wouldn't be able to stand him blathering on about Italian postwar neorealist cinema all day. *Yes, I saw* Umberto D., I'd have to scream, *and it was the most depressing movie of all time! Now go make me a freaking smoothie!*

I sat down in my Aeron chair and looked contentedly around the room. It was bigger than my West Hollywood bedroom and much, much cleaner. That first day, when Kylie walked me around the Metronome halls, seemed like a lifetime ago. If anyone had told me that I'd have my own office with my own little sign on the door (TAYLOR HENNING, CREATIVE EXECUTIVE!) just four months later, and with a marquee project to boot, I would never have believed them. Never, ever, ever.

I turned on my Mac Pro. I'd made plans to meet Luke for lunch on Larchmont, but maybe I'd send him a quick e-mail. My new computer was gorgeous—sleek and white, with a crystal-clear twenty-four-inch flat-screen monitor and an ergonomic keyboard that promised to make typing feel as good as a hand massage.

There was a knock on the door.

"Come in," I called, leaning back in Melinda's six-hundred-dollar chair. My lower back practically sang out in joy.

Julissa walked in, looking approvingly around her. She was wearing pigtails, and she looked about twelve. "Nice," she exclaimed. "You did it! Congratulations."

"Thanks." I smiled gently at her, trying not to seem too wildly overjoyed at my new digs. I didn't want to be gauche.

"Iris wants to see you." She raised her eyebrows a little.

Surely Iris was just calling me in to congratulate me. Maybe she'd bought me a plant for my office so I could turn mine into a primeval forest too. "Now?"

"Yeah." Julissa nodded and ducked out again.

Walking down the hall to Iris's office in my sleek black dress, I felt like a totally different person than I was in September. I felt smarter, more confident— hell, I even felt taller, though that was probably just the three-inch heels. I breezed into the outer room, where my old desk seemed small and abandoned.

Kylie sat typing in an exquisite mocha silk wrap dress, her votive flickering on her desk. Her back was perhaps just a bit straighter than usual, and her nose was elevated just a few inches higher. Clearly it was important to her not to wear her defeat too obviously.

"Good morning, Kylie." I figured I might as well start off on the right foot. What, after all, was the point of being uncivil to someone beneath me?

"Good morning," she replied coolly. She didn't stop typing.

It was about as friendly a response as could be expected. I thought I could get through all this resentment, given a little time, but I wasn't going to dwell on it now.

I peeked past a miniature orange tree into Iris's office. "You wanted to see me?"

Iris sat hunched over her desk, her head in her hands, fingers slowly massaging her temples. "Close the door, Taylor," she said without looking up.

I shut the door tentatively. Through the window behind her, I could see a gigantic Christmas tree, complete with fake presents, in front of Soundstage 6. "How was New York? Did something happen?" Maybe she'd had a turbulent flight or had gotten bumped from first class and had to sit next to a really fat guy in coach. Or what if Holden had thanked her for requesting the meeting? After all, I'd told Iris the face-to-face was *his* idea. Not that these were real problems, though—the good news of the Deming project would overshadow any of it.

Iris finally looked up. Her mouth was pursed as if she'd just tasted something bitter, and her face was a strange, sickly color of gray. "How many times have you met my daughter?" she asked.

A lump formed in my throat. Quinn. What had she done? "Your daughter? What do you mean?"

"Don't play dumb with me," Iris said coldly, taking her glasses off and tossing them onto the desk. "How many times? Once? Twice?" Her voice was cold and hard.

I was at a loss at first. "What are you getting at?"

"I'll show you what happened. After you packed me off to New York."

She tilted her twenty-two-inch plasma screen so I could see the TMZ.com web page. And the headline.

When the Cat's Away, Her Kitten Will Play

Can anyone say *rehab*? Quinn Whitaker, the sixteen-year-old daughter of Metronome honcho Iris Whitaker, let it all hang out on Saturday night (consider a bra next time, Quinn!), throwing the party of the year while Mom was out of town. Hollywood celebretards Rumer Willis, Vanessa Hudgens, Hania Barton, and Quinn's boy toy, actor/DJ Blake Miller, joined Quinn in sucking down the SoCo and stripping down in the hot tub. Who's the most effed up rich kid in L.A. now, Jamie Lynn?

I swallowed. "Oh my God," I said. I knew Quinn was no angel, but I didn't think she had it in her.

"Do you know that I have never *ever* let her stay at home for a weekend before? Her father was on location in Vancouver. And when *you* called and said that this was the last time I could meet Holden for this big movie, I thought, Okay, she's a big girl. I can trust her." Iris tapped her fingernails on her BlackBerry, and underneath the desk I could hear her kicking something with her foot. She was so agitated that she literally couldn't sit still. "In one night, all of that hard work—of being home with her, of having dinner every night, of making sure she didn't turn into yet another Hollywood casualty—all of that was gone." She got up from her chair and turned her back to me. "What you did was unconscionable."

I felt horrible for Iris, but I didn't see how it was my fault. Quinn had thrown a party—what did that have to do with me? "I don't understand," I said.

"What did you think was going to happen? That she just wanted some quiet time to *herself*?"

Suddenly I wanted to sit down, but I was strangely afraid to. I didn't like where this was going.

"She told me everything, you know. All about your little deal." Iris turned around and shook her head at me in disbelief.

"The fact that you would use a teenage girl like that . . ." She paused. "You know, in all my years in Hollywood, this is the *lowest* I've seen anyone stoop."

I couldn't meet her gaze—I stared down at the floor. I felt nausea creeping up on me, as well as a dawning comprehension of what sort of trouble I might be in. I couldn't believe Quinn had told her everything. Hadn't we agreed it was a secret?

"And this is the best part. I got a call from Michael Deming this morning."

I looked up in hope. Things were bad, I understood that—but the Deming thing was going to make it all better, wasn't it?

"He hated you," Iris said.

It took a minute for the words to register, and when they did, I felt like I'd been punched in the stomach. "What?" I gasped, fighting for breath.

Iris put up her hand. "Let me see if I can remember here. He said you were presumptuous. Arrogant. And 'the epitome of why he left this business,' as he put it. Apparently you crowed about what a big paycheck he was going to get. That's just how Metronome likes to woo its talent, by the way. Appealing to their wallets."

Still, I waited for the good part. Deming didn't have to like me—he just had to like the movie I was offering him. "But he's going to do *Evolution*, right?"

"No, Taylor, he is not. And now Bob Glazer is threatening a boycott against this entire studio." She smiled thinly. "Holden will never work with us again. Not after he turned down a twelve-million-dollar deal with Judd Apatow to do a movie that never existed in the first place." Iris narrowed her eyes, and I saw where Quinn had learned her deathstare. "So not only did you ruin the project and embarrass me, you embarrassed this entire company."

When I could breathe again, I simply started to cry. I stood there in front of Iris's desk and felt the tears fall hotly down my cheeks.

"Fortunately Kylie's project with Troy Vaughn is hanging on by a thread and might just pull through," she said coolly. "Otherwise this would be a complete disaster. So could you please send her in on your way out?"

"Of course," I struggled to say. I had never felt this awful in my life. But I told myself as I wiped my nose on the sleeve of my lovely Rebecca Beeson dress that this was part of being in Hollywood—the life of a creative executive had its up and its downs.

"Oh, and you're fired, Taylor. You'll leave the lot immediately."

With that final shock, I opened the door and was only just briefly aware of Kylie staring at me before I ducked my head and hurried past. I pointed toward Iris's office on my way out. "She wants to see you," I whispered.

Then I walked down the pulsing hallway to the office that had been, for five minutes, mine. Amanda looked up from her desk, ready to hand me my cappuccino, but upon seeing me, she froze. She opened her mouth and then shut it again, and I thought I saw understanding flicker across her face. I could not say that she looked sad to see me so broken.

She didn't know the details, but she would in about a minute. In fact, I heard an IM ping on her computer that I would have bet anything was from Kylie. In another two minutes, Cici, Wyman, Tom Scheffer, and everyone else would know, and I wanted to be gone when they did. I grabbed my bag and coat from my desk. I saw a security guard coming down the hallway, but I didn't need him to show me the way out.

CHAPTER THIRTY-ONE

Three hours later, I guided my car into a diagonal spot on Larchmont Boulevard, right near where I'd first found Quinn at Pinkberry all those weeks ago. I turned off the ignition and stared, exhausted and sick, through the windshield. Since leaving my former office, I'd driven aimlessly around, trying to figure out how everything could have gone to shit so quickly. Now my mind had finally reached overload, and I could barely even cry anymore.

I looked into the rearview mirror and flinched. My eyes were bloodshot and red-rimmed, with pink bags blooming under them, and my cheeks were blotchy. My nose seemed larger somehow, and even my lips looked swollen and terrible. If Luke didn't run screaming at the sight of me, I was going to have to offer him an explanation for the state I was in. And what was I going to say? Should I tell the truth and face his inevitable anger and disappointment? Or should I pretend I had some horrible allergic reaction to a sheepdog I'd been walking? It was a sign of my obvious distress that I seriously considered the latter. But I realized that it was time to come clean. I'd have to frame the story in a way that didn't make me seem like a stalker and an evil seductress, and then, after I explained that, I'd be able to tell Luke about my day. He would help me, I was sure. He would know how to make it right again.

I dabbed some powder on my nose and a little MAC gloss on my lips and then climbed out into the brisk day and set off toward Le Petit Greek. Larchmont Boulevard didn't look as appealing to me as it had that day I struck my deal with Iris's backstabbing daughter. Under a steel-colored sky, the miniature Santa and reindeer above the crosswalk looked garish and cheap. Luke had been right: L.A. just wasn't meant for Christmas.

I passed by a lingerie store and a sneaker emporium and finally turned into the simple green and white dining room of the eatery. There were baskets of lemons picturesquely placed here and there, and the walls were hung with large photographs of the Greek countryside. Most of the tables were full, and waiters brushed past me delivering platters of souvlaki and gyros. I had a hard time spotting Luke, and I craned my neck uncomfortably and squinted my puffy eyes. A waiter cleared his throat and I stepped out of the way. Then I saw him, at a table for two against the wall. But he wasn't alone. There was a woman with him, and it only took me about one more second to figure out who it was and what she was doing there.

I raced over to the table, my heart in my mouth. "This is my date," I hissed.

Kylie turned around and smiled sweetly, as if she were expecting me. "There you are. We were just talking about you." Her smile turned into a sneer—clearly she had not been saying nice things. "I was just explaining to Luke that we work together. Or rather, we did."

I glanced desperately at Luke. He looked at me blankly and then turned away. Kylie must have told him everything. But how had she known he was here? And how had she even known that I knew him? When I figured it out, I felt like the dumbest person in the world yet again. Mark Lyder. *Never burn bridges, Taylor,* he'd said. *Especially not in Hollywood.* He'd told Kylie about me and Luke, and Kylie had obviously managed to get Luke to agree to meet her.

I hadn't thought it was possible to feel worse, but it was. "Please leave." I lowered my voice. "Luke has nothing to do with this."

"Of course he does," she said in her mock-innocent tone. "He was just another way to get to me. Admit it."

Luke looked down at his plate. "That's enough, Kylie," he muttered.

But Kylie wasn't done with me yet. She looked like she could stay and rub all this in my face forever. "And I assume you were the one behind the whole thing at Chateau?" She nodded her head and didn't wait for an answer. "I figured as much. Really classy."

It was killing me to listen to her, but what could I say? Everything she accused me of was true. I stood there, clenching and unclenching my fists. I couldn't cry, I couldn't—not in front of Kylie, even though it was the only thing I wanted to do. Luke fidgeted in his chair. He still wouldn't look at me.

"Fine, Kylie," I said. "The damage is done. Are you happy? You can go now."

Kylie stood up and straightened her silky mocha-colored

dress. "All this time you thought you were better than me," she said almost gaily, picking up her bag. "Well, take a long look in the mirror. Because *you* make *me* sick." She gave one last triumphant smile, then hoisted her Kooba bag onto her shoulder and threaded her way past the crowded circular tables to the door.

"Luke, please let me explain," I began, sitting down. I could feel the tears starting to come again, and I blinked to hold them back.

"Is it true?" he said to the table. His voice sounded hoarse.

I took a deep breath. There could be no more lying now. "I never was a personal groomer or a dog walker, it's true. I came here to L.A. because I wanted to make movies. There was nothing else I wanted to do with my life."

Luke snorted. "You know that's not what I'm asking."

I wanted to reach out and touch his hand but I was afraid he would pull it away. So instead I grabbed a napkin off the table and balled it up in my fists. I hated having to say what I was going to say. "I made that first lesson with you because yes, I did want to hurt Kylie." Luke began to nod, still staring down at the tablecloth. I wanted to stop there— I hated how much I was hurting him. Having to say it made me realize how awful I'd been, and how I was this close to losing something that had really begun to matter. I took a deep breath. "And then I did sort of arrange for you to catch her with Mark Lyder, but that was before I really got to know you and—"

Luke finally looked up at me with those sad, beautiful eyes. But his voice wasn't sad at all—his voice was hard, like Iris's had been this morning. "I don't want to hear any more. I can't trust you. I thought you were real."

I dropped the napkin on the floor and reached for his hand. But he took it away before I could touch it. I could feel the desperation rolling off me in waves. "I *am* real. The other night, with you in Venice, that was *completely* real to me."

Luke snorted. "Except I spent it with a different person than the one sitting here right now." He pushed his chair back from the table and stood up. "I have to go."

I tried to reach for his corduroy coat, but he pulled that away from me too. "Luke, I'm not Kylie. I know I did some things wrong, but . . ." I was begging, but at this point I didn't care. "I *am* that girl from the other night. Please."

"Right now, I don't know who you are," he said, his face stony and resolute. "And I'm not sure I want to." Then he turned and walked away.

I buried my face in my hands, and when I looked up a few minutes later, I was staring at a plate of fried squid, their poor little bodies drenched in olive oil and lemon juice.

"The gentleman ordered it," the waiter said. "Will there be anything else?"

"Just the check," I whispered. Just the check and a whole new life.

"Excuse me, where is the cafeteria?"

The young girl I'd stopped wore a stained gray kilt and tights; she looked curiously at me and then pointed down the hall behind me. "Down there and to the left," she said, adjusting her wide cloth headband. "And it's not a cafeteria; it's a *lunchroom*."

"Whatever," I muttered, turning around to retrace her steps down the hall. True to its ritzy name, Carleton reminded me of an oversized mansion instead of a girls' school. Ivy-covered white colonnades marked the perimeter of the main building, and even the floors looked like marble. I felt a little guilty sneaking around Quinn's school, but luckily no one stopped me. I probably just looked like a stylish private school teacher, the one that all the girls liked.

I turned down the hall and saw an open set of ornately carved wooden doors. A cacophony of gossiping teenage voices spilled out. Hesitantly I stepped across the threshold and found myself in the middle of a cafeteria—sorry, *lunchroom*—that put the Metronome commissary to shame. There were no flat-screen TVs, but what the room lacked in hi-tech entertainment it made up for in ambiance. Sunlight filtered in through double-paned windows that stretched to the ceiling, and the girls had a choice of gilt-pedestaled tables or plush, velvet couches along the wall for where to eat their sushi or salads.

I finally spotted Quinn holding court on a couch, eating a Fage Greek yogurt, her kilted henchmen seated at her feet. Just seeing her smug, self-satisfied face sent a wave of rage washing over me. As I had sat at the table in Le Petit Greek, staring at the squid carcasses in the wake of Luke's departure, going to see her had seemed like the only rational thing to do. I wanted to hear her explain why she sold me out.

I stood up a little taller and approached the red couch on which Quinn sat like a pasha. One of the girls noticed me coming but didn't say anything. She just stared at me until I was right in front of them—until I spoke.

"I need to talk to you," I said.

Quinn sneered. "What the hell for?" One of the girls on the ground giggled, and I could see others turning to look. I was obviously out of place in this room of uniformed adolescents, and suddenly I was attracting a lot of attention.

I tried to keep my voice down. "I did what you wanted. I risked my job for you. And then you sell me out to your mom? How could you do that?" My voice quavered, though I was trying desperately to stay cool.

"Easily." Quinn stood up and tossed her yogurt into the trash. "*It's never your fault.* Didn't I teach you anything?" she asked with a smirk. "I do what I want to do. You know that. So why expect me to be different for *you?*"

I didn't have an answer for that. Because Quinn was right. This entire time Quinn had never deviated from who she really was: a girl who would use, cheat, and betray anyone in her path. It was why I'd asked for her help in the first place.

At least she knew who she was, I thought. Luke had said he didn't know who I was. But the truth was, neither did I.

"Are we done here?" Quinn said, and before I could answer, she was gone.

Her gaggle of girlfriends remained for another moment on the couch, each of them staring at me—some with pitying looks, others with scorn—and then one by one, they stood up in their short skirts and breezed on by me too, leaving me alone in the middle of a high school lunchroom.

Hollywood is like high school, Mark Lyder had said. And he was right. But as for which one was worse, I couldn't really say.

CHAPTER THIRTY-TWO

Merry Christmas, emporium! Merry Christmas, you wonderful old Building and Loan!"

For the first time that I could ever remember, Jimmy Stewart's final run down the main street of Bedford Falls failed to make me tear up. In fact, I barely felt a thing. I hit Pause on the DVR and rewound the scene.

I reached down from the couch, where I had been lying for the last six days, and picked up another Philly Steak & Cheese Hot Pocket from the plate on the floor. I ate it without sitting up; I had perfected the art of prone digestion.

I had also perfected the art of being awake without thinking about anything. The key was television. I'd read somewhere that the brain is more active asleep than it is watching TV, and after a pleasantly anesthetized week, I was here to say that yes, TV was the next best thing to a lobotomy. And it was certainly cheaper and easier to come by. As long as I stayed on the couch, in front of the flickering screen, I could spend an entire day without seeing Iris's steely glare, Luke's sweet smile, or Kylie's triumphant smirk. I could also tune out the memory of Quinn's cutting voice and the humiliation of a day that had begun with being fired and ended with being escorted out of the cafeteria—no, *lunchroom*—by a burly woman in a hairnet who told me I should find girls my own age to play with.

It was only when I went to bed that all of those images flooded my brain. So for bedtime, there was ice cream, numbing my mind along with my taste buds and sending me into a sugar-filled stupor.

Magnolia stood over me, her pretty brow furrowed and that awful Cabbage in her arms. "You sure you're all right? Do you need anything?"

We'd made up after our fight—she'd offered to dry-clean my Calypso dress, and I'd apologized for suggesting she was one step away from knitting dog-hair sweaters. We had agreed that we were both under a lot of stress (Magnolia, for instance, had had a particularly hairy round of customers that day) and had sealed our friendship over an obligatory meal of Poquito Mas.

Jimmy Stewart was just starting his jog when the scene froze. Remote in hand, Magnolia perched on the arm of the couch. "Taylor? You there?" She waved a few manicured fingers in front of my face.

"I'm fine," I said to the TV.

"Are you getting any responses?" She pointed to the laptop that lay next to the Hot Pockets. "Any interviews?"

"Oh." I sat up. "I'm sure I am. I just haven't checked in a while."

Magnolia cleared her throat and said gently, "I don't mean to sound like your mother or anything, but you can't get a job if you aren't even really trying."

I twisted my head around so that she could see me roll my eyes at her. "I don't see what's so great about having a job. I mean, you can't stand yours. I couldn't keep mine. I don't see why I can't just lie here for another month. I've learned a lot about cleaning rain gutters from HGTV, for example. Also I now know a lot about cuttlefish, thanks to PBS. Did you know that some of them can turn all the colors of the rainbow?"

Magnolia sighed. "You sound like a crazy person, Taylor."

I didn't answer her. I *felt* like a crazy person. I crossed one leg over the other and at that point noticed that I was wearing not just two different socks but two different *shoes*. I kicked the shoes off—what did I need footwear for? I was never going to get off this couch.

"We could go get a drink somewhere," Magnolia offered. "I could buy you a bloody bishop or something."

I laughed mirthlessly. "I hate those things," I said. "But thanks. And really, I'm sorry if I was a bitch before. I know I'm a drag now. I wish things had gone differently. That's all. Now that my whole life has gone up in flames."

Magnolia put Cabbage on the floor and grabbed my hand. "Hey, stop with the violins. Things aren't that bad."

"No, they are," I said. "What happened at work is all over town, there's no way it's not. So I can forget about another job. My boss thinks I'm the scum of the earth. Even my gay boyfriend dumped me." It was true—I hadn't heard from Brett since I'd bailed on our Sonoma weekend with so little explanation. Apparently, hell hath no fury like a gay boyfriend scorned. "Oh and I almost forgot," I continued, holding up my fingers to finish ticking off my imaginary list. "The guy that I was dating—or starting to date—the guy I actually really liked . . . thinks I'm terrible." I was too depressed to cry.

"Hey. Things will work out for you. I know it. You're good, Taylor, and good things will happen to you. You just have to think positively."

I waved my hand in the air dismissively. "Empty assurances," I said. "They give better advice on *Days of Our Lives*."

Magnolia giggled. "See?" she said. "You can still be funny. That's something." She stood and scooped up Cabbage again. Then she called for Woodstock and Lucius, who came scrambling out from who knows where in a cloud of flying hair and meaty breath. God, those animals were disgusting. Then again, I was no picture myself.

"We're going for a walk," Magnolia said. "You need anything?"

I rolled over and put the uneaten half of my Hot Pocket on the plate. "No thanks, sweetie," I said. "See you later."

With Magnolia gone, I could settle back into my schmaltzy Frank Capra movie. With a sigh of satisfaction, I hit Play.

Nothing happened. Jimmy Stewart remained frozen in midstep. I pressed play again, and suddenly he was inside his house, surrounded by people, and I could hear the ending music swelling.

"Shit," I said. Had I watched the DVD so much I'd destroyed it? It was possible.

Like an arthritic, half-crippled old man, I eased myself off the couch and went in search of another DVD (amazing how quickly coordination and muscle tone can go). Magnolia had only dog movies, so I went to my trusty stack of five. And there it was, *Journal Girl*. My favorite.

I didn't pick it up though. Instead I went to my bookshelf,

where I picked up a copy of Dana's script. It was the only paper around, and at this point, I had no use for it anymore.

I pulled out the brads from the script and turned the pages backwards. Grabbing a pen from beside my bed, I started to write.

Dear Michael,
I'm so sorry.

CHAPTER THIRTY-THREE

Okay, is this for the Blue Balls or the Crack Is Wack?"

The man on the other line gulped nervously. "Did you say Blue Balls?" he asked in a wavering voice.

"Oh, it's just the name," I said brightly. "Don't be scared. And just so you know, we've got a special on the Woolly Mammoth this week. So if you're going to do the butt, you may as well do the back." These were words I really never thought I'd say to a stranger, but as the new receptionist at Joylie, such blunt enticements were part of my job.

"All right, I'll take it all," the man said in a hushed voice. He was probably at work. And really, who would want their co-workers to hear them scheduling an appointment to have all their private hairs ripped out by the roots? I marked the appointment in the oversized ledger, grabbed another handful of Tootsie Rolls from the dish on my desk, and tried to tune out Wham!'s "Last Christmas," which the radio seemed to have on an endless loop. The holiday was only a week away.

At least I had a job. Magnolia had been nice enough to offer me the position after Kitty, the old receptionist, ran off to Vegas to marry one of Joylie's hirsute clients. (It had been quite the proposal. The man—a Ducati-riding banker Magnolia called the Hairy Carpet Man—had asked Magnolia to wax his chest hair into the shape of a heart, after which he walked into the reception area with a diamond ring taped to one of his nipples and got down on his knee in front of Kitty. "And she said *yes*," Magnolia had screamed, clearly scandalized at Kitty's bad judgment.)

So here I was, in a pink lab coat, answering phones just like I'd done at Metronome, but for half the pay and none of the glory. I hadn't been able to tell my parents about my miserable failures— I wanted to postpone disappointing them until after Christmas. I hadn't called any of my friends from college—not that I spoke to them much these days anyway. I hadn't even signed onto IM recently, because I was afraid Brandon would IM me again, and I'd be forced to tell him what had happened. I couldn't afford to have Brandon know; I'd be able to hear the gleeful "I told you so" all the way across the country.

I looked at the cars driving past the plate-glass window and sank my head into my hands. Outside, a guy in out-of-season linen pants and a wrinkled Oxford shirt paced on the sidewalk, obviously pleading into his cell phone. He had the look you see in the hallways and waiting rooms of casting calls—that smiling, eager desperation. Like a dog that's been kicked, Magnolia would say, but that keeps hoping that someone will eventually pet it.

I felt like failure was contagious and that an epidemic of it was raging in West Hollywood. All around me were the actors, writers, filmmakers, and everyone else who, like me, had fallen out of favor with the Hollywood gods. They became visible the minute you fell through the cracks—they were there in the coffee shops, on the treadmills at the gym, on the hiking trails in Runyon Canyon. Ground zero was the Whole Foods on Santa Monica and Fairfax, where they seemed to linger all day, eating their takeout salads with a copy of *L.A. Weekly* in front of them. It was starting to dawn on me that people could live their entire lives in this city *waiting*—waiting for work, waiting for love, waiting for that proverbial big break that had a snowball's chance in hell of coming. It was enough to keep you from getting out of bed in the morning, if you thought about it too hard.

"How're we doing?" Magnolia asked, coming out from her waxing suite to look at the book. She leaned over my shoulder. "Oh no. Not this guy. He doesn't *bathe*."

I smiled wanly. "I could call him back and tell him that showers are a prerequisite for service." I took a sip of coffee—*free* coffee from the Joylie break room. No more five-dollar mochaccinos for me. "Hey, do you think George Michael has somehow bribed America's deejays? I mean, this song. Over and over and over. Why? Is it like this every year?"

"Last year it was 'Grandma Got Run Over by a Reindeer.' For some reason all the dudes on KIIS FM seemed to think it was hilarious." Magnolia glanced at her watch. "You can take lunch if you want. Half an hour."

I stood up and grabbed my purse. I hadn't realized I was starving. "Thanks. You want something?"

"Besides a nose plug? Nah, I'm good."

She took my seat, and I stretched a tight hamstring. "Another week with no Buddha Ball and I'm going to fall to pieces completely."

Magnolia put a pencil in her mouth and looked at me thoughtfully. "You're doing a really good job here, you know. They taught you well at the prison camp." She grinned. "Have you ever thought about getting your aesthetician's license? I'd be happy to train you. You can watch me anytime."

I gulped and smiled my best fake smile. It was very sweet of Mags to offer, but no way was I going to apply hot wax to Hollywood's genitalia. "Let me think about that. I'll be back in twenty."

Things had not gotten that desperate yet, thankfully. I had a bit of money in my checking account and a closet full of designer duds that I could, if things got really bad, sell on eBay or something. Quinn may have turned on me, but she was never going to ask for her clothes back.

It was sunny and crisp outside, a lovely, anomalous winter day. I zipped up my corduroy jacket against the wind. Whoever said L.A. never gets cold was a liar: these days I was usually freezing. Then again, it might have been less about the weather than the fact that I'd dropped ten pounds in the past three weeks. My initial post-Metronome diet of Hot Pockets and ice cream had turned me off of food completely for a while, and now I could fit into the skinniest of skinny jeans. At least being miserable had its perks.

I headed down the block toward the Afghan Kebab house. The falafel platter lunch special for five-fifty was the best deal in town. Afterward, I'd browse through the beauty supply at the corner drugstore, as if I had a reason to wear makeup anymore. No career. No boy. What was the point?

I thought of Luke and felt a tightness in my chest. Every time a white Jeep Wrangler drove down the street, every time I looked at my darling tennis dress in my closet, every time I passed a freaking *sushi* restaurant, the sadness came in like some kind of terrible tide. I'd found the perfect guy, and just like that, I'd lost him. There was nothing I could do to convince him that I wasn't a horrible phony, though I had tried. I called, I e-mailed, I texted, but never did I get a response. I'd stopped short of stalking him at work, but believe me, I'd considered it.

When a little more time had passed, I'd write him a letter to explain myself and drop it off at his house. That way he'd know my side of the story, and he'd also know how sorry I was. I would also call Iris. Not just because of my career, but because she had been the best, fairest boss I'd probably ever have in my life, and I owed her that much.

I picked at my falafel as I walked down the street. The one person I'd managed to pour my heart out to was Michael Deming, though I assumed he never got that missive either. (*I was an asshole,* I'd written. *I wanted so badly to tell you what your films mean to me. But I was too embarrassed. . . .*) I shook my head at my incredible stupidity and said, "Idiot, idiot, idiot" to myself. A homeless guy in a red vest and dirty purple hat looked at me sympathetically, probably thinking I was crazy, and asked me if I was famous. For this minor and insincere compliment, I gave him a dollar.

And then of course, there was Dana McCafferty, the innocent bystander in all of this. After a hesitant, stop-and-start conversation on the phone, I'd finally gotten Dana to meet me at Urth Caffe three days ago. She showed up sans backpack, but the fifth-grade-boy look was pretty much the same. The meeting was, naturally, awkward. This time Dana did little except stare at the ground and nod, and I certainly couldn't blame her. She had been on the verge of signing with Ingenuity when the deal had fallen through. Now she couldn't get anyone to return her calls.

I felt so awful, I was unable to drink the green chai latte in front of me. "I never meant to screw up your life this badly," I'd told her.

Dana had only nodded and played with a pink Sweet 'N Low packet. "At least I got close," she said in her small voice.

"You'll get an agent, I promise." The words had sounded hollow, even though I meant them. Because really, what did I know?

The only bright spot had been patching things up with Brett. Inspired by my Deming and Dana confessionals, I'd called him in tears, apologizing breathlessly for ditching him, being such a bad person, the whole nine yards. "Snap out of it, drama queen!" he'd cried. "Yeah, you flaked, but apology accepted. Consider us kissed and made up." He'd even invited me out to El Guapo a few nights ago, but I couldn't handle the possibility of running into people from Metronome. I gladly took a rain check, though. Brett Duncan was the only friend I'd made in L.A., and I intended to keep him.

I walked on down the avenue, chewing the lunch I barely tasted. I should have given the homeless guy my lunch too, because thinking about my mess of a life had taken away my appetite.

"Taylor?"

I turned around and almost dropped my falafel on the sidewalk.

Iris Whitaker took off her Chanel sunglasses—I was pretty sure they were the same pair Quinn was wearing when we met at the Malibu Country Mart—and gazed at me. In her eyes was not the scorn I was expecting but a kind of thoughtful bemusement. I wiped chickpea crumbs off my chin and smiled a very hesitant smile.

"Where are you off to?" she asked kindly. *Kindly.* What was going on?

I thought about offering an answer that didn't involve hair removal: *I was just going to the drugstore,* I could say. Or, *I have a friend in the neighborhood.* And in a way the latter excuse was true—that homeless guy really liked me once I gave him some money. But something about Iris's expression—quizzical, friendly—made me decide to be honest. That, and I'd learned what lying could do to a girl. "I was just getting a little lunch." I gestured to my falafel, and then pointed down the street to Joylie. "I work over there."

Iris gazed at the storefront. "I was just on my way in."

"You were?" Nervously I slipped my falafel into a nearby garbage can. No way could I stuff my face in front of the seventh most powerful player in Hollywood. "I can get you a discount." I cringed even as I said it. Iris could certainly afford a bikini wax, or whatever it was she was after.

Iris chuckled. "I wasn't going for an appointment. I wanted to see you." She pulled her beige sweater coat closer around her.

I looked at her with wide, disbelieving eyes. "You did?"

"I got a phone call from Michael Deming's agent this morning. The one you met with—Arnie?"

"Arnie Brotman." I winced, remembering how pushy I'd been with him, how stupidly sure of myself. I wondered what he thought of me now. Not that it mattered.

"Odd fellow," Iris noted, smiling a little. "Anyway, it turns out that Deming has reconsidered. He wants to do the project."

"Pardon?" I leaned toward her like someone hard of hearing. She couldn't have said what I thought she said.

Iris laughed. "He wants to do the project," she repeated.

"He does?" The shock made my knees weak, and I looked around for a bench to sink down on. There was nothing, so I steadied myself against the sticky side of the trash can. *Gross*— but I really didn't care.

"Yes, he does. Apparently something made him change his mind." Iris gazed at me closely, as if she suspected that I had done something to redeem myself, as hard as that might be to imagine. "Do you have any idea what that might have been?"

I shook my head. It was all beyond my comprehension, really. "No. I don't." I thought about Deming's weird cabin, his tuna sandwiches, his habit of filming squirrels and foxes. God knows I would never understand the guy. "He *is* supposed to be kind of unpredictable," I offered.

"Yes," Iris said, nodding. "Well, I put in a call to Bob Glazer to tell him the good news, and"—she paused dramatically— "Holden is still in."

The homeless man I'd given money to shuffled by, grinning—whether at me or the voices in his head, it was impossible to say. "You're kidding!"

Iris smiled warmly. "His schedule is still free, thank God."

I could have cried with joy—I could have jumped into Iris's arms—I could have kissed the homeless dude on the lips. The heavy cloak of guilt that had been resting on my shoulders ever since I'd screwed Iris, Metronome, and pretty much everyone involved seemed to lift instantly. Everything had worked out. I hadn't done any lasting damage. I was *free*. "Iris, that's incredible!" I held out my arms as if I could hug all of West Hollywood. "I'm so happy for you!"

Iris held up one manicured hand. "There's a catch." Her eyes seemed to bore right through me, and the wind blew tendrils of wavy auburn hair across her cheeks.

"A catch?"

"Deming will only do it if you're working on it too."

This was another thing I wasn't sure I heard correctly. "Me?" I said stupidly.

Iris fiddled with her sunglasses and smiled. "He told Arnie he wants the girl who's been writing to him all these years . . . and I assume that's you?"

Surprise, surprise—the U.S. Postal Service had come through for me. I could hardly believe it. I nodded. "That was me all right."

"So you two have been pen pals?" Iris asked with an arched brow.

I felt myself blushing. Seven years of postcards. How gushy and bubbly the early ones had been—how silly and naïve. I felt sorry for the old Taylor; I wished I could go back in time and tell her to be less of a wide-eyed innocent. "Kind of. I mean, I wrote him and . . . well, it's a little hard to explain." It wasn't hard, of course, but I didn't want Iris to get the stalker vibe from my story.

Iris nodded. "Well, whatever it is, you've made some kind of impact."

Then her smile faded for a moment, and I remembered how she had given me the deathstare in her office. Once again I felt my nerves jangling. I bit my lip and waited for her to go on.

"Just so it's very clear, Taylor, I still don't like what you did."

I hung my head—I couldn't look at her. "I know."

"Or how you got my daughter embroiled in all of this. You're going to have to make me forget that. *But*"—she held up a finger—"you're smart. You're ambitious. You have excellent taste. And we need a hit."

Still I stared at the sidewalk and waited for her to come to her point. I was glad she thought I was smart and ambitious, but being smart and ambitious didn't pay the rent these days— booking Brazilians and Crack Is Wack specials did. Speaking of which, I was going to be late getting back to my desk. I looked back toward Joylie nervously.

Iris straightened up and put her hands on her hips. "You have your job back. You start after the holidays," she said brusquely. She pushed her sunglasses back onto her face and turned on her heels. "Oh," she said, turning around. "And I almost forgot. Merry Christmas."

"You too, Iris." I realized that suddenly I was grinning like an idiot. This was the best Christmas present I could have hoped for.

I watched Iris walk against the wind, her hair flying off her shoulders, toward her silver 700 Series Mercedes. So maybe movies weren't totally fake after all, I thought to myself. Sometimes in real life there *were* happy endings. I pulled my iPhone out of my bag, and a moment later, a familiar voice picked up.

"Hello?"

"Dana? *Guess what?*"

CHAPTER THIRTY-FOUR

Shara, the raven-haired receptionist who had never, ever been nice to me, smiled cryptically as I walked through the spa-like lobby of Metronome Studios and swiped my ID through the scanner. On the other side of the big glass doors I passed the CE offices that had so awed me on my first day. Everyone was busy on their phones and their BlackBerries. As Kylie would say, *Quel surprise*. Cici tossed her hair over her shoulder as I passed her desk; Wyman stared at me through his black-framed film-nerd glasses. I held my head up very high and looked straight ahead. Whether they were glad I was back or not was something I didn't really care to know. I passed Lisa Amorosi in the hallway. In the month I had been gone, she had apparently discovered the wonders of the flatiron, and her normally frizzy hair was shiny and pulled back into a sleek ponytail. She did a double take when she saw me and then offered me a slim smile.

Part of me wondered if it was my clothes: a plum-colored long-sleeved top with a pretty flower appliqué from Forever 21 and a pair of black tweed pants from Banana I'd bought on sale. Nothing on my body cost more than forty dollars, which was definitely bucking the Metronome trend. But screw it, I told myself. Did I really need to be decked out in an outfit that cost as much as a down payment on a car?

I continued on down the hall, past the open mouths, toward Iris's office. At least now I would have Kylie's desk, and Kylie would be on the other side of the floor, in Melinda Darling's office. I had no idea what to say to Kylie. I'd stayed up half the night trying to formulate the most civil hello I could think of, but in the end, what I said didn't matter nearly as much as how I said it. Quinn had taught me that much. And anyway, from now on, I wasn't going to think so hard about how to act around people. I was just going to be me. Maybe that was a corny philosophy—certainly Quinn wouldn't approve—but it was the best one I had. And after I made nice with Kylie, I would simply settle down into doing my job. I would be the best first assistant Iris had ever had.

But when I walked into the little area outside Iris's junglelike office, someone already sat at Kylie's desk, answering the phones. I cleared my throat, and the chair swiveled around.

"Taylor?" Julissa cried, standing up.

"Julissa!"

I ran over to give her a hug. With her hair back in a chic knot and kohl smudged around her eyes, Julissa looked ten years older than she did the last time I'd seen her. "Wow, you look great." I took in her cute little smock dress and suede ankle boots. "Very Metronome."

"Thanks." She blushed and sat back down, suddenly almost shy. "Welcome back."

"It's good to be back." I glanced down at Kylie's desk. Dime-store photo strips of Julissa and her friends joking around had replaced the jeweled frames, and a giant bobblehead of Dwight Schrute replaced the aromatherapy candle. Stacks of scripts were everywhere. "Wait a sec. Are you——"

"Yep." Julissa grinned. "As of last week."

"Oh my God, Julissa, that's great!" I did a little hop of joy, which made her giggle. "Congratulations!"

"Believe me, I was totally surprised," Julissa confided, reaching up to play with her hair and then stopping herself. "But when Kylie got promoted, and you were gone . . ." Her voice trailed off.

"Well, you deserve it." I picked up my four-year-old navy J.Crew coat and turned to look at my old desk, bare once again. "I guess I'll call IT to get me booted up here."

Julissa furrowed her brow at me. If the look on her face hadn't been so good-natured and so bewildered, I'd have said she reminded me of Kylie in that moment. "What?" she said.

"To get me situated here."

"Wait, didn't Iris tell you?"

"Tell me what?" I felt a rising tide of panic—had Iris changed her mind? Had I just walked down that ridiculous screen-saver hallway with my head held high only to be told that I had to turn right around again?

"You're not sitting in here."

As if on cue, Iris breezed into the office, Burberry coat on her arm, venti mocha in hand, Louis Vuitton doctor's bag swinging. "Good morning, Taylor."

"Iris." I shook Iris's hand, not sure what else to do. "I guess I was just about to sit down here."

Iris smiled her warm, crinkly-eyed grin. "Well, I'd love to have you, but this is not where you're sitting. You're over there," she said, pointing in the direction of Melinda's office.

"But what about—"

Iris turned to go into her office. "Julissa, would you please escort Taylor to her new digs?"

Julissa sprang out of her chair. "Come on, Henning. Follow me."

As we walked down the hall, past the nap room, past Cici doodling at her desk (who also looked at me with a strange, unreadable expression), past the copy room and the kitchen, I leaned down and whispered, "What happened to Kylie?"

Julissa smiled a slightly nasty smile. "Let's just say Kylie didn't pan out."

I stopped in my tracks. Wyman breezed past us in a cloud of Axe body spray. "What do you mean?"

"*Creative differences* was the term they used. Translation: she effed up. Thought she had a commitment from Ingenuity when they never intended for Troy Vaughn to do the project. They talked him into doing another film with Owen Wilson." She tugged impatiently on my arm. "Come on, let's get you to your office."

As I followed Julissa to the office I had so briefly occupied once before, I thoughtfully sipped on my coffee. It wasn't so hard to figure out what had happened: as payback for the Chateau fiasco, Mark Lyder and his cronies had screwed Kylie over in the end. I contemplated this for a moment and decided that yes, I almost felt sorry for her.

As we came upon the office I'd soon be occupying, a girl looked up from her desk.

"Sheila," Julissa said, "this is Taylor, your CE. Taylor, meet Sheila, your new assistant. She's fresh out of Grinnell, and of course she loves movies."

Sheila had short dark hair and enormous brown eyes. Long gold earrings brushed against her shoulders as she stood up and shook my hand. "It's great to meet you."

"You too," I said. To Julissa I whispered, "What happened to Amanda?"

Julissa hissed back that Amanda had requested a change of assignment and now would be assisting Lisa Amorosi. This was very good news. I wanted, as Quinn had suggested, a faithful assistant, not one capable of sabotage.

Sheila opened a drawer to her desk and took out a key and handed it to me. "For your office," she said, smiling.

I took it from her like it was nothing—like it wasn't the culmination of months of blood and sweat and tears. I squeezed it in my hand. If I ever moved to another office, I was going to have this key bronzed.

"There's a ten o'clock staff meeting," Sheila said, reading off a notepad, "and then you have a lunch meeting with Bob Glazer and Holden MacIntee. Is the Ivy all right?"

"Sure," I said, trying to sound blasé, as if I ate lunch every day at a place where the Caesar salad is to die for and everyone who is anyone sips Pellegrino and trades Hollywood dish.

Then I opened up my office. The Lucite desk and Herman Miller chair were still there, and someone had put a vase of brilliant pink gladiolas on the bookshelf. There was the beautiful Macintosh computer, and there was my very own view of a parking lot lined with palm trees.

"We just had it painted for you. And I'll be bringing some

catalogs for more furniture later. Your budget's three thousand, but I'll see if I can get more."

Three *thousand*?? "Um, that's fine."

Sheila went back out, and I plopped my bag on the desk and turned on my computer. It gracefully blinked awake. Then I sank down into my chair and contemplated putting my feet on my desk but decided it was too cliché, like the final scene of *Working Girl*.

Sheila popped her head back in. "Do you want anything to drink?"

I smiled at her eagerness—I remembered just what that was like. "It's okay, Sheila. I can get it myself."

She smiled back and vanished. From the other side of the room, I heard Julissa sigh.

"Taylor, you've got to use your power," she said, pretending to be exasperated. "Make the girl get you a smoothie. One of those muddy-looking ones Tom Scheffer likes so much." Then she giggled. "Or not."

I threw open my arms, as if I could hug my beautiful new office. I thought about kissing the desk, but wasn't sure that would look right. "I really don't know what to say," I said. "Look at this place!"

"Oh, Taylor." Sheila walked back into the office holding something large and rectangular, covered in brown wrapping paper. "Someone sent you some décor for the office."

"Who?"

She propped it against the wall. "Don't know. But it's already framed and everything." She slipped out.

Julissa raised her eyebrows. "Presents already! But hey, I better get back to the desk. Congrats again." Julissa gave me another hug. "And feel free to lord it over me, since you're now a CE."

"As if."

When Julissa closed the door, I crouched down in front of the package. When I took off the paper, I sat back on my heels and felt tears come to my eyes.

It was the original movie poster for *Journal Girl*. And at the bottom was an inscription. *To Taylor, My favorite writer. Best, Michael Deming.*

I stood and looked out the plate-glass window. "Thank you," I said softly to the Hollywood Hills in the distance.

CHAPTER THIRTY-FIVE

ut!"

Michael Deming took off his headphones and popped another stick of Doublemint gum into his mouth.

"Dana?" Michael craned his head toward the cluster of director's chairs behind him. "Dana? I need you."

"I'm here!" she squeaked. Sitting beside me in a director's chair that was three times her size, Dana McCafferty slid to the floor on her Keds. "Taylor, can you hold these for me?" she asked, handing over her headphones.

"No problem." I took the headphones, hung them about my neck, and took another sip of coffee.

Dana rolled her eyes. "He's so needy," she said, but she was smiling as she padded off toward Deming, who was pacing behind the cameras, hands thrust in the back pockets of his jeans.

It was my third day on the set of *The Evolution of Evan*, and I was still a little unsure what was expected of me as the supervising studio exec. As far as I could tell, everything was going well—they were still on schedule, under budget, and aside from perhaps maybe one too many huddled conferences with Dana McCafferty, all seemed to be moving along. I shaded my eyes against the setting sun and pulled my Old Navy faux-sheepskin jacket closer around my shoulders. It was almost May, but up here, north of San Francisco in bucolic Marin County, it still felt like winter. Below me I heard a little yelp.

"Jerry, shh," I said, reaching down to pick up my new puppy. The shelter had said that he was a shepherd mix, which basically meant they had no idea. I got him to replace Lucius, Cabbage, and Woodstock, all of whom had been miraculously adopted. He squirmed a little bit—we were still getting to know each other— but I patted him down the back like I'd seen Magnolia do a million times. "Jerry Maguire, I want you to be a good boy," I cooed, talking into his ear.

Jerry stared at me with his imploring brown eyes and whined.

"Yes, I know it's hard being a doggy," I said, lapsing into the baby talk that I couldn't control. I hadn't pegged myself for a cooing baby-talker, but I'd stopped trying to fight it. And Jerry seemed to like it, though it was hard to tell what was going on in that pea-sized brain of his. As soon as I got back down to L.A., I was going to watch *The Dog Whisperer* with Magnolia and enroll him in some obedience training. The other night he had an accident all over my shoes. Thank God they were only old ones.

"Taylor!" Michael Deming gestured for me to come over. He stood with Dana and Holden, a few steps from the cameras. Behind him was a little park that we'd populated with assorted extras—a man walking an Italian greyhound in a little sweater, a woman reading a newspaper—and illuminated with lights. In the center of the scene was the park bench where Holden and his love interest, played by a young unknown with naturally golden hair and bee-stung lips, had to break each other's hearts on camera. I'd been paying attention to the filming, but watching take after take got a little monotonous, and I'd turned my attentions to the crafts service table, which was laid out with an array of delectable sandwiches and cookies for the cast and crew. I was debating about helping myself, but it was only eleven—too soon, really, to start pigging out on lunch.

I carried Jerry over to the trio. "What's up, guys?"

"I think Evan would be crying in this scene, you know?" said Holden, looking extremely handsome in a cashmere sweater and two-day-old stubble. "It's a breakup. And he's a sensitive guy."

"No, no, no," Michael said, shaking his head. "No tears. Absolutely not."

I had told Michael he could make the movie he wanted, and I meant it, but I thought we should have a third opinion. "What do you think, Dana?"

Dana grimaced. "No crying," she said. "I don't think that's the character."

I turned to Holden, who looked a bit miffed. "Let's try it without the tears," I said. "Sometimes subtlety is the most powerful weapon in the actor's arsenal." I smiled. It almost sounded like I knew what I was talking about.

Holden kicked at the ground and nodded his head; he could be gracious in defeat (sometimes). "Well, okay," he said, brushing his hair back. "I guess that's okay."

As we walked back to the chairs, Dana whispered, "He's kind of a prima donna."

"At least he listens to reason," I said as Dana clambered back up into her chair.

She picked up her notebook—she was already working on another script—and looked over at me. "And Deming loves you," Dana said. "I mean, you don't have to be here every day, but whenever you aren't, he looks lost."

I looked back at him pacing with the cinematographer, discussing a shot. It was weird, but I actually felt proud of him. During preproduction, as we cast the film and worked on locations and a budget, Deming was patient, modest, and even instructive, though it was patently clear I didn't know what I was doing. We'd gone out to dinner numerous times, laughing, bullshitting, comparing notes on new releases—he admitted, with some embarrassment, that he loved the latest Will Smith vehicle—and had become, I thought, genuine friends. Once he'd had me over to the apartment he'd rented across the street from the filming and made me a tuna fish sandwich "for old time's sake." He even wanted to set me up with a writer he knew in Oregon.

On that count, I had demurred. I couldn't help still thinking about Luke, even though I'd never heard from him, not even after I sent the long and hopefully not too pleading letter explaining my side of the story. But I told myself it was all part of the process of growing up and making your way. Along the path of your life, some people just slip away.

Of course, I'd only been on one date with the guy, so I shouldn't be so moony, but I let myself indulge in my nostalgia. After all, what was the point in pretending to be different than you were or pretending to feel something other than what you really felt?

Anyway, most of the time, I felt great. The past few months of putting together the movie had taken all of my time, and it was just as crazy and wonderful and frustrating and satisfying as

I'd hoped it would be. Throughout it all, I'd followed only one guideline: *fake nothing.* So far it had served me well. It turned out that asking questions wasn't so terrible after all.

At my feet, Jerry began to whine and tug at his leash, reminding me that I hadn't taken him for a walk since before breakfast. "All right, little muffin face," I whispered. *Muffin face?* Seriously, I was embarrassing myself.

"I'll be right back," I told Dana, grabbing the end of Jerry's leash. "I'm going to take the monster for a quick stroll."

Before Dana could answer, one of the grips, a hulking guy with strawberry blond hair and an earnest, dopey look about him, approached. "Are you Taylor Henning?" he asked. "There's someone here to see you." He hooked his thumb over his shoulder toward the parking area.

"Who?"

He shrugged. "Some guy."

I pulled my windblown hair back with an elastic from around my wrist and took out some Chapstick from my pocket. It was probably the production exec, coming to trade shifts with me. I made my way past a group of trailers, then the crafts service table, from which I swiped a chocolate chip cookie. The wardrobe girl, Heather, waved at me and I waved back.

I turned the corner around the audio trailer, and then I pulled Jerry to a stop on his leash. In front of me stood Luke Hansen, in jeans and a Carhartt jacket and work boots, looking more like a cute teamster than a professional tennis instructor. The cookie almost fell out of my open mouth.

"Oh my God," I said, swallowing.

"Hi." He stuffed his hands in his pockets and grinned at me shyly.

"What are you doing here?" I blurted out. At my feet, Jerry barked once and then sat down on his haunches, whimpering.

Luke looked down at Jerry and then back up at me quizzically. "Cute dog," he said and then smiled again. "I have a wedding up here tomorrow, in San Rafael. One of Tom and Julia's friends. And when I heard they were shooting your movie around here, I thought, you know, there might be a chance you'd be here." He glanced at Jerry again. "Is he yours?"

"Yep," I said. "My roommate's dog obsession rubbed off on me. Well, not the obsession part, really. It's not like I have a coffee mug that says 'I heart my mutt' or something, but I do like dogs now, and so I . . ." I let the rest of my sentence trail off. I didn't want to start babbling just because Luke was suddenly here and apparently not hating me anymore.

Luke laughed. "What's his name?"

"Jerry. As in *Jerry Maguire*," I said. It was kind of an embarrassing name, really, but it was better than Magnolia's idea, which had been to name him John, after John Cusack.

Luke bent down and petted him, and Jerry rolled on his back, tongue lolling out in ecstasy. "So Magnolia finally got to you?"

"Huh?"

Luke stood up. "I ended up going to that salon you mentioned. Joylie. And I found out you actually did work there."

I smiled uncomfortably. "For a little while."

"Anyway, I met your old roommate, and she kind of set me straight on a few things. She's the one who told me you'd be up here."

I looked up at him hopefully. Had Magnolia accomplished what my letter had not? Had she been able to convince Luke that I wasn't the world's most devious person? Mags had excellent communication skills with creatures of the canine persuasion, that was true, but I wasn't sure how that applied to tall, handsome tennis instructors.

"Did you have anything done there?" I teased, because joking made me feel like I was still in control of my fluttering heart, when in fact I most certainly was not.

Luke laughed. "I do my own personal grooming, thank you," he said. "So how's the movie going?"

I glanced back at the set. Michael Deming was directing the motion of a dolly for a long tracking shot. "It's going really well," I said honestly. "I still can't believe it's happening, after . . . after everything." I didn't want to remind him of my failures, but it seemed that there was no way around it. Anyway, it was important to clear the air. I paused. "Did you get my letter?"

Luke looked away. "I did," he said. "But I didn't read it. I threw it away. I'm sorry."

I nodded. That made sense to me. "I understand," I said. I picked up Jerry, who licked my face. "I was kind of a shit."

A breeze swirled up, and petals from a nearby apple tree fluttered past us like snowflakes. Luke's eyes were the color of the sky.

"You were a shit," he said. "But I get it. I mean, I know you're not that person. You just got a little confused."

Yes, I thought, I'd been confused. But I wasn't confused now—I knew what I wanted, and it was standing right in front of me. "You can say that again."

Luke reached out and knuckled Jerry's head. I caught a whiff of the warm, clean boy smell of his hand. "Well, I just got up here and I'm staying in a house twenty minutes away with Tom and Julia, if you feel like taking a break. And . . . I'm sort of out a date for this wedding. But if you have work to do, I totally understand."

I stepped closer to him. Over the PA I could hear the assistant director call for everyone to be quiet on set.

I looked around at the scattered crewmembers getting ready for another shot and at Deming sitting back in his chair. Dana was at his side, her little body bouncing up and down in excitement. Really, I'd never met anyone more hopeful and enthusiastic. Holden stretched his hamstrings while waiting for his cue. He'd told me how much he missed Buddha Ball, and we'd talked about going to yoga here in Marin together. He was great, really, when it came down to it. Everyone and everything was great.

"I think this can go on without me," I said.

The hand that had been petting Jerry reached down and touched my wrist. "You sure? Because you're a big-shot movie executive now."

I laughed and shrugged. My skin tingled where he touched it. "It's just a job."

Then I set Jerry down and took Luke's hand, and we walked off together, the spring wind blowing and a tiny dog yipping at our heels. Behind us, the cameras rolled.